BLIND JUS'

No part of this book may be used or reproduced in any manner whatsoever without the express permission of the author and publisher. Brief quotations, with attributions to the book's title, may be used in a review. Published in the United States.

Publishing Consultant
The Pierce Agency, LLC, USA
www.ThePierceAgencyLLC.com

Cover Design Courtesy of Sassi Creative, Inc.

Printed in the U.S.A.
ISBN -13: 978-1-7346754-0-5

For reprint permission, or to use text or graphics from this publication, e-mail your request to cj.mccall.author@gmail.com.

Acknowledgments

In addition to my children, I wish to express my appreciation for the never-ending patience of my brother Jerry and my friend of 30 years, Marlene Davis, who graciously provided valuable input and never-ending encouragement, despite her discomfort with some of the language. Each had to listen to unending comments about drafting ideas, general complaints, and comments through 10 drafts.

I would be remiss if I didn't include the unlimited patience expressed by my editor, Rebekah Pierce. Among other things, she did what I believe editors are supposed to do. They see things that an author doesn't see and offer comments, suggestions, criticisms, and, often as not, complete rewriting and changes. It would be totally misleading to suggest that my drafts did not require all these inputs! While I did not originally agree with some of her input, invariably, she was correct. While there were times that we disagreed, we never had disagreeable moments.

One of the most material attributes of our relationship was the availability for us to have a really intellectually open dialogue, even if we didn't necessarily agree. This was especially true regarding some of the language and subject matter in *Blind Justice*. It was very supportive and reinforcing when she inserted editorial notes indicating she sensed my discomfort. I sincerely thank her.

Dedication

This book is dedicated to my children, Jay, Kelly, Katy, and Max. Not many authors would choose to have their children review a draft of their novel. However, they are all young adults, very bright, astute readers, and good writers. And they were raised in an environment where they were encouraged to engage in critical thinking and, with respect, freely express their opinions, which they did without reservation.

Individually and collectively, they were patient, encouraging, gave their opinions, their time, and effort in reviewing my draft. Most importantly, their observations and comments were insightful and illuminating, and, at times, challenging. But I would never have agreed to their reviewing my draft if I did not have confidence in their analytical ability and respect for their opinions.

As any author knows, if they had expressed agreement with everything in the draft, it would've been a disservice to them and me. I thank them.

BLIND JUSTICE

CHAPTER 1

Snow drifted serenely to the ground. Andrea Bocelli was singing softly in the background when a fucking talking head suddenly appeared on the television screen. Scott fumbled for the remote. A "Talking Head" was Scott's cynical label applied to lawyers acting as Independent Counsel when, yet *another* public figure had gotten into yet *another* mess. Even though he had managed to mute the sound, he could do without a reminder. Talking Heads comforted the public, but for him, they stirred up negative memories.

Dinner tonight was grilled salmon, small red bliss potatoes, steamed asparagus, a mustard sauce with capers and a nice, moderately dry white wine. Increasingly, as he matured, he had broadened his palette and developed his cooking skills. Most women he met interpreted his statement that he could and liked to cook as meaning he "grilled." When the occasion arose where he could "cook" for them, they were always pleasantly surprised to have erred. While not a gourmet cook, he was a lot of fun in the kitchen.

The finer elements of presenting a dinner table weren't his forte, but Scott wasn't the least bit embarrassed or hesitant in seeking advice; in fact, he appreciated a woman who complemented his skills. They, in turn, enjoyed preparing a meal together, which he always enjoyed. He had been successful enough to satisfy his wish for a commercial-style kitchen with all stainless-steel appliances, a Zero Degree refrigerator, a natural gas range, solid granite counter tops, and all the various utensils and appliances that a "chef" needed from time to time.

Notwithstanding his personal and marital history, he was rather proud to count himself among a small minority of men who, in addition to the usual male appetites, liked and enjoyed women as people. As a result, Scott had a number of very close women friends in whom he confided and whose advice he both sought and valued.

Although he had lived and practiced law in the DC area early in his career, he had been away for many years before finally deciding to return 15 years ago. He had always loved the area. For the most part, he had a very pleasant history here. Gravitating back, then, had been fairly easy for him. Traffic and congestion were sometimes annoying, but at the same time it was invigorating living in the nation's capital knowing that some of the most important events in the world were being decided at that moment around other fireplaces in the city.

He was also extremely fond of all of the restaurants, the diverse ethnic and cultural ambiance, and the opportunity to buy so many different types of foods to prepare whether he wanted to cook or buy some prepared goodies. Dean & DeLuca on M Street in Georgetown was a favorite.

His guest for dinner on this particular night was a woman he'd known off and on for a few years since his divorce and return to DC

Normally, he would wait until his friend arrived so that they could have Grey Goose martinis with a lemon twist, although the absence of vermouth caused it not to be a real martini. However, it had been a good, but long week, and a drink was very much in order. As he finished the prep work, he decided to have a glass of wine in front of the fireplace. The combination of the falling snow and the crackling fireplace led his mind to drift off to memories of his first few years practicing law.

Maybe it goes back to the time when our ancestors lived in caves when there was little to do at night but silently stare into a fire. In any event, it was comfortable for him because growing up in a small community, life for boys centered around the Boy Scouts and spending an enormous amount of time in the woods staring into blazing fires.

Gazing at the burning coals, his mind drifted back many years to when he first "arrived" in Washington in 1971. His views of life and exposure to the real world were vastly different from many of his colleagues. He had done and experienced many uncommon things in his youth. And it was this history that had compelled him to do everything in his power, when the time came, to ensure that his children would never know life as he had. While he was naive about many things, especially when he first arrived in Washington, he did bring with him knowledge far beyond his years about the darker sides of people and the wicked things they could and would do.

CHAPTER 2

An odd and improbable set of circumstances evolved in 1971 offering Scott Carmichael the possibility to move to Washington to work for a United States Senator from his home state. Although he had yet to graduate from law school, there were many things in his background that instilled him with confidence. Fundamentally, because he had been working since the age of nine, he had come to believe that he could do just about anything if someone showed him how. Shy, retiring, and subservient were labels no one applied to him.

Two members of his law school class, Sam and Raymond, were his good friends. Each had worked for a United States Senator from his home state before enrolling in law school. From time to time, they would encourage Scott to go to Washington and work for the "Senator." But Scott was apolitical.

His marriage to Sandy had been on the rocks for a number of years and had continued well into law school. At that time, they had lived together for only about three of the five years of the marriage. Ultimately, not from his friends' urging, but seeing it as a possible environmental change and solution to his marriage woos, or, at least, a new beginning, in the early spring of 1970, he applied for employment in the Senator's office. They were gearing up for a very important reelection campaign for the first serious challenge the Senator had experienced in 20 years. It was said that his office was going to hire two lawyers and two MBA-types. Scott was due to graduate midyear of 1971, so after submitting his application, he gave it no more thought.

One week before the Christmas holiday, he had a 48-hour take-home income-tax exam. He was asleep when the phone rang that Friday morning around 8:30 a.m. It was a call from the secretary of the Senator's AA in Washington. He had no idea what "AA" was and had to ask her. "I am Secretary to the Senator's Administrative Assistant."

He quickly incorporated "Beltway" lingo (another term he didn't know) into his side of the conversation by using the "AA" reference. Later, he learned that some AAs merely ran the office while others had a strong power-base because they were an advisor in their Senator's state politics. This Senator's AA was the latter.

"We received your application, and we are trying to set up an appointment for the AA to interview you. We want to set it up in Tulsa, OK." Tulsa was about a hundred miles from where Scott went to school. Sleepily, he agreed to the interview, hung up the phone, and then got up to have some coffee.

After a few sips, his mind began to emerge into the light; he was certain that she had made a mistake and called the wrong person, so at about 10:00 a.m. he called her back.

"It's been almost a year since I sent the application. There must be some mistake. You called the wrong person."

"No, I did call the right person and we want to set up an interview." Again, they confirmed the appointment. "I will call back and tell you the time that the AA will be available."

Since it was during a Congressional recess, the AA had a meeting at the airport and that's where she wanted to arrange Scott's interview. Scott mentioned that he had a 48-hour take home exam but let her know that he could work that out.

Later, she called back. "The AA had received an invitation to go pheasant hunting. Could we change the place of the meeting to Oklahoma City?" It was about 220 miles from his school.

He reminded her about his exam and that he was running out of time. Not exactly overwhelmed by it all, he replied rather sarcastically, "Are you going to be calling back in another two hours to change the meeting to a location that's even further, you know, like Dallas?"

She reassured him: "There will be no further changes."

He hung up the phone slowly. Not only was he shocked by the call, but he believed there was not even a remote possibility of him even getting the job. There were three reasons for his concern.

First, Sam, who persuaded him to apply for the job, was, to say the least, a bit of a rebel. The Senator was really big on education because he himself had only graduated from high school and had never attended college or law school. Even today, in some states, an individual can study law under the tutelage of an attorney and sit for the bar exam, which was the path the Senator chose. Nevertheless, he was a supremely accomplished attorney and a widely known world figure. He demonstrated unquestionable skill, talent, and tenacity in responding to every challenge.

He was from the era when there was no prohibition against a Senator serving on multiple major Senate Committees. Thus, he, as well as many of his colleagues, served on several, if not all, of the five major committees, often chairing or being the vice chair on one or two, as well as chairman of a subcommittee or two. In those days, the Southern Senators controlled the major committees and subcommittees, and were referred to as the "Southern Block." They had real horsepower!

Sam was suffering stress and fatigue from full-time employment with the Senator and going to school at night. Although the Senator did not have a close personal relationship with minor staff members, he was interested and inquired from time to time how things were going for them. After all, he had given them a job that paid more than enough to live on and go to school. One day, in a very casual way, the Senator inquired about whether Sam knew the Senator's grandson who was also attending George Washington University (GW) as an undergraduate.

GW is a major university with a tremendous number of regular full-time students, not to mention all of the night students from government and industry in both the undergraduate and graduate schools. Sam had barely been more than introduced to the grandson, but he casually indicated that he had not seen the grandson on campus.

Given the Senator's rural background and limited knowledge of going to a major university, he found this curious. The Senator did not realize that GW did not have a "campus" with grass and so forth as he had envisioned. Rather, it was an urban university, and the streets were the campus. His suspicions aroused, the Senator had one of his staff check on Sam's class status only to find that he had dropped out. It didn't matter that he only skipped a quarter. To the Senator, this was a falsehood, deceptive, and a betrayal of the purpose of giving him a job. Suddenly, there was one fewer staff member! Moreover, Sam had the dubious distinction, according to him, of being the only staff member the Senator ever personally fired! In this distinction, he enjoyed a perverse pleasure, a viewpoint no doubt communicated in some fashion to the Senator and the AA.

Second, Raymond was from Texas. West Texas, where the land is flat to the horizon and people drive … like they damned well pleased! That is to say, they never drive less than 100 miles per hour, except at intersections prohibiting cutting across the corners. And, if that wasn't enough, the sin of all sins, he was also a liberal! It's a wonder that the staff member who hired them did not lose their job.

In any event, Scott was fairly certain from Raymond's description that he was not considered to be one of the office's prime staff members and that if he were to be asked by a potential employer if he would be rehired, it was a no-brainer that the answer would be no. And thinking it would help him to get the job, before he appreciated the detrimental impact of the relationships, Scott let it be known that these two were his classmates *and* friends!

Finally, the most important reason why Scott did not believe that he would be hired was because he was, given a fairly distinctive history growing up in small town America and experiencing the effects of the stereotypic, hypocritical, Southern Baptist mentality, to become and remain most of his adult life, a liberal *and* a rebel, with a cause! But, then again, liberals and rebels always believed they have a cause. Exacerbating his "mental" deficiencies, he was also quite fond of his long hair, mustache and sideburns, or "Pork Chops," as they were called.

After graduation, Raymond had accepted a job with the Law Student Division of the American Bar Association. Because Scott had become quite active in the Law Student Division as well, he was going to Chicago on a monthly basis. So, while on his trips, Scott stayed with him. It also gave him relief from his dead marriage and time away from Sandy. Two-day meetings stretched into four to five days trips. It would have been longer if he had met a woman, but, for him, Chicago really was the Windy City with the coldest of winds blowing in off Lake Michigan.

One thing Scott always liked about Chicago was that you could always get a good meal and a drink on Sunday. On one trip, they were having lunch at a local bar before his plane left. He was scheduled to meet with the Senator the next day for an interview at the Senator's "down-state" office. Although his meeting with the AA had gone well, months had passed without follow-up contact. He felt one reason might be because when the secretary had asked how the AA would recognize him at the airport, Scott indicated that he had long hair and a mustache. A long pause had ensued. He felt the AA was trapped but he kept the interview with Scott anyway.

Most people would have cut their mustache and hair. It was, after all, a wonderful opportunity for him to get a good job and to get the hell out of Dodge.

But, oh, yes! He did have one thing possibly going for him. In the second telephone conversation with the AA's secretary, she said she had noticed the name of his hometown. She asked him: "Do you know a girl named Ann Padgett?"

"Yes." Hey! We are talking about a town of seventy-five hundred!

"Ann is my first cousin," she said.

In knee-jerk fashion, void of any diplomacy, Scott blurted out, "Wait a minute! Ann's my first cousin also! Who the hell are you? I never heard of you."

It turned out that she was a cousin on Ann's mother's side, a family name he hadn't heard often, but recognized immediately. That made the AA's secretary his second, third, or some kind of cousin. He wasn't really sure which. It was a weak connection, but what the hell!

Ann's mother, Cindy, was always one of his most favored people in the world. She was, in some ways, more of a mother to him than his own mother. Throughout the years, all the times he told stories about her, he had always described her as looking and acting like the Grand Ole Opry star, Minnie Pearl, only without the hat and 10 times as nuts.

As Scott and Raymond waited for their flight, he asked Scott, "Are you going to *cut* your mustache and *trim* your hair?"

"Not only no, but *hell* no!"

"You know you don't have a chance of getting a job with him if you don't at least trim your hair and cut your mustache?"

"One way or the other, I don't expect a job, so why should I bother trimming my hair or cutting my mustache? When I interviewed with the AA, I didn't do anything to my long hair or mustache. I feel that it mustn't have mattered, or I would not be having a follow-up interview with the Senator."

Scott just wasn't thinking very responsibly. Although he was telling Raymond, and himself, he really didn't care, he did. He simply did not have any experience at bending and didn't want to even know how.

Time came for his meeting with the Senator and Scott could tell from the first moment the Senator walked into the room and saw him that the Senator instantly wanted to be somewhere else. Anywhere else! Within 30 seconds after the interview started, the Senator began looking at his watch. "I will be leaving soon because I promised my wife I would see her to the airport." Considering that the Senator had at least one chauffeur and he had been married a lifetime, Scott really didn't think it was urgent that he see his wife to the airport. Naive, yes! Stupid, no!

In fact, Scott was so naive about Washington that he did not know about available jobs. While sitting in the interview, it occurred to him that because he had been so disinterested, he had never discussed with his friends any of the details about what they actually did in the Senator's office. Even when he was in Chicago having lunch with Raymond before the interview, the topic never came up. The focus of the conversation had been Scott's hair and mustache.

As the Senator asked more questions, Scott's answers became vaguer. The more the Senator's questions were met with vagueness, the unhappier he became and the more frequently he looked at his watch. Finally, Scott knew there wasn't a prayer of his getting a job, but he couldn't understand why the Senator was becoming so irritated. Scott was soon convinced it wasn't really his hair or mustache, but rather, his answers were without substance.

When Scott knew that all else was lost and he didn't have a snowball's prayer, all he wanted to do was get the hell out of there. He began to think of some way to tell the Senator that whatever his impression was of him, he was wrong. Great job interview technique for sure! Tell a senior United States Senator that he was wrong! Needless to say, Scott was not so naive or stupid to think that he should do that. So, how could he get the message across without doing just that? As much as a liberal and a maverick as he was, he had not been raised to be discourteous to people, especially, senior citizens. And he certainly was not going to be discourteous to someone as accomplished as the Senator, at least not intentionally.

Because he had been unresponsive or generally vague in his answers to most of the Senator's questions, he began to get the impression that the Senator thought that all he wanted was a 9-5 job. That goal was what Scott called "being on the government tit." Given the Senator's background, if Scott were right, he could easily understand why, to the Senator, Scott was "waving a red flag in front of the bull."

So, at the appropriate time, Scott spoke up. "Senator, I'm not sure how, but I feel that I have given you an *incorrect* impression about what I want to do in Washington. I do not know much about Washington, don't know about the types of jobs available, and I do not know a lot about what jobs are even available in your office. I do not necessarily like coming in to work at 9:00 a.m., nor do I like leaving at 5 p.m. Essentially, I don't mind working hard, long hours, but I really do not do well with a regimen or being on a rigid schedule."

To this day, Scott still doesn't know or understand where that little speech came from or why he included comments about coming to work, a regimen or a rigid schedule. He knew it made no sense at the time and that it wasn't connected to the conversation. Maybe it was just because it was straightforward, honest, and he owned up to the fact that he had no idea what the hell he was doing. But what he did know for sure and was clear about explaining was that he was willing to work hard, long hours, something he'd done all of his life.

Unexpectedly, the tone of the interview shifted from frigid to very warm and congenial.

"Have you met my Legislative Assistant?" asked the Senator.

"No."

"Let me call him in. I do have to run to the airport, but he can talk to you while I am gone."

The Senator introduced him to the Legislative Assistant and left for the airport. The "LA" (now Scott was really into Beltway talk) and Scott talked.

Things were on a roll! Then it came time for him to graduate; it was January 1971. Scott's income-tax professor gave him an F. He truly deserved a D, not because he had earned it, but because he was a graduating senior, and it would have gotten him the hell out of law school.

He had gotten through undergraduate French after leaving the Army, but that was because of a tall, blond TA who had agreed with him that he had no chance of passing, but she would give him a D so that he could graduate. She had even agreed with him that, under the circumstances, there was no need to go through the charade of even taking the final. At the time, he had been admitted to dental school, but that is another story.

Anyway, this professor had a hard on for him because Scott detested income-tax. He would sit in class listening to him drone on and on about income-tax. The professor was getting an erection and Scott was fearful of chronic flaccidity if he did not get out of there. The classroom was a slim rectangle with built-in tables, anchored by iron pipes, on each side of a long center isle seating about three or four students per side. To leave the class, Scott had to walk up that center isle directly facing the professor and go out the door in the corner to Scott's right. And there was no such thing as subtlety in leaving that classroom. If skin truly could scream or crawl, Scott's would have done that so many times. When he could take no more, he would just get up and walk out.

Later, when he went back in the summer of 1971 to take the bar exam, his classmates all made it known that it was common knowledge that his tax professor had flunked him to get even for repeatedly walking out of his class. One of the times after he had left, the professor slowly moved his head from side to side and told the entire class, in a slow drawl, "Something has to be done about that boy!"

After his professor had flunked him, he thought his whole life had come to an end. Some of the older law students, his crowd, had been in the service or held jobs, sometimes both, before enrolling in law school. They hung out at a bar called Maxine's. The bar probably wasn't more than 18 feet wide and about 60 feet long. It was the kind of dark bar with dark wood and really cold beer that made for a great place to hang out. In the front part, usually at the tables, were the regulars who were all retired railroad men. Most still wore their railroad bib overalls and hats with their paraphernalia and railroad memorabilia pins on their chest. In the middle part of the bar were the red necks, and in the rear, was his law school crowd. Anyone who has ever experienced being in bright sunlight, opening a door, staring into a dark bar and all they could see were neon signs and the whites of people's eyes, has been to a "Maxine's."

So, there he was, 28 years old, married, with a baby daughter, and things were not going well at all. Scott spent the next three days at Maxine's getting drunk, feeling sorry for himself and talking to a guy about being a co-driver on a tractor-trailer to Mexico to pick up a load of midwinter watermelons. Both were more appealing at that time than anything else he could think about.

Whenever life handed Scott a bag of lemons, eventually, he always figured out a way to make lemonade. He already knew that in times when he was down, he was not out! Understandably, he knew these things just had to run their course even if during the morass he couldn't see his way clear to a solution.

After a few more days of feeling sorry for himself, Scott started recovering and thinking about what to do. Historically, once a solution presented itself, his recovery morphed very quickly into his being very proactive.

His attention became riveted on salvaging a job with the Senator's office. It hadn't been offered, but he thought maybe he could make something happen without them finding out about the F. Although there was no definite start date, he still felt that he could get a job.

His effort began with making an appointment with the Dean of the law school. The Dean appeared to be uneasy with the situation. He made it fairly clear, without saying anything directly, that he was aware of the situation. Scott sensed that the Dean knew that the professor had flunked him out of retribution. Nevertheless, the Dean indicated that there was nothing that he could do. Scott explained his opportunity in Washington, but still, he would not budge.

"I am very sympathetic and fully understand your circumstances. However, there is still nothing that I can do. But the Dean of the George Washington Law School is a personal friend of mine. If you are admitted and take any course that you have not taken before and make at least a C, I will accept it and you can receive your degree in the spring. You may use my name when you call the school."

So, on a cold Thursday afternoon, Scott called the AA. "Has the decision been made about hiring anyone?"

"Sorry, Scott. No decision has been made about hiring anyone yet."

"I would like to come to Washington right way to work for the Senator and finish law school there. I heard that you have jobs you can plug people into while they are in school."

"You mean a patronage job?" the AA replied.

"Yes, that's exactly what I mean!"

"We don't have any patronage jobs right now because we just gave out the last two we had to another senator, but I will check around because a number of senators owe us favors. Also, since the Senator is a very senior Senator, he generally gets anything he wants. I'll call around on the job question and you take care of admission to law school."

Scott's next step was to call the law school and talk to its Dean about admission. His call was taken by the Dean's secretary. He introduced himself and explained the circumstances of the income-tax course and liberally sprinkled the conversation with his Dean's name. They went over the spring schedule and talked about a couple of courses that he could take that were offered at night.

"That is all well and good, but I need to talk to the Dean," Scott demanded.

"Why?"

"So, I can be admitted to GW law school,"

In a matter-of-fact tone, the secretary told him, "There is no need to talk to the Dean. *I* just admitted you!"

Welcome to the ways of Washington! That was Scott's first introduction to the power a personal secretary could use for, or against you, as well as a brief, *very* positive introduction to a new kind of woman. After that experience, he never again took for granted, or underestimated a woman whose occupational label included the word "secretary."

On the following Monday, Scott called the AA back and told him that his law school mission was successful, and the AA told him that they had a job for him.

"I will be leaving Tuesday morning and, barring an accident, I will see you Friday morning at your office."

He packed up a few belongings, loaded his 1969 Pontiac Le Mans, and kissed Sandy and his daughter, Debbie, goodbye. But just as he was preparing to leave, she asked, "When will we be coming up?"

"I don't know."

And he drove away.

CHAPTER 3

Scott's route to DC was due east through Tennessee on I-40 where it connected with I-81 running southwest to northeast up through the Shenandoah Valley in Virginia. At the time, neither interstate was completed. Travelers still used two lane state roads in many sections of an incomplete Interstate system.

It was an arduous trip complicated by the fact that he was trying to adjust to new hard contacts. It was a miserable experience to say the least. He had forgotten to take them out the night before the trip and slept with them in. Consequently, driving that morning was horrific as he suffered through burning eyes and blurred vision. Wearing his glasses didn't improve anything either. Further complicating matters, he was racing Northeast in front of a fast-moving ice storm.

Driving up through the Shenandoah Valley on I-81, he turned east on US211 at Luray, Virginia, and headed east toward Washington. At that time, I-66 only extended from the D.C area to Gainesville, Virginia. He picked it up there and headed toward the Beltway at Tysons Corner. So far, it was a very normal route.

Both then and now, no local would ever follow his ill-advised arrival route into the DC area. In blissful ignorance, he proceeded counterclockwise on the Beltway toward Springfield, Virginia, arriving due south of Washington, at the infamous, nightmarish, multiple highway intersection area known as the "mixing bowl," which was perpetually under construction. Worse yet, it was February 8, 1971, dark, snowing and rush hour!

From there, he headed north to DC on what was then I-95, now I-495. By the time he reached the intersection of Glebe Road and I-95, he was totally exhausted. He pulled into a Holiday Inn. For some 30 years, it or another flag hotel stood in that spot. For many years afterwards, driving north past that location, Scott always had flashbacks of his first trip to the area and that hotel.

The next day, he went to the Senator's office. He didn't have any place to stay, so the AA arranged for him to stay temporarily with Andy, another member of the Senator's staff who was somewhat younger than Scott. Andy lived a couple of blocks from the Capital at 1st and D SE. It was an efficiency apartment with one bed, so Scott slept on a cheap, flimsy, folding aluminum cot, which was "somewhat" uncomfortable. It had a broken spring with a sharp point about where Scott's crotch was so that there was always a rude awakening if he turned over on his stomach, especially in the morning!

He didn't know anyone, and all the members of the Senator's staff were also younger, so he didn't have much in common with them. However, one night, Andy invited him to a party above Georgetown on upper Wisconsin near the Old Europe Restaurant. The Senator was a very conservative southern Senator and Scott was shocked to walk into the party and see most of the young members of his staff smoking grass. It was also a double shock for Scott because he had never even seen it!

Since he was separated from Sandy, it was a fairly lonely and unhappy time. But he did not broadcast his status and kept a low profile. He didn't care much for the bar scene and, although he was not opposed to female company, he had never picked up a woman in a bar in his life. In this arena, he was simply inept. He didn't know what to say. If he was introduced to somebody at an apartment party, he was OK, but the bar scene was not his thing. He still had youthful energy, but no one began socializing until around 10:00 p.m. In fact, no one thought anything about going out until then.

From 1st and D SE, he walked a couple of blocks up to the local restaurant and bar scene on the 2nd and 3rd blocks of Pennsylvania Avenue SE, beginning catty-corner from the main Library of Congress building. It was referred to as going up on the "Avenue." In that block, were two bars he liked: Duddingtons and the Hawk and Dove.

On the corner at the end of the 300 block was Roland's Grocery, a small neighborhood grocery where even the police double parked and didn't bother you when you did. Often, they were double parking *with* you. At that time, at 1st and Pennsylvania SE, the entire block on which they later built a new Library of Congress building catty-corner from the Capital, was a clay parking lot. It became a mud hole when it rained; but parking places were scarce as hen's teeth and people were desperate for a place to park, so they took their chances parking there.

Andy introduced him to that area. Being a creature of habit, he continued going to the first place Andy had showed him – a bar called Duddingtons. It had a restaurant upstairs and a bar downstairs where you could also get food and dance. It was named Whitby's Underground, but to everyone in that area, it was just the "Underground."

Outside access was a separate street-level doorway on the left next to Duddingtons. You walked downstairs with a wall on your left. At the bottom of the stairway there was a bar area to the right. The bar was horseshoe-shaped. As you turned to your right, the curved part of the horseshoe was away from you to your left and the open bottom part was nearest to you. It was closed off for the servers to place and pick up their orders.

Walking to the right, past the closed part of the bar, to the far wall and turning around, the view was of the far wall at the bottom of the stairs where you entered. It was covered in wallpaper about eight by twelve feet. There was a blowup picture of a Boeing 727 in a "flare" landing position, i.e., nose up, gears down, flaps down, landing almost straight at you with big puffs of smoke coming from the tires as they touched the runway. Being an aviation buff and frustrated fighter jockey, Scott loved it!

He had his routine when he went to the Underground. He never came in without going to the far wall and turning around to look at the mural. No matter what music was actually playing at that time, when he looked at that mural, he always heard the piercing sound of jet engines and screeching tires touching down at the beginning of the Beatles' "Back in the USSR!"

At that time, Scott had no way of knowing that the Underground was to become a significant part of his personal and professional history!

CHAPTER 4

The next four years of Scott's life were separate two-year chapters, at least from a working and school standpoint. Since his arrival in Washington in February of 1971, his life revolved around his patronage job at the U.S. Capitol, working on constituent matters in the Senator's office, and finishing law school at GW that spring.

A few months after living with Andy and finishing law school, Scott found a townhouse in the 2100 block of N. Brandywine St. in Arlington, Virginia near the intersection of Lee Highway and Glebe Road. For a brief two months in the summer before he took the bar exam, Sandy and Debbie came to Washington. Sandy had barely stepped off the plane in June when she announced, "My father told me that if things didn't work out, to call him and he'd pay our way home."

It didn't exactly create a warm atmosphere for a "new beginning." In any event, after taking the bar examine in July, they returned to DC They didn't even make it through August. Scott came home one afternoon and told her: "I think it's time for you to call your father!"

After she left, he found himself in a two-story townhouse with a pine paneled basement. The first floor was completely bare except for a sofa bed. The second floor had a double bed, a single bed, and his gray Samsonite suitcase.

There were some meager kitchen items that were given to him by his mother when he got out of the service in 1964. In her haste to take all of the wedding gifts, Sandy neglected to take the blades for the still unused GE electric carving knife. They would remain in his kitchen drawer for the next 20+ years, absolutely brand new, still in the plastic sleeve. He used them with guests as a humorous way to start a story about his failed marriage.

A short time after Sandy left, two female friends entered his life. Susan dated Scott's friend Sam in law school and Cynthia was a friend of hers. They had come to Washington to work for the Senator on one of the subcommittees he chaired. The three of them were all on their own in the city and a little bit lonesome. They were comfortable spending time together and did not worry about having to date just so they would not be alone. In fact, the girls rented an efficiency apartment in the same building where he stayed with Andy. And, coincidently, they also had a sofa bed. He used to stay over quite often with nothing happening but sleeping.

One Saturday morning, Susan went shopping around eight o'clock. Cynthia and Scott stayed in bed asleep. Suddenly, they were awakened by Susan speaking in a frantic, whispered tone: "You have to get up! I ran into a friend from school. She insists on saying hello to Cynthia!" The girls looked like they were about to lose it. This was a problem.

"What are we going to do with Scott?" asked a now panicked Cynthia.

Those were not the days where men slept over platonically and you certainly did not want anyone to know if it wasn't platonic, especially since there were two of them. Either way, they were *screwed*!

Since it was an efficiency apartment, the only other room was the bathroom. Quickly and quietly, Scott grabbed his clothes and shoes and dashed into the bathroom and got into the bathtub behind the shower curtain. It all happened so quickly that there was no time for him to get dressed or do anything else. So, there he was, nervously standing clothed only in his Army boxer shorts, holding his shoes and clothes in his arms!

He could hear them talking outside. He almost had a heart attack when he heard, "Can I use your bathroom?"

There was no time to react. Susan and Cynthia couldn't refuse. The next thing he knew, the door opened, the unwanted guest came in, and closed the door. His mind was in a panic, racing, and bouncing back and forth between his fear and their fear out in the apartment. He was terrified to even breathe because there was absolutely no noise whatsoever in the bathroom and he felt if he even so much as breathed, it would be impossible for her not to hear him. If possible, he panicked even more when he thought about how women were so nosy about other women's bathrooms and their housekeeping habits. He was certain when she finished, she was going to look behind the shower curtain. He was completely trapped!

His heart was racing 90 miles an hour and he was wondering what he would say if she looked behind the curtain. "Hi or Boo!" And, if it wasn't awkward enough already, he had never heard a woman going to the bathroom! Nevertheless, he was grateful she did, and he took advantage of the noise to take a slight breath. As she was finishing up, he realized it was show and tell time! Fortunately, she washed her hands and left.

Immediately after they said their goodbyes, Susan and Cynthia let him know it was safe to come out. It was a toss-up as to which of them experienced the most intense panic during this episode. They all needed time to catch their breath. But after exchanging their respective sides of the adventure, each ended up hysterically laughing. And then they all noticed something. Throughout this exchange, Scott was still standing there in his Army boxer shorts, holding onto his clothes and shoes. And his grip was so tight, he could barely let go and get dressed.

For a while, he dated a woman of Italian heritage who was a tour guide at the Capital. She introduced him to grass and porno movies! Years later, every time he saw Elizabeth Vargas on ABC, he thought of her because of the strong resemblance between the two women. She had a friend who was the assistant manager at the Translux Theater on 14th St. NW, one of two porno theaters in DC Despite strait-laced Nixon being in the White House, the strip club, night club, cheap bar, prostitution, and porno district were all a mere two blocks down New York Avenue NW from the White House.

She and her friends used to like to go to porno movies as a group, usually as couples. It was very interesting to learn that the theater had portioned off the balcony upstairs as a private viewing area with couches and lounge chairs. And that area was enclosed with a large Plexiglass window at the edge of the balcony through which people could watch the movie. It was a very interesting experience for Scott.

Working at the Capital was an eye-opening experience for him as well. The people that worked around the Senate galleries included plainclothes policemen, uniformed Capital Police, full-time employees on the payroll of the Secretary of the Senate and patronage people from various Senators' offices.

At that time, there were no legalized lotteries or off-track betting parlors. Nevertheless, every morning, one of the plainclothes police officers would come around and take everybody's numbers bets.

One of the regular employees working with Scott was a young fellow who was what was known as an "accommodation" drug dealer. That is, he couldn't afford to buy marijuana for himself, so he would buy a pound and quickly sell all but an ounce to get his money back. The profit would allow him to have his ounce for free for his girlfriend and himself. Then he would repeat the process, often two or three times a week. Labeling him as an accommodation drug dealer did not change the fact that right at the Senate gallery doors in the United States Capital, Scott was, in fact, working with a number's runner and drug dealer. At least, if there was ever a problem, that certainly would be the way it would read in the papers.

Susan and Cynthia had never seen a porno movie. Before going to see them with his Italian friend, Scott had only seen old, jerky, blurry, black and white home movie type porno films. So, one Saturday afternoon, they decided to go to the Translux. Although it is very common for men to wear trench coats to the movies, as it happened, that day, it was actually raining. Aside from the oddity of each of them coincidently wearing trench coats, the awkwardness was compounded by the fact that they were the only women in the theater. Even though it was their first time ever being in a porno theater, it was rather obvious from the equal spacing of all the men what was going on with them.

No doubt they generated even more attention since they were good looking, and they were with him. Without thinking, Scott simply went down to the middle of the aisle and picked seats in the very middle of the row because that's where he might normally sit in any theater. It was, to say the least, very interesting to sit there with two young attractive women, one on each side, in a theater of men who were there alone, for obvious reasons. After the movie started, the trio was very quiet, but Scott could hear his friends' respective breathing deepen, as did his. Coincidentally, after the movie, although none of them smoked, they each had a ravaging appetite!

Back to the real world, one Sunday afternoon, Susan and Cynthia wanted to go to a regular movie and do some shopping. Since neither had a car, as usual, Scott drove them. He had seen an article in the *Washington Post* about using wagon wheels covered with Plexiglass as coffee tables. He happened to comment on the article and how he thought that was especially neat, so they bought him a wagon wheel for $20 in appreciation for his taxi service.

Nevertheless, Scott still found himself most nights in his townhouse with only two beds and the Samsonite suitcase on the top floor. Odd as it sounds, he had adjusted to having no furniture and living out of a suitcase, literally. That continued for another year. A sofa bed and that wagon wheel were all that was on the first floor. The pine-paneled basement, with shag carpet, contained his television and a small desk.

Eventually, in early 1972, he decided it was time to do some "decorating." Susan had a nice figure and would not have impressed someone as being very strong, but she was actually athletic and quite strong. They began moving the sofa bed to the basement. It was an extremely heavy king-sized sofa bed. They had it about halfway in the kitchen and halfway in the narrow basement stairwell when it decided to spring open.

So, there they were. She was in the kitchen and he was in the basement stairwell. They were at such a bad angle that he thought she was going to have to call the fire department to come and get him out of the basement since it blocked the whole doorway, and they could not get the bed closed. That was the extent of his "decorating."

Such as it was, being in the basement felt like being in a house full of furniture with the things one would expect to see in a den. Only when he came up out of the "man cave" did he realize he was still in a townhouse with two virtually empty floors.

Somehow, he got the idea to enter graduate law studies at GW. He was unable to be admitted straight out into the Master of Law (LLM) program on his undergraduate grades; however, GW had a program that admitted students on a provisional basis. Thereafter, if their work were satisfactory, they would be admitted into the LLM program. He began taking night classes and was doing well.

There were several young ladies living next door that had parties on their patio, but he was so much into his studies that he was oblivious to an evening party, even with his windows and back door open. However, he made a major mistake when he was finishing up his studies the following summer when he was getting his divorce by working *and* taking 14 hours. He made a D in a course, which lowered his GPA, and he was unable to finish and obtain his LLM. Time got away from him and he never did return.

The next year floated by uneventfully with the exception that he somehow got it into his head that there might be some hope for his marriage, notwithstanding the fact that they had been separated more than they had lived together. In any event, in the summer of 1973, he contacted a small university back home and obtained a part-time teaching position to begin in the fall of 1973. He was going to teach labor law, insurance, real property and business law. He was very excited about it because he had always wanted to teach. It was his intention to return to his home state, salvage his marriage, teach college, and obtain a job with a law firm.

Unfortunately, the idea of getting an LLM was unimpressive to anyone with whom he interviewed. His original choice was to focus on income tax just to show his former income tax professor, however, he couldn't bring himself to do it, so he chose Government Procurement Law. It is the study of government contract law, which is doing business with the Federal government. When he interviewed, they did everything but yawn when he mentioned an LLM in Government Procurement Law.

At that time, doing business with the Federal government was essentially limited to the large metropolitan areas and large law firms. It didn't matter that he was taking courses under Nash and Cibinic, the recognized authorities in Government Procurement Law who literally wrote the leading law book on the subject! Today, doing business with the Federal or State government is big business everywhere. But, for Scott in 1973, it represented just another example of bad timing.

As the time approached for him to return for yet another run at salvaging his marriage, teaching college, and getting a job, the stress became excruciating. Finally, one day in late August, he realized that there was absolutely no way that he could return to that marital nightmare! So, at high noon, he went over to the Senator's office and got on the Federal Telephone Service, which was free anywhere you called in the world, and he told Sandy that he was not going to come back.

"You have never kept your word about anything ever and I cannot afford to invest any more of my life with you," he stated matter-of-factly. As he spoke, he was so nervous, he was trembling. He couldn't understand why. There had been so many breakups but none where they had a conversation like this. Nevertheless, his mind was absolutely crystal clear, and he decided that this time, it was different and a done deal, not out of anger, but he was through!

At last, unlike all the other separations they had experienced during their tumultuous marriage, he had emotionally broken free. He experienced a physical reaction equivalent to taking off a large pack. But this also meant that he had to give up his teaching job.

Since he had planned to go back home, he had also given up his job with the Senator. His hair wasn't as long now, but he still had the mustache. Even though he had been hired, these physical characteristics, the dim view taken of his marital situation, and no doubt some of his own personality traits, had left Scott without any support within the Senator's office for other employment. Being a senior Senator, it was no more than an aide making a casual phone call to the Justice Department or wherever for a good position, but no phone calls were made on his behalf. While his position was one of the Senator's patronage slots, technically, he was carried on the payroll by the Office of the Secretary of the Senate.

After a few hours, the euphoria of severing the cord subsided. And then he began to panic when he realized that he had burned all his bridges, without any thought of his financial circumstances. All of his money consisted of $3.15!

In desperation, he went to the Secretary of the Senate and explained his situation. They had had their run-ins before since patronage personnel were not regular employees under his authority. In the final analysis, sometimes patronage personnel were the tails that waged the dog. Going to school, they often missed most late sessions and created friction with full-time employees, especially, when sessions ran late toward the end of a term. If the sessions ran longer than two hours after the classes were over, they were supposed to return to work. But often, the patronage people did not return when it was obvious their classes were over, Scott included.

Tourists from all over the world come to the Capital. Sometimes Scott pretended to be a Secret Service Agent, security personnel, or something or other. It really didn't matter, and he knew it. Young women were impressed by the mere fact that he was there and obviously belonged. It didn't take much for him to generate a fixated stare if he was interested because he was already looking at them. But if he was really interested and intent on meeting them, he used his "stare" technique. The whole idea was to make them nervous, of which he took full advantage. Once he made eye contact, he became the tiger fixated on the limping deer.

His favorite target zone was a small seat in an alcove by a window directly across from where he usually stood. Women frequently sat there. Typically, after establishing eye contact, he would just walk over. Having already seen him across the wide hallway, they knew he belonged. Sometimes, he would just walk up, silently stand there and stare, just for effect. Then, he might inform them they were not supposed to be sitting there or asked them if they had identification. With foreigners, he was quick to ask for their passport. It was a pea picker's delight! Dates were easy and Scott had plenty of his own late-night sessions to attend.

Nevertheless, to his surprise, despite their history, the reception by the Secretary was warm and sympathetic to his circumstances. "I don't have any positions available like the patronage position you've had, but I do have a job running an elevator." This would be a real job on his payroll and Scott would be under his control. In his old position, Scott was paid close to $9,600 a year for an average workday of four hours. That was very good money for even a full-time job in 1971-73. "The elevator job does not pay as much as the other job you had, but it does pay about $6,500 a year. But you could work in the morning and look for a job in the afternoon. Also, the hours are consistent and there will be no late-night sessions." Scott thought to himself, at least not the kind that meant staying at the Capital.

So, on Monday, September 25, 1973, Scott was a 30-year-old licensed attorney with 24 hours of completed course work toward a Master of Law degree in Government Procurement Law at GW, separated, with a four-year-old child, and working as an elevator operator! Was life good or what?

CHAPTER 5

Scott was in the Underground on business on Thursday night, September 28, when he first saw Jennifer. The Underground had become his neighborhood bar. A week before, on Tuesday night, he was really down and had come in for a beer. Expecting only a few locals to be there, he was shocked to see it packed elbow deep. They were playing 50's music and immediately his spirits were lifted. Some of his office staff were there, so he had a chance to dance a lot with the new hire just up from Dallas. The music was fantastic, and it was especially fun because she danced the way they did back home at the University.

Later, he learned that a Georgetown student by the name of Nard had collected about fifteen hundred 45 rpm records and had worked a deal with bars to play music on their weekday "off" nights, usually meaning Tuesday, Wednesday, or Thursday. Many people on the Hill and DC worked well beyond five o'clock, so dinner hour and entertainment cranked up later than in most towns. Nard did several bars at the same time. So, whoever was playing the music, Nard got $50 and the music operator got all the beer they could drink. It was, without a doubt, a roaring success!

Scott had an idea to produce musical cassettes and market them to places like the

Holiday Inn to play on their off nights and pack their bars. For this to happen, he was back to talk to Nard. What he learned was, depending on whether the bar offered food and had somewhat of a dinner hour, they adjusted the kind of music they played. With a dinner hour, they began with slow music, low key and in a lower volume. Gradually, they would build up the tempo as people finished dinner.

Scott and Nard talked while Nard played records. After the business conversation was finished, around 10 o'clock, Scott decided to stick around for a while to see if all the excitement generated by the oldies was genuine or just a fluke for the night. He hadn't had a drink since he was there for business, but a crowd was building up, so he decided to order a drink and just stand around and check it out.

He noticed Jennifer immediately when she came in with a group of about a dozen girls and one guy. She was strikingly attractive, wearing tight jeans, a homemade-looking patch quilt type blouse, which she filled in a noticeable, abundant fashion. And although Scott had seen her first, he started dancing with her friend Carol instead. Carol had cameo beauty but had absolutely no interest in Scott and the conversational skills of the Sphinx!

After giving up on the Sphinx, Scott approached Jennifer. Seems the guy and the girls had all known each other from the same group of townhouses where they all lived. The guy had married one of their group and they now lived out of town. He was back on business, so they were all out to celebrate.

The moment they slowed danced and he felt her against him was the most erotic experience of his life! He desperately tried to maintain his composure. Things were going well at first.

"What is your name?'

"Jennifer ..." Her voice was very soft and sexy. As she spoke her name, a heavy beat of the music distorted her last name. They continued dancing, so there was a delay before he asked her to repeat her last name. During the delay, they continued slow dancing; he got carried away and kissed her on the ear. That *really* pissed her off! She refused to repeat her last name.

"Would you repeat your last name?"

"You *won't* need it!"

A young Marine started talking her up. Scott was still on his first drink and very sober. He was painfully aware that he was bad in this scenario! Consequently, he had consciously, consistently, avoided even trying. But he was *obsessed* with her! And, at the same time, he was aware of and yet ignored the fact that he was making a *total* fool of himself.

Sitting at the horseshoe-shaped bar, Jennifer had Scott on her right side and the Marine on the other. Not because that was where they had been sitting. When she and the Marine sat down, Scott just planted himself by her. She was working hard and succeeding in paying attention to the Marine and ignoring Scott. In fact, he mostly saw the back of her head. She did turn her head his way, not to talk to him, but to see if he was still there. And each time she turned his way, Scott immediately attempted to start a conversation. He felt like the little Puerto Rican dog stupidly bobbing its head in the back of a car whether anyone was looking or not!

Finally, after being in the Underground for only an hour and a half, he tore out a piece of the yellow pages, wrote his name and phone number on it, and handed it to her.

"I know you think I am trying to pick you up, but I am not. Here is my name and phone number. I would like for you to call me."

She looked at it and then at him. "You *must* be joking!"

After assuring her that he wasn't, he left, with his tail between his legs.

Scott was absolutely a disaster at remembering people's names. But for some reason, he remembered the Sphinx's name and that she worked for a congressman. Despite the disastrous experience with Jennifer at the bar, he was driven! The next day, the Sphinx was easy to locate through the Capital telephone operator. Speaking with Carol, he used the implausible excuse about a friend coming into town and wanting to get him a date with "Jennifer," but he did not remember her last name or have her phone number. Of course, he didn't care, but, at the same time, he was well aware of the awkwardness of his call. To his surprise, she gave him the information. Apparently, Jennifer hadn't mentioned the kiss.

He started calling the number right after five o'clock. There was no telling how many times he dialed the number. It was continuously busy until she answered around 10:30 p.m.

Even though he felt like a total fool, it was the last thing he was going to let her sense. There was absolutely no mention of how long he had been calling. Despite his nervousness, he acted very casual. "I'm glad I was able to catch up with you. I got your name and phone number from your friend, Carol." He never mentioned his nickname for Carol and never referred to her by that name during the course of the conversation.

"I know we didn't get off to a very good start last night. I'm sorry about that. But I really would like to go out with you. And I hope you can see how obvious it is that I was not trying to pick you up last night." Remembering the kiss on the ear, he started to say something but just didn't have the nerve. He did his best to dance around that subject. After more small talk, amazingly, he was able to convince her to go out with him the next night, Saturday!

They went to the Red Lion next to the GW campus just off Pennsylvania Avenue a few blocks from the White House and to his place for more drinks afterward. Later, they came back into town and had dinner around 2:00 a.m. at a place on Pennsylvania Avenue NW called Lil Abner's. It had pinball machines with short legs so you could eat on the glass top and play. They were having a really good time. As though the rocky start had never happened, conversation was easy and casual. He took her home at 4 a.m.

He was deliriously happy that she had agreed to have a second date the next night. She was to drive over to his place. He knew that this really meant she wanted to bring her car so she could leave if she wanted to. He was ready to spring the trap and she knew it. And he knew she knew it!

The next night, he cooked Cornish Game Hen, peas, and potatoes. He warmed that damned Cornish Game Hen until it was the size of a sparrow and those damned peas until they resembled raisins the size of bird shot! Much to his surprise, or not, she stood him up!

Beginning at five o'clock on Monday, Scott began calling her home. Again, he called for five hours until, finally, she answered the phone. She was nonplused about the Sunday night date.

"What happened to you last night? I had dinner prepared and everything."

"I did not think it was firm." Without really pressing her, because he didn't want to make her mad, he repeated some of the conversation to illustrate that it was a firm commitment.

She was as sweet as could be, and was lying through her teeth, but he wasn't about to tell her he knew so. He was in a full-court press for about 25 minutes trying to convince her that they should go out for a beer.

Scott was still living on Brandywine in Arlington. She lived along the river in DC at an apartment building named Tiber Island. She attempted to convince him it was too late, he was too far away, and that it would take him at least 45 minutes to get there. He assured her that he was not all that far.

"All I have to do is zip down Lee Highway to Spout Run, hit the GW Parkway, go over the 14th Street Bridge, and I can be there in ten or fifteen minutes," all of which was an even bigger lie than she had told him about Sunday night. But he would say whatever it took to get her to go out with him again.

Then, he had the audacity to tell her that she should because "it might be the smartest move you will ever make!"

She didn't directly respond to the comment, but she did give in. "Okay, I will go out with you."

"Good! I'll be over there in about 15 minutes."

Ironically, playing on the radio as he was driving was The Doors, "Light My Fire!" He drove so fast that his ears were pressed against the side of his head even with the windows up. No doubt, he was across the 14th Street Bridge in ten minutes. When he reached her building, he could not wait on the elevator, so he ran up the stairs, two steps at a time. He was out of breath when he reached her door on the fifth floor but was so elated to be there.

When she opened the door, it was the first time he really got a look at her in good light. She was gorgeous! She was about 5"4', had shoulder length auburn hair, big green cat eyes, very striking cheekbones, and a nose that reminded him of Italian genes similar to Sophia Loren. He already knew from the night before that she was very busty, but in the light, she was more imposing. Even more noticeable in the light was how well her clothes fit. They weren't tight, but there was no extra material anywhere! They were truly form fitting.

Without all the noise background from the Underground, Scott also was able to hear her voice. He already knew from the night before her voice was very soft, sexy, and feminine. Absent the noise interference, he felt the impact even more. She was a sight and sound to behold! His heart was racing!

They drove over to the Avenue, which was only about a mile away from Tiber Island. He thought it better not to return to the Underground. Instead, they went to a bar called Up Your Alley next to the Hawk and Dove for drinks. From that night on, they were inseparable. They would talk on the phone five or six times a day, often meet for lunch, and could not wait to get into each other's presence. Anything and everything they did was wonderful!

She was beautiful and any man would describe her as the kind of woman who had a body to kill for! She also turned out to be a clothes horse. She probably didn't own a dress that cost less than $80-$100. No telling how much a complete outfit cost. She bought them, had them tailored, and if she gained two ounces, refused to wear them. Her taste and selection of colors was impeccable!

Both of them really enjoyed eating out. They spent a small fortune in restaurants. One of the things that Scott really enjoyed a lot was when they were out for dinner and Jennifer would get up to go to the restroom. He not only enjoyed watching her, but he noticed that both men *and* women watched her coming and going to the restroom. This scenario really pumped Scott up because he knew that she was coming back to *his* table!

Even though Scott experienced enormous pleasure in all this, as they spent more time together, he became abundantly aware that as beautiful and alluring as she was, she was equally smart, had a really good head on her shoulders, and was far more intuitive and perceptive about people than he. She was intoxicating on many levels.

They dined out regularly at very fine restaurants; they also relished food from dives, joints, and other specialty food locations. One of their favorite things to do was for Scott to buy a sub from Mario's in Arlington, a Mario's Special, and a six-pack of beer for lunch. Needless to say, it was a challenge for them to get through the day without seeing each other. Scott would pick up Jennifer at her office near Capitol Hill and they would go down to East Potomac Park on the river and sit across the river from National Airport and watch the planes coming and going. Jennifer had purchased an air band radio that they used often so they understood all of the controller's shorthand for what was happening with the air traffic and on the ground at the airport.

Another one of their favorite things to do was to buy a hot pastrami sub and a couple of beers, which they put in her oversized purse. Then they would go to a movie. Most often, they went to the theater on Tuesday, Wednesday, or Thursday and Saturday afternoons, which was dollar admission to the theaters. At the time, it was about all Scott could afford! They used to giggle because they knew the people in the theater could smell the hot pastrami and hear them popping the pop-top on the beer.

Within five days of becoming an elevator operator, one day after meeting Jennifer, he found a job working for an airport lobby group. He did that for two years. It wasn't much of a job, but he did benefit from some significant professional experience when he became involved in administrative proceedings before the Civil Aeronautics Board (CAB). They regulated the airlines travel routes and their airfares. The airlines had applied for fare increases to cover the cost of the initial emergency regulations establishing armed guards and baggage service personnel. The armed guard personnel were airport employees and baggage service personnel were airline employees. The problem was an emergency surcharge for each leg of a traveler's journey; it was to produce the money for both services, but it was collected by the airlines who were not reimbursing a number of his group's member airports.

Scott knew the real action was in the Federal District Court and the CAB preceding was nothing more than his employer being able to put in its newsletter that "we are attacking on all fronts." He had absolutely no experience in this line of work. In reality, he had no experience at anything!

The first time he walked into a meeting before the hearing actually started, he counted 54 lawyers in the room. Since they represented the airlines, they were from the largest law firms in the country. It was an extremely rocky time for Scott. As much as he had confidence in many other areas, this was not one of them. He was the epitome of the young lawyer who couldn't find their way to the courthouse.

But since he knew his material so well, he elected to sit up right next to the Administrative Law Judge's bench. His plan was to watch what the other lawyers did and learn from them. He was also a little hard of hearing, so he would have trouble hearing the judge if he were too far away. Scott decided to sit next to the Administrative Law Judge with him to Scott's left and all the lawyers in front and to the right of Scott.

At the beginning of the hearing, once the preliminaries were taken care of, the very first thing the Administrative Law Judge said was, with a waving motion of his right hand towards Scott: "Let's just start right here with Mr. Carmichael!"

Scott nearly died! Not having a clue what he was supposed to be doing and void of any learning curve from observing the other attorneys, Scott picked up a prehearing order that the judge had entered. The airlines were going to be questioned alphabetically. So, he started with Allegheny Airlines. Since they were paying his members, he thought that would be a friendly witness. Wrong! That's when Scott was rudely introduced to the fact that his clients, the airports, were not part of the "aviation club." The lawyer representing Allegheny was difficult and Scott had absolutely no experience to challenge any witnesses, let alone an attorney.

After a very bumpy start, he worked his way down to Braniff Airlines. They were represented by United States Supreme Court Justice Abe Fortes' old law firm. Suddenly, the Administrative Law Judge jumped all over Scott! "Mr. Carmichael, why are you asking all of these questions?"

"Well, Your Honor, Braniff Airlines has only answered about half of the questions as instructed in your prehearing order."

"What? What?" Quickly flipping through the pretrial order, the Administrative Law Judge was surprised and reluctantly confirmed Scott's statement and allowed him to continue. Even though Scott enjoyed the moment, he was painfully aware he had no clear path to where he was heading or trying to accomplish.

Not long after that, Scott was informed by one of the attorneys that he had a phone call from the General Counsel for Western Airlines in California. Inexperienced, yes, but stupid, no! Scott knew immediately that he had caught all the airlines with their pants down, had gotten their attention, and they were adjusting presenting their case. Scott went to the phone and took the call.

"What evidence would you like us to put in in our case in chief?"

"Just answer the questions that were requested in the prehearing order." Scott was really pumped up and full of confidence after that.

Four days later, things took a dramatic turn for the worse! The Administrative Law

Judge leaned over, looked at Scott, and said, "Tell me, Mr. Carmichael, other than contractual, can you tell me any legal basis why these airlines owe your clients any money?"

"Well, your Honor, I'm not prepared to address that issue." Scott was too off balance to think of responding that that was not an issue before the hearing. Having petitioned to intervene as a party, and been approved, that legitimized his clients' interest in the substance of the hearing, which was an airline rate increase.

"Well, *most* lawyers I know, at least most *good* lawyers, would have an answer." As rattled as Scott was, he had the presence of mind to think that *that was a real chicken shit thing to do to an inexperienced lawyer.* There was no call for that. Concluding his soliloquy, the Administrative Law Judge summarily informed Scott: "Mr. Carmichael, your presence is no longer required, and you may leave! The Board's Bureau of Economics can ask all of the questions that you have been asking."

Scott gathered up his papers, and began walking toward the door, suffering yet another humiliating exit, with his tail between his legs! Scott wasn't willing to accept this treatment without a fight! He convinced his organization to file an appeal, but within a few weeks, he was officially fired!

His former employer was represented by a major DC law firm. Although he had only been introduced to the lead attorney, Scott knew he was the most recent General Counsel of the Federal Aviation Administration. He was one of those "revolving door" lawyers that go in and out of government service and back to a major law firm that does business before the agency. He was handling all of the corresponding *real* emergency regulation litigation in the Federal District Court. Scott knew of no one else to call. He was suddenly unemployed and needed a job. There was no logical reason to call this attorney and Scott knew the lawyer either knew or would find out that he had been fired, but he just had to do something.

As luck would have it, another client of the law firm had been looking unsuccessfully for three months for an acceptable assistant corporate counsel. The lawyer regaled Scott with all of the highlights of the job. Then, he gave Scott the bad news. "I know you want to stay in DC, but the job is in Miami. These people own land in the Bahamas, the Canary Islands, and 4,500 acres in the mountains above Los Angeles. At the moment, your prospective boss, who is a lawyer about your age, is in the Canaries."

Being keenly aware at the moment of his stubbornness and the consequences of some of his poor decision-making skills, Scott quickly analyzed the situation. The lawyer giving him the advice and the opportunity was a 38-year-old graduate of the University of Virginia Law School and a partner in a major DC law firm that represented General Motors and Howard Hughes. Scott was 32-years old and unemployed. Scott was going to Miami!

A year after they met, Jennifer's apartment lease was up, and she had let it be known she wanted the two of them to start living together. By the time this opportunity came along, they had been living together for close to two years. Suddenly, he had the opportunity to quickly escape unemployment with a great job in Miami working for a major Caribbean land developer. First, he told Jennifer the good news about the job opportunity. She was very excited for him. Then, mimicking the lawyer's strategy, he dropped the other shoe.

"There is only one problem."

Silence.

"The job is in Miami."

Long silence. *Oh shit! She is **not** happy!* She was from Texas. By now, he knew she was the epitome of the common perception of a woman from Texas: an iron fist in a velvet glove! Calmly, but in her soft, determined manner, well known to him by that time: "You're moving to Miami?"

Silence.

"Yes."

"Let ... me ... see ... if ... I ... have ... this ... right? You're moving to Miami?"

"Yes."

After another awkward moment of silence, she summarily and firmly informed him:

"Well, if *you* are moving to Miami, then *I* am moving to Miami!" Even though it scared him, her confidence warmed him deeply.

CHAPTER 6

The move to Miami was filled with joyful anticipation. Scott was transitioning from a do-nothing, frustrating job for which he received absolutely no training or instructions. He had a secretary who caused him to break out in hives when she cussed him out in front of everybody and he didn't even have the authority to fire her. And he was transitioning from a job from which, ultimately, he had been fired, to a job that offered enormous potential.

He went from a small office to an office on the nineth floor, three times as large, and with a couch and seating area. His office had straw wallpaper. His view out the window was of Nixon's Florida White House on Key Biscayne. His secretary would go downstairs in the hotel and bring him his breakfast and lunch. Vice presidents, 15 years his senior, had to come to him for all sorts of approval, which caused a lot of resentment on their part.

Suddenly, Scott found himself "supervising" five employees and responsible for processing contracts for the annual sale of $30 million of resort properties and deeds transferring title to $20 million of property annually! Ironically, this position did not give him any formal training either. He was expected to go to the head contract processor, a lady from

Columbia who spoke with a heavy accent, and have her teach him *his* job.

As for Jennifer, things didn't work out so well for her. The lawyer from the company's outside law firm interviewing Scott observed that Miami *really* needed a lot of professional women. Jennifer was only 25-years old, but she had already worked for a United States Senator and was a one-girl-office managing a $100,000 budget for an education lobbyist. When Scott found out one day at lunch the dismal salary they were paying her, he prepared a brief outline that she took back to her boss. He gave her a 50% raise on the spot to keep her from quitting until he could get approval from the board for a substantial raise. The board ended up doubling her salary!

Scott had shared her background and experience with the Miami lawyer. As time went by, it became apparent, at least to Scott, that the professional women the lawyer had in mind were the ones that worked the Miami Beach hotels. Miami didn't embrace beauty *and* brains. Thus, Jennifer was without a job for a long time, putting on some weight, which only exacerbated the situation, and was very depressed. Finally, after Scott chopped her resume down so much that she could keep her tits out of the typewriter and answer the phone, she got a job as a receptionist.

Concurrently, Jennifer and Scott also were made aware of the discrimination against "snowbirds." Even though they both had American Express, Diners Club, and other cards, they were unable to obtain a local department store charge card.

Not long after that, she had the opportunity to interview for a real job over on Miami Beach. The job was with a well-known financier who was one of the earliest corporate raiders. Only, he didn't break up companies; he kept them.

When she went to the interview, he kept her waiting for 30 minutes. When she was finally brought in for the interview, he was in silk pajamas with a silk bathrobe, as in Hugh Hefner. He informed her that he'd been watching her on closed-circuit television. When recounting her experience, she made the comment to Scott that she was glad that she had followed her mother's advice: "Never scratch in public. You never know who's watching."

All in all, they enjoyed their time there. The company had two floors in the Sheridan Four Ambassadors Hotel right on Biscayne Bay. It put them up for two months in an apartment on one of the floors. Then, after a couple of months, Jennifer found them a place and they moved to Coral Gables.

Unlike the Washington area, where they could leave town and go hiking on the Appalachian Trail for a weekend or a few days, they felt trapped in Miami. North, there was 50 miles of condominiums, to the West was the

Everglades, to the south was nothing until you got to Key West, and, obviously, to the east was the ocean. If you weren't into sun, sand, and surf, there just wasn't a hell of a lot to do in Miami.

They had gone from reading two to three newspapers a day in Washington and watching the news for each minuscule change to being relegated to reading the *Miami Herald*. The national and international news were demoted to three or four pages buried deep in the paper. It seemed that the headlines were always about the bodies being found in the multitude of canals that surrounded Miami. The canals were Miami's version of New York City's East River.

The British faction of Scott's company's Board of Directors had always been extremely frustrated with the American contingent. They felt they were too extravagant and loose with money. After serious maneuvers, the British gained control of the corporation and starting firing vice presidents right and left. Scott was far too down the food chain for anyone to bother with him, but, after a period of bloodletting, the British faction recognized that they were firing all the people who knew how to run the corporation and scaring the hell out of everyone else. Recognizing their mistake, they began approaching individuals and offering them a six-month bonus if they would not leave the company for at least six months. For Scott, this was the case. As well, they also asked him if he would like to move to the Bahamas to work there. Certainly, it seemed like a good idea. And Jennifer and Scott were up for it.

Ironically, after these changes, Scott went from a 70-hour week and being as happy as he could possibly be, since he had gotten his act together and was no longer "loose as a goose", to only working 40-hours a week and not too hard at that. Not because he had grown lazy, but the workload had diminished dramatically. Increasingly, though, he became dissatisfied.

The administrative assistant in his office, Darrell and his wife, Elsie, had become Jennifer and Scott's good friends. Elsie was from Longview, Texas. They had met in Laos when he was a Canadian Army officer and she worked for the "State Department." Elsie cussed more than any five-men Scott had ever known in his life. The four of them did a lot of drinking and commiserating. Drinking was egged on by the fact that they had several mature producing fruit trees in their backyard. They had an orange tree, avocado tree, grapefruit tree, and a key lime tree. They would buy two quarts of vodka, sit on the patio, and try to keep up with the tree dropping 100 key limes a day. Impossible, but they gave it a good try!

Fourteen months after their arrival in Miami, in January 1976, Scott and Jennifer were happily married. But only after she had given him an ultimatum and informed him that, "You have had long enough to make up your mind!" Before the ceremony, when she thought he was getting cold feet, it really ticked her off when he told her that for the preceding six months, every time he had a few drinks, he had to fight proposing to her.

By the summer of 1976, Scott was so frustrated with work that he walked in one day and quit. Shortly after that, Darrell also quit. They each still received large bonuses for staying. After that, they concocted ways to go down to the unemployment office and collect unemployment. For the most part, the two couples' evenings were spent trying to keep up with the key lime tree and in the mornings, Darrell and Scott began their mornings with cold pizza and cold beer out on the head boats fishing in the Gulf.

One morning returning from the Gulf, after six weeks of drinking and fishing extravaganzas, Scott walked into their duplex on Ponce de Leon. Apparently, he had a look on his face. Then again, Jennifer could *always* read him. Without his saying a word, she looked at him and said: "Time to go back to Washington?"

"Yes."

Returning to the Washington area in the fall of 1976, they checked into a Holiday Inn south of DC in Springfield, Virginia at the intersection of I-95 and the Beltway. Ironically, once again, Scott found himself at the infamous "mixing bowl."

Immediately, they reviewed ads for an apartment. Knowing the area made it easier to narrow their search and get around. Embarrassingly, on their first outing, however, they were rudely awakened to the fact that, although he was a lawyer, he was an *unemployed* lawyer! Renting an apartment required an embarrassing phone call to his former employer to confirm to the rental office that he had been given a substantial cash payment when he left his job. Scott felt like a recent college graduate with a new job having to call his parents to co-sign a lease.

Finally, they rented an apartment on the 11th floor of Cameron Run Terrace, a three-building complex just south of Alexandria at US-1 and the Beltway. Jennifer was afraid of fires. She was reassured, as was he, because the 11th floor was as high as the fire department ladder trucks could reach. Their building was only about 150 feet from the Beltway.

Even though it had a balcony, they were unable to use it or sit on it long enough to have a drink because it was noisy as all Billy Hell! Neither of them could hear the other over the din of rush hour traffic, nor could they read lips.

Having previously worked for a Senator and a lobby group, Jennifer had no trouble finding a job. Within two weeks, she was working under former Vice President Hubert Humphrey on a subcommittee of the Senate Foreign Relations Committee and the FBI was conducting a security check for her Top Secret clearance. The security check created quite a stir in her small Texas hometown. When she heard from her high school friends that the FBI had come to town asking about her, it puffed her up something awful.

Scott was proud and happy for her. He was not so lucky, though. He had not been a top student, had not graduated from an Ivy League school or even an East Coast law school, and although both of them had worked for a Democratic Senator, now the Republicans were in charge.

For Jennifer and Scott, it was, respectively, a very exciting and discouraging experience. She was off and running with a new and rewarding job, while he continued to be frustrated, disappointed, and unable to find employment. Circumstances had unexpectedly flipped from Miami. Scott was painfully aware of having been an assistant corporate counsel of a major land corporation with an 11th floor office looking out over Biscayne Bay's where he saw parts of the movie *Black Sunday* being filmed with the Goodyear blimp.

Also, he had been accustomed to supervising five employees, having vice presidents 15 years his senior come to him with questions and responding to purchasers' complaints under the Interstate Land Sales Act. He missed his personal secretary going downstairs to the restaurant and bringing him his breakfast and lunch.

Once, he even "bought and sold" two company airplanes worth more than a million dollars. Even though it was an intra company transfer, it was exciting. He was given one day to complete the transaction, which was impossible. He asked his boss three times if he could have just three days to complete the transaction. "I've never bought and sold airplanes; however, I know I can do it." After the last try Scott said, "When am I going?" The very next day, he flew to an island in the Caribbean and delivered a check for $485,000 to the majordomo of one of the principles of the company, even though the transaction had not been completed.

On the other hand, the whole episode had made him unpopular in some quarters. Scott discovered that one plane, belonging to a major stockholder worth $1 million by itself, had been illegally flying around the country and to Europe for *three* years. It was a simple matter of the pilot failing to return an annually required IBM computer punch card to the FAA. When Scott telephoned, according the FAA, the plane no longer existed. "There's no such tail number registered!" they had told him.

The investigation also revealed that the airport being used was on a private island in the Bahamas, the length of the airstrip was two thirds of the recommended minimum, and the airframe was designed for 550 hp engines, but 750 hp engines had been installed to increases the performance specifications.. Further complicating matters, Scott had no information on whether the instrumentation had been recalibrated or the airframe and wings strengthened for the oversized engines. And, if this wasn't enough, it had an American insurance policy, which specifically *excluded* landing on private airstrips. Whoever was responsible should have purchased a Lloyd's of London policy.

Later, when Scott asked his boss what he thought of the memorandum he had written describing the problems and the solutions, Scott was summarily informed that if the owner of the plane knew about the memorandum that he would fire Scott. Scott was incredulous! "Why? I did a really good job and solved a lot of problems! Why would he fire me?"

"You told Jonathan he couldn't fly his plane. Jonathan does *not* like to be told no!"

CHAPTER 7

So, while Jennifer masterfully succeeded in her job search, his professional life had collapsed, and he continued having no luck at all as time went on. With absolutely nothing professionally to do, except what he really wanted to do, for reasons no longer remembered, he learned to make stained glass. He learned a lot about the process, not the least of which was that cutting glass had to be exactingly precise or you spent an awful lot of time sanding edges recovering from imprecision. In the future, he came to understand and reflect on this interesting parallel to practicing law.

In the middle of winter, a very cold winter, he opened the window in the spare bedroom where he worked. Noisy Beltway traffic was overwhelming as he sweated profusely from sanding. Eventually, he did finish a simplified Tiffany-styled lamp and a very delicate bleached, white-veined leaf encased between two pieces of clear glass surrounded by 1 inch, angled, cream-colored glass on the top, sides and bottom with triangular jade colored glass on the corners. Those were the only projects he ever completed. Not much to show for seven months of work!

It had been so long ago that he no longer remembered how he happened to contact a group of lawyers who were looking for an addition to their office sharing arrangement. Perhaps it was just an ad in the paper offering to rent a single office that attracted his attention. In any event, after nine months, even though Jennifer was making good money at her job, his severance funds were diminished, and it was time to find something to do. In truth, what he really always wanted to do was go into private practice. And, although he was a very gutsy guy, it had been too intimidating an idea for him.

His search led him to two lawyers sharing an office with a part-time lawyer who worked for the Arlington County School Board. They would never have moved, but their current location had been sold and was going to be renovated to become the Japanese consulate or something. Although Scott would've preferred to be in the older office building because of lower rent, the time had come to make some choices, move forward, and associate with other lawyers to learn the local terrain and generate some business. Being in an office with established attorneys would ease the transition. Also, it offered the possibility of professional support and some referrals.

It was now the fall of 1977. They found office space near the Arlington courthouse in an older building, the Arlington Executive Building. It was going to require refurbishing of the suite. In the end, it was a harbinger of the future dynamics of the group. They had to hire an interior decorator because the only thing that they could agree on was the color of the carpet, and that was only after she selected the samples. He never did know for sure, but later formed an opinion based on the personalities involved that the decorator wasn't the source of the samples.

The colors were atrocious, at least to Scott's taste! But being the new kid on the block, he wasn't going to say anything. The carpet was a combination of a tightly woven, subdued orange and green. The walls were a slightly darker variety of lime green. It reminded Scott of a dress belonging to Sandy. She liked solid bright colors. It was a very similar green, slightly brighter, with a 6-inch wide, white-fringed, yellow band around the waist. When he was a child, his eye doctor told him that because he had astigmatism, he did not like bright colors. He had hated that dress! He named it her Easter Egg Dress.

The lawyers were, without a doubt, an eclectic, hodgepodge group of characters. One, Kevin, specialized in civil service work. He was Jewish, exceedingly organized, or otherwise known as anal. He was so bad with houseplants he had even killed a cactus! Later, as it turned out, he was not altogether kosher either.

Everyone agreed to share the cost of a small library. Kevin had his own secretary. Scott and the other two lawyers, Shep and Don, shared a secretary. By default, Scott managed their joint common expenses for the office, including the library. One day, their secretary, Nikki, pointed out that the library had "acquired" a copy of the Arlington County Code. When confronted by Scott, Kevin responded that *every* library needed a copy. Perhaps, except that in that office, only *he* did code work. Additionally, a bill for repair costs for a typewriter used by his individual secretary also appeared as submitted to Nikki as an office expense. Despite the fact that he had turned the bill over to her, he maintained that it had been an oversight.

Shep was a former insurance adjuster with a practice primarily confined to domestic and personal injury work. His idea of preparing for trial was to read some of the Virginia Code related to his cases and a treatise, or rather, a limited portion of a treatise on the subject of his case the day before trial.

It was absolutely impossible for him to sit down and engage in a lawyerly discussion or analysis of a legal issue. For reasons Scott never understood, he simply could not concentrate or focus on things that long. He had been a WWII B-17 pilot, shot down twice in North Africa. Scott never was sure if either crash involved a head injury or not.

Often as not, despite Scott's genuine effort to discuss his case or even when Shep approached Scott to discuss his own case, Shep would abruptly divert from the topic of conversation and launch into telling a very detailed, sophisticated joke, all the while frustrating Scott because of the interruption.

Scott never had any idea what he was talking about or where he was going with the joke.

Despite the aggravation, he was the greatest raconteur Scott had ever heard and impeccably mimicked accents. Although it drove Scott absolutely crazy, it never failed that, despite his inability to engage in a sustained intellectual conversation on anything, the punch lines of Shep's jokes, once *finally* reached, were incredibly on point about the legal issue that they had been discussing. Even with this unique ability, he never overtly tried to tie the point of the joke into the point they had been discussing or exhibited recognition that he even knew that he had made a point. It just always seemed to come out that way much to Scott's frustration and consternation!

Don worked part-time for the school board. Earlier in his career, he had become what lawyers called a "one client lawyer." He wasn't the most energetic lawyer and through a friend, a contractor, he was fed a steady diet of real estate closings for people who purchased homes in the contractor's subdivisions. It wasn't really legal work, but it generated a steady source of good income.

A number of years before Scott started practicing, a purchaser in Northern Virginia had complained about a fixed price for an attorney's real estate settlement fee, which at the time, rather than a sliding scale, was a standard 1% of the sales price. The purchaser sued the developer, and the case went up on appeal to the Virginia Supreme Court. It culminated in a ruling that lawyers were not immune to antitrust law.

Prior to that time, the Virginia State Bar had a fixed fee schedule for certain types of standard legal representation, and it was an ethical violation to charge anything other than what was on the fee schedule. All of this was based on the premise that lawyers were not subject to antitrust rules. Thereafter, an attorney's real estate fee became competitive and prudent lawyers adjusted their fees to a competitive price. Don refused to do so and gradually lost his practice. Ironically, he gave Scott a hard time because Scott used a timekeeping system. It wasn't until Scott pointed out that Don got at least 10 short, less than six minutes or 1/10 of an hour phone calls a day, which he did not bill, that Scott figured out Don was losing an hour of billable time each and every day. Once he multiplied 22 working days a month by 12, it was clear he was losing about $16,000 a year because he was too lazy to write them down! He had a timekeeping system within three days.

The fourth member of the group also took on domestic relations and personal injury cases. He and Scott were the only two in the office that practiced both in Virginia and the District of Columbia. He was by far the most professional attorney in the office. His first name was James, the same as Scott's father. Some months later, Scott learned that they were from the same state and he was from a town so small Scott had never heard of it and had to look it up on the map to even get an idea where it was located.

When a new attorney in an office sharing arrangement starts what is, in effect, a solo practice, his initial revenue goal is to make enough money to pay his share of the rent, the secretary, and the phone. Accomplishing that the first time is a milestone! Of course, the initial hurdle to get over is to find clients of any kind. Or, more correctly stated, clients of any kind who have some money.

Scott did bring expertise that no other lawyer in the office possessed, criminal defense experience. In the spring of 1978, about four months prior to entering the office sharing arrangement, Scott finally had enough of stained glass and took some affirmative action. He went into DC and began to take court-appointed criminal cases in the Superior Court of the District of Columbia, which is the equivalent of the District's state court system, and in the United States District Court. Naturally, in the United States District Court, the prosecutors are Assistant United States Attorneys (AUSA). Because the District of Columbia is a Federal enclave, the prosecutors in the Superior Court of the District of Columbia are also AUSAs.

The upside of it all was that the respective courthouses were only about two blocks from each other, and it was very easy to pick up daily case assignments in each court. It was a simple matter to get two cases, sometimes even three a day. An even more important upside for Scott was that he was out of his cave, out of his funk, and he was developing a new self. Feeling able to exercise self-determination was very encouraging and he wasn't looking back.

On the other hand, the downside was that the pay was not very high, and the compensation documents required time-keeping accuracy to the minute. And, they were examined by over-the-top bean counters looking for any discrepancies and overlapping time periods. It wasn't uncommon to receive a letter six weeks after submitting the forms denying payment because an activity time period, for example legal research, had overlapped by one or two minutes a different activity time period, for example, conference with a client. One would think they would just dock the time and get on with it. Talk about a waste of government time and money!

In the Superior Court system, arraignment hearings were held in a courtroom that a few years earlier was the actual courtroom in which the burglars were arraigned after they were arrested for breaking into the Democratic Headquarters at the Watergate Apartments. It later appeared in the movie *All of the President's Men.*

Near the exit to the judge's chambers beside the judge's bench, the doorjamb to the doorway to the judges' chambers was splintered from several bullet holes. Of course, at that time, there was no security for weapons. Each time Scott was in the courtroom, he noticed the holes and was always puzzled as to why they were never repaired. He wasn't sure if it was just an inefficient bureaucracy or a point of pride as a reminder of stressful situations that sometimes confronted the court.

For hearings in the Federal District Court, he was restricted to hearings before the Magistrate. They were bond hearings for those recently arrested. Their procedure was to check you out before they would let you go up to the level of hearings before the Federal District Judge. In short, they were not going to let you screw anything up at the Magistrate level and they definitely were not going to let you go upstairs to the big courtroom before a Federal District Judge until you proved that you would not screw it up.

Scott had only been taking court-appointed cases four months before the office sharing arrangement presented itself. During that time, he represented hookers, accommodation drug dealers who had gotten caught and various misdemeanors. In some instances, he even represented people charged with very serious felonies.

Scott was very naive about certain things. He once whispered to a young hooker, as they both leaned against the holding tank bars just like in the movies: "Why do you do this sort of thing?" She gave him a withering look that made him feel like a blithering idiot and then smiled.

"Because I *like* doing it!"

One afternoon, he was in the Magistrate's courtroom. He had finished his assigned case and the Magistrate asked him if he would be willing to take what was called a "late starter", that is, a case which had come in late, was unassigned, and all the other attorneys who had finished their cases had already left the building. Naturally, the opportunity to get another case was always welcomed.

The Magistrate's courtroom was very small, not much larger than the average living room. There was a door through which the defendants entered the courtroom. The door opened and in walked one of the most beautiful black women he had ever seen. She had the striking facial features of Dionne Warwick. He noticed that she was wearing well-fitting, expensive clothing; her jewelry was very tasteful natural gold; she was well groomed; and, scared totally shitless! If there was ever a person exemplifying the phrase "a deer in the spotlight," she was it.

After the arraignment, he met her out in the hallway. As he was talking to her, she appeared puzzled and confused. Suddenly, she looked at Scott. "Who *are* you?" She had been so frightened in the courtroom that she had never even looked at his face.

As it turned out, she was an employee of the U.S. Post Office on the House side of the Capital. It was a contract post office used by the House of Representatives. She was about 35, with three kids and a husband. Her husband was a carpenter with a drinking problem and money had become tight. When things failed financially, basically, she lost it and started writing postal money orders out of her own personal drawer at the post office. She made no attempt to disguise or hide anything. She wrote money orders to pay for her credit card bills and even sent her father a $300 money order.

The way the system in a post office worked was that an employee had their own drawer filled with a certain amount of money and a certain number of stamps. When they ran out of stamps, they were to go to the appropriate person in the office and buy more stamps. It has its own built-in checks and balances system. In short, they are never out of the money and never run out of stamps for long, unless they get sticky fingers. It's such a simple system that one would think that no one would mess with it because it's so easy to get caught. But when you lose it, rational thought goes out the window.

The postal inspectors determined that she had embezzled approximately $7,700. She was charged with 99 counts of forgery, uttering, and embezzlement. Each money order she had filled out and cashed involved one count each of forgery for writing it out, uttering for negotiating it or cashing it, and embezzlement for actually taking or giving the funds. Needless to say, they had her by the short hairs and had caught her with her pants down, so Scott struck a deal. The prosecutor agreed to allow her to enter a plea to one count of embezzlement of $300.

After the deal had been struck, the postal inspectors came to Scott's office. "We have investigated further and determined the amount of money she embezzled was twice the original amount. We have presented this new information to the AUSA and, were, in effect, thrown out of his office. We were told if we had done a good job in the first place, we would've known that she embezzled more money. But a deal has been struck and the AUSA is not going to go back on it."

Scott couldn't understand why they had shared that new information with him, especially the part about the AUSA's reaction to the request. Maybe they were trying to scare him into cutting a deal, even though they had lost their opportunity with the prosecutor. Maybe they wanted him to think that they were going to go back for another try at increasing the charges and he should cut a deal while he could. *But* they never offered a deal. Moreover, Scott felt that if that were their purpose, they never would have told him about the prosecutor throwing them out of his office.

But, even more to his surprise, that wasn't all the information they shared with him. The practice in the Postmaster's office was to keep a substantial amount of cash, at times, upwards of $35,000, in a desk drawer in a very old, ordinary wooden desk; they relied on the built-in lock in the desk drawer for security. The key to the desk drawer, if there was one, as well as all other keys for the office, was kept on a large metal ring hung on a nail on the wall. At night, part of the janitorial staff was allowed to come into the office and make copies to earn extra money. The nail on which the key ring hung was beside the copier and available to *anyone* all day long and, at night!

Proving embezzlement requires a finite starting point; that is, how much money was there in the beginning. In regard to his client's personal drawer, there was a finite amount of money and a finite number of stamps from which they could determine the imbalance. The practice of keeping undetermined large amounts of cash in the desk drawer had been going on for years. No one even knew how long it had been the practice. Thus, determining a finite starting point was impossible. In short, there was a void of records, and anyone could have been tapping into that slush fund for years without anyone knowing.

It did not escape Scott's attention that they were looking for a scapegoat and trying to clean up the entire issue of the slush fund. Moreover, once they shared the history of the "cash in the drawer," Scott understood both why the prosecutor had thrown them out of his office and the impossibility of their making any case involving any cash not related to her personal drawer. It also did not escape his attention that they had not provided any accounting records or copies of money orders to substantiate any additional embezzlement.

Years later, when Representative Dan Rostenkowski became embroiled in "Stamp Gate," it brought back a lot of memories of the disorganization of the House of Representatives Post Office. In Scott's mind, it raised even more serious questions about if anybody ever knew what the hell was going on! It was entirely possible that they could not prove that it happened, but Rostenkowski couldn't prove it *didn't*. It is, after all, the prosecutor's job to make even the most innocent things into ominous transgressions.

In the end, a Presentence Report was prepared. Scott learned he needed to ask the U.S. Marshall's Office if he could use a copy of it to present to the House Subcommittee overseeing the House Post Office so they could use it in their consideration of the issue of restitution.

The Marshall looked at him as though he had asked to go home and sleep with his wife!

"Is there a rule against that?" Scott asked.

After a long pause, the Marshall responded, "No, but, to my knowledge, a Presentence Report had never been released prior to sentencing in the District of Columbia." Again, Scott inquired as to whether there was a rule or law against it. "No, but the report belongs to the Federal Judge. You will have to ask him for permission to do that."

Scott didn't feel very encouraged about that because the Federal Judge was new to the bench and previously had been the U.S. Attorney for the District of Columbia. But after he explained to the judge what he wanted to do and why, he surprised him and told Scott he could use the Presentence Report, *but* he was to advise the subcommittee that it had to remain confidential. Naturally, Scott agreed, but in his mind, he thought if it weren't a contradiction in terms asking a subcommittee on the Hill to keep something confidential, he'd never heard one!

The next step was to present it to the subcommittee, which was no easy task. Everyone on that subcommittee was diving for cover because they did not want to be associated with the disorganization of the Post Office. Most of them probably had never even been there or were unaware where it was located. He was encouraged by following his instincts and was really beginning to make some headway. He had the Presentence Report and now could talk to the

Postmaster of the House Post Office as well as the members of the subcommittee.

In Washington, there is a phrase known as the "August Doldrums." This phrase refers to the month of August when Congress is usually in recess and there is very little news to report. Word reached Scott that the *Washington Post* and *New York Times* were sniffing around about this story. He didn't need that to further complicate the subcommittee's reluctance to talk with him and reach a deal. To date, no one had responded to him. If this got in the papers prior to his striking a deal on restitution, it would be over.

Restitution from the court's standpoint is different from restitution the subcommittee might require. And a committee representative could always show up at sentencing to save face and present their position that they wanted restitution for the entire amount, which could include the additional amounts discovered by the postal inspectors. The court lacked any authority for the additional restitution since his client hadn't been charged. But Scott had no illusions about the United States Attorney beating the drums loudly and the sound would not fall on deaf ears. The court's goals in restitution and the committee's, then, actually would conflict with the latter deemed politically motivated. Regardless, the court would be forced to take notice and, undoubtedly, take it into consideration at sentencing, without a doubt, to his client's disadvantage.

One morning, Scott was drinking his coffee as he opened the *Washington Post*. The headlines screamed about Jimmy Carter's friend, Bert Lance, and his banking escapades before he had come to Washington. Scott felt a sense of relief, instantly recognizing no one would be interested in hooking his minnow when they could harpoon a whale! He continues to have a warm place in his heart for Bert Lance to this day.

CHAPTER 8

Being a hungry young lawyer, the lawyers in the office gave Scott a few cases, too small or bothersome for them. Nevertheless, he vigorously pursued them as though they were landmark cases. At the same time, he shared his background of having worked with inmates during a law school summer internship while living at a prison, and that he had four months experience with court appointed criminal defense cases. In particular, they were aware of his recent success with the House Post Office embezzlement case.

As it turns out, James' law partner in the District owned a taxicab company and they knew a lot of *interesting* people. Being the only one in the office with any criminal defense experience, a few months into the office sharing, James approached Scott about a young man he knew who had been arrested. Scott was naturally grateful and enthused about any work the lawyers referred to him. That was especially true of James, right up until he told Scott the charge was rape!

"Oh, and by the way, he's black!"

Instantly, Scott's pulse quickened, his stomach constricted, and painful images flashed through his mind. They stirred up memories he did not like to think about. All he could think of was escaping this dilemma. But James was insistent! "I know this young man. I know his family. I know that he could not possibly be guilty." Scott continued to sit there in total silence. He didn't challenge James at all.

Finally, after James had finished his pitch, Scott responded. "I won't take the case, but I will speak with him and try to get a feel for how much trouble he is facing. After the interview, I'll let you know about my decision."

When Timothy came in for his first interview, Scott remained reluctant to take the case. Aside from the personal discomfort due to the troubling nature of the case, he had other deeply personal, emotional, conflict issues. Having grown up in the South, Scott had virtually no personal contact with black people. That was a time when black men were either called "boy" or their given name preceded by the word "nigger." In that world, the adult white world, which filtered down to their children, at least one unspoken rational- there was certainly no need for a spoken rationale - for this practice was that "nigger" preceded their name so when white people were discussing them, they would know who they were talking about amongst themselves. For example, in Scott's life, there was a "Nigger Earl" and a "Nigger Roy." His father had white friends and their names were Earl and Roy.

Scott's maternal grandma owned a lumber company. His maternal grandfather died when Scott's mother was 16 years old. Before the

Depression, the family owned three lumber companies, timber lands and a sawmill. Scott's paternal grandfather also died when Scott's father, James, was 16. But James' family was what was commonly referred to as "dirt poor." However, James had married into the lumber business and worked hard.

It was also the era when men worked for a company most of their lives. Cleo and his wife, Audi, both worked there. Their houses next door to the company. Cleo began work at the lumber company when he was 16 years old delivering lumber in a wagon for Scott's grandfather. Scott's Uncle Burton, his mother's brother, had worked there all of his life, too. Scott and his brother each received a $2 weekly allowance. It doesn't seem like much in today's world, but back then, movies were 10 cents. Popcorn and a coke together were 25 cents.

James had grown up so poor, he had to pretty much fend for himself. But years later, after hard work and toil, he had done well. He was making $6,000 a year at time when the average salary in America was $3,000. He regularly hunted and fished. He played golf at the country club. So did Scott and his brother. Long weekends were routine. He had two weeks paid vacation a year. He always told his brother and Scott that if they wanted extra money, they could mow lawns in the summer and rake leaves in the fall, which they did. On their own, in the fall, they made potholders by hand with small metal looms and sold them door to door for 25 cents. When they ran out of them, they just sat down on the curb and made some more.

James let it be known, with obvious pride, that they didn't need the money, but if Scott wanted to make some money, he could work at the lumber company, which he did, starting at the age of nine. At first, about all he could do was fill orders for nails, which were sold by the pound, and pick out paint and put the can in an electric shaker. That was fun!

At age 10, he was taught to make aluminum screens from scratch. By the time he was 11 or 12, on Saturdays during school and full-time in the summer, he was expected to be there early to open all the doors and turn on the lights, all by the 7:00 a.m. opening time. When he was 12, he was allowed to back two trucks out of out of the shed where they had been locked up for the night. One was a three-quarter ton with five forward gears, and the other, a two and a half-ton with five forward gears with an overdrive effectively making it 10 forward gears. Very heady stuff for a 12-year-old!

His father paid him 50 cents an hour. The men were paid 75 cents an hour. His father explained that they had families and it would be unfair to pay him the same amount, especially since his family owned the lumber company, which, without saying so, was why he had a job, and he was a kid. Scott understood perfectly and appreciated his father explaining that to him; his appreciation grew even more so as he got older.

Scott worked with a man named Osco Williams, a master carpenter, who was very patient and who was the one who taught him to make the aluminum screens. Some of the other men who worked for Scott's family were named Hoyt, Champ, and Herbert.

Because Scott's dad had grown up poor, he decided that his family would eat very well. He'd buy a calf and a sow pig. He made a deal with Hoyt, who lived in the country, that he would buy the calf and sow pig and provide the feed if Hoyt raised them. In exchange, Hoyt got half the cow and half the pig when they were grown. They would get the sow bred, retain one female piglet from the litter, and use the money from selling the other piglets to buy another calf. Later, the female piglet would be bred, and the cycle would continue.

Everything was butchered and his dad made sure all steaks and chops were one and one-half inches thick. That was a big deal for James because when he was growing up, being able to buy an inch and a half steak was the gold standard and something he had been unable to do. Scott's family had a large freezer loaded with beef, pork, fish, squirrel and ducks. It had a separate compartment with two five-gallon paper containers of ice cream, one each of chocolate and vanilla. His father loved milkshakes. Scott has no memory of his father ever saying his brother and he, or they and their friends, ate too much ice cream. Only of him saying, "When that runs out, we will just buy some more!"

The men taught Scott how to pick No.1 2x4s when someone wanted them and to use the crooked and cracked ones if they were going to be cut into stakes for holding the boards framing the poured concrete for foundations. They even attempted to teach him how to pick up lumber correctly when loading it without gloves to avoid getting splinters in his hands.

But no black man ever worked there!

The one black man Scott knew was a man by the name of Earl Dodd. Earl worked part-time around the house for his grandma. His wife's name was Pauline, and she was the housekeeper for their friend, Joel, whose dad was the family doctor. Scott learned to treat Earl with respect because his grandma treated Earl with respect. Scott's mother and father treated Earl with respect as well. His Uncle Burton and Aunt Cindy treated Earl with respect. Every summer, when his mother's two sisters came to visit with their husbands and children, they all treated Earl with respect. Scott's aunts and uncle had all grown up with Earl around the house and treating Earl with respect was the way it was done in grandma's house.

Earl was a very friendly, soft spoken fellow, but Pauline scared the living crap out of Scott and his friends. When they would go over to Joel's house, they would take the shortest path from the front door to his room and shut the door, which would have been "before the dust settled," except there was no dust in that house; you had better not track in dirt! She was in charge of that house, and you did not mess with her.

Earl was the most prominent black person in Scott's young life simply because he was the one whom he was around on a regular, personal basis. He was always very nice to Scott and made him feel comfortable being around him. He was always happy to see Earl.

It was common in those days for black men to have a "stench" about them. Generally speaking, the thought was that they were not very clean. Earl had that stench, except there's no question that Earl was a clean person. He always wore leather shoes, pleated pants, and a long-sleeved white dress shirt with the collar buttoned tight, even when it was inappropriate for summer weather.

He wore a Fedora. Maybe it was the expected dress for black men at that time, or maybe they were just trying to dress like white men to fit in, in a fashion. When he was working, he always wore a brown paper grocery bag rolled up to make a paper hat. Perhaps it was meant to soak up the work sweat.

One of Scott's clearest memories of Earl was when he was about 10 years old. Earl was sitting on a small stool eating his lunch on his grandma's plain, well-worn Formica covered kitchen table. His grandma had a very large home with six bedrooms. Her kitchen was not very large for the size of the house, though. It was adjacent to what would be called the family dining room. There were cabinets between the kitchen and the family dining room with French windows on both sides, so the China, glasses, and silverware were accessible from both rooms.

Although she had a formal dining room, Scott had no recollection of ever eating in it. The only story he remembered about her formal dining room was that when his maternal grandfather died in 1926, he was laid out for viewing on the dining room table, which was the custom. On Thanksgiving, Christmas, or other special occasions, Scott never asked about or missed eating on that table.

Scott lived two blocks away from his grandma. She made the best homemade bread in the world. She would just throw flour on the countertop, which barely had any pattern left from years of use and make a bowl like depression in the middle. Then, she would crack an egg and put butter and vegetable oil in the depression and start mixing it with her hands. It always puzzled Scott that she never measured anything! Every time she made bread, it was as though it was the first time he had ever seen her do it. He would ask her about it, and she always smiled and responded softly, "I have been doing it for a while and know what I'm doing." Even today, he still has a very clear image of her standing at the counter mixing everything with her hands, kneading the dough, seeing her smile, and hearing her soft voice.

Regularly, she would either call him to let him know she was baking, or he would put in a request. He knew the bread was her "bait" to get him to visit and he felt warm knowing all he had to do was ask her to bake "his" bread. Usually, she baked two loaves. Either way, the important information for him was, when was it coming out of the oven? And even though he didn't wear a watch, he would show up like clockwork at the kitchen door at the back of the house! He was an odd kid because then, as well as now, he liked the heels, which is where he started cutting. Next, was spreading Welch's Grape Jelly on the hot, fresh bread.

Later as a young adult, his mother told him a story involving grandma's sister, Floy. After being widowed and married once or twice, no one seemed to be sure about those details, Floy came to live with his grandma.

Scott remembers when he was about 12 getting a hug from Floy. She was a very busty woman of substance! In describing Floy throughout the years, Scott enjoyed people's reaction when he described her by telling them that, "When she took you to her bosom, light, air, and the world as you knew it disappeared!" Scott learned to take a deep a breath before she hugged him. On the other hand, it was great in the wintertime when his ears were cold! Often as not, his listeners smiled as they recalled their own "Aunt Floy."

Seems she complained once about Scott cutting the heels off the loaves of bread. "Bertha, you shouldn't let that boy cut the heels off the bread. It will dry them out."

His grandma was a salt of the earth person, the epitome of a passive woman. Nevertheless, as the story was told to him, she responded, "Floy, I bake that bread *for* Scott! It *is* Scott's bread! Scott *can* cut the heels off! Scott *can* cut the bread down the middle, sideways, or *any* other way he chooses!"

Floy never again spoke about *Scott's* bread!

Family members never knocked on grandma's door when they came over and it was never locked. They just called out for "grandma" to let her know they were in the house. So, that is how he came in one time for "his" bread and noticed Earl eating his lunch in the kitchen. His grandma used China and her silverware for every meal. He can't recall which he noticed first, but instantly, he noticed that Earl was eating the *same* food that Scott was going to have for lunch, using the *same* silverware Scott was going to use and the *same* China Scott was going to use.

To this day, he doesn't know why that struck him as strange. Maybe it was the first time he had ever seen Earl eating anything at his grandma's. But he does remember the shock of seeing a "nigger" eating in his grandma's kitchen, even if it was Earl. Immediately, however, he remembers concluding that it must be alright because Earl was there, his grandma had served him, and it obviously was just the first time he had seen it.

In any event, now in a totally different frame of mind and from a different viewpoint, after surveying all of this, something else caught his attention. Earl was drinking iced tea out of a quart Mason jar! Suddenly, the contrast riveted Scott's attention. It made no sense that he was eating the *same* food on the same China with the *same* silverware, so there certainly wasn't an issue of eating or drinking after a "nigger." So, what was going on? Out of the mouths of babes will come anything!

"Earl, why are you drinking your iced tea out of a jar?"

"Well, when I finishes my lunch, I can take it back with me to work."

It made perfect sense to Scott, and he was on his way! After that, it was perfectly normal for Earl to be eating the *same* food in his grandma's kitchen, on the *same* China, with the *same* silverware, and drinking *his* iced tea from a quart Mason jar.

One of the most indelible memories of Earl was Scott's father coming home for lunch and telling his mother in an excited tone that Earl showed up at the Plymouth dealership to buy a new car. The owner told Earl that would be happy to sell him a new car and would work with him putting together a payment plan. Politely, befitting his status, he reportedly responded by telling the owner that, "If you doesn't mind, I's jus soon pay cash!" The story spread like a wildfire around town because there were few people in town, especially the white people who were so impressed by all this, who could pay cash for a new car. After that, people looked at Earl in a different light.

Although at the time Scott was growing up, he never thought anything about it, the "black" area in town was only a half block from his house. He lived right on the edge of another society and never thought or knew anything about it. They rarely saw a black man walking down their street and when they did, they never gave that a thought either. From his house, he and his brother would walk left half a block to the corner, take a right, walk a block, take a left and go about 75 feet to Jesse's Barbecue to pick up some for dinner. Everyone who went to Jesse's brought a small saucepan and Jesse would put barbecue sauce in it. It was always a treat to go to Jesse's.

Next to Jesse's was a nightclub. A few doors up, across the street, there was a church. In the summertime, Scott's family would sleep with the windows open and have the attic fan going. Sometimes, they could barely hear the music from the nightclub waffling through the night air. He did not recall a single person ever complaining about anyone from that neighborhood, the music, or the nightclub.

Scott's father had a fishing partner, Harlan, for about 30 years. Harlan and his wife, Armelda, used to visit on a regular basis and his father would cook fresh fish, French fries, and his mother would make homemade hush puppies. Also, there would be fresh tomatoes, cucumbers, scallions, and fresh sliced onions. In the summer, there would be iced tea and watermelon. His father had converted the garage into a sort of den, small kitchen, and eating area by closing off the front of the garage. He nicknamed it the "Doghouse."

Whenever he cooked, there was a ritual before Harlan and Armelda would leave. His father would fill two brown grocery bags with generous portions of fish, French fries, and hush puppies. One went to Armelda's father, Hanley, who liked to eat his cold for dinner the next night, and the other went to Earl and Pauline. They lived two blocks from Scott.

He and his brother would usually walk over and deliver the bag to them. It didn't matter about the "neighborhood" that they were walking through or that it was after dark. They were never told to be careful or watch out for anything or anybody! They never gave it a second thought. Obviously, neither did their parents.

Another black man in his young life, but not in as personal a way as Earl, was a man by the name of Roy Jenkins. Roy also dressed in the typical fashion of a black man at that time, at least to those who were not laborers. Roy also wore a Fedora. He also was a very pleasant, nice fellow. He rode a bicycle with a basket on the front and delivered prescriptions for a local drugstore. He had a sideline of selling homemade hot tamales. They were made with seasoned meat and corn meal and were wrapped in corn husks. Boy, they were delicious! They were 75 cents a dozen. This doesn't sound like much today, until one remembers that grown white men working for the lumber company earned 75 cents an hour. So, Roy had a pretty good sideline gig going.

One thing was for sure, when Roy was spotted on his bicycle two or three blocks away with his hot tamale box on the front, everyone knew he wasn't delivering prescriptions, and Scott would run home screaming and yelling that Roy was coming with hot tamales so he could get some money and buy some. They came out of the box steaming hot, wrapped in half dozen bunches tied with corn husks.

Well into adulthood, Scott's recollection was that Earl also waxed floors. No telling how many times he had told the stories about Earl doing floors, Roy's hot tamales, and his brother never once mentioned that it was not Earl who waxed the floors, but a black man by the name of Dave. Scott thought it funny how one's memory played tricks on you. He didn't remember Dave's last name, but he was a very pleasant man. And it helped that Scott's father had no white friends named Dave. But even more so, Scott had no memory of Dave ever eating in his house.

When he first came to Washington, it was somewhat of a shock to see so many black people, which he still thought of as being "niggers." Although he had a black classmate in law school, he never got to know him well, even though his group invited him to Maxine's to drink beer with them on several occasions and he did. Turns out, Charlie Pride was his cousin! That was a shocking revelation and left them speechless because early in his career, no one outside of the Grand Ole Opry circuit knew that Charlie Pride was black. He did see a black law student, several in fact, at Northwestern University in Chicago. He was speechless at listening to them discuss cases.

Well, maybe he did have more personal experiences with black people before he came to Washington. One was a very positive experience and, the other, for certain, one of the most shameful and embarrassing experiences of his life. Neither, for various reasons, has he ever shared with but a few, with the reason for the latter being rather obvious after he related the incident.

The positive circumstance was easier for him to talk about. When he was in Chicago, Raymond had arranged, against his wishes, that rather than Scott staying as usual at Raymond's group house off Lake Shore Drive near Michigan Avenue, for him to stay with a law student that Scott did not like whose family name was internationally well known. Suffice it to say, his initial impression of him was that he was a very wealthy, aloof person. After all, the first time he came to Scott's attention was in Dallas when Raymond told Scott that this fella had his Corvette flown from Chicago to Dallas for a law student event because he didn't want to drive a strange car! That is when Scott asked, "Just who the hell is this guy?"

Raymond proceeded to tell him just 'who the hell' this guy was. As it turned out, this fellow wasn't aloof that all, but was a nice guy who was painfully shy and was very uneasy always being viewed as just a rich kid.

His host had a crush on a Swedish-looking nurse at Cook County Hospital. He had a date with her that night. He and Scott went to a bar and waited for her to come in after her shift was over at 11:00.

Cook County Hospital was in quite a different neighborhood from anything Scott had ever been around. Before his friend's date showed up, a guy came in the door and spoke a name to the bartender. "You know him?" The bartender acknowledged that he did, and the guy casually announced that a half block down the street, someone had just blown his head off with a shotgun!

Scott hadn't even begun to digest that news when something else totally unexpected happened. Scott thought his friend's date was going to come alone, but she showed up with a girlfriend, another RN, a black RN! Since he had already received the cold shoulder from the Northwestern law students, all of them, including the white ones, for, he supposed, being from the South, he expected a continuation. It was racial and geographically based, but he felt prejudice for the first time in his life. Of course, it was nothing like real racial prejudice in the South, or anywhere else for that matter, but Scott had never felt any prejudice, so it was disproportionately uncomfortable.

Scott was extremely uneasy. Suddenly, once again, he was the outsider, the minority. Much to his surprise, she started talking to him. It was the first time he had ever spoken to a black girl, or one had spoken to him, much less engaged him in a conversation. That would've been unheard of in his hometown. Talk about catching him off guard! She shocked him when she stood up and asked him to dance, *slow* dance. Everything was happening much too fast for him and he couldn't think. He was too embarrassed to make a scene, so he lamely got up and went to her on the dance floor.

Everything he had ever heard or believed about a "nigger" girl was a contradiction to what he was now experiencing. She drew him in close; she smelled very nice, felt very nice, and her hair, which he had always been told was like steel wool, was as soft, fresh, and sweet smelling as he could possibly imagine.

But Scott had the bad taste to tell her things he had been told about black women and how he had come to realize that everything was not true. He told her how nervous he had been when she appeared, and then asked him to dance. Her reaction conveyed she had poise, class, and style! He made it clear that he really appreciated her being so nice to him. It was becoming an incredibly pleasant experience!

The next night, his host and the Swedish nurse were invited to a Polish wedding so far south of Chicago, he thought it was in Indiana. The Swedish nurse told his host that she was bringing her black friend who liked Scott. And she told her Swedish friend to be sure and tell his host to be sure to bring Scott along. They had a great time! Scott was never really good at remembering names well, but he still remembers her full name because she had the same name as a white girl he knew in the Chi Omega sorority where he was a houseboy in college. Looking back on some of the women he has known that he still holds in high regard, she was one of them. That small group he has always wished and hoped life was good to them.

The shameful and embarrassing experience is a horse of a different color and uncomfortable to relate. He was in Dallas at an annual meeting of the American Bar Association. Again, Raymond was involved. Scott's marriage was on the rocks and he was drinking too much, too often. Somehow, Raymond ended up talking with a group of black lawyers. Raymond was a flaming liberal and probably started talking to them with Scott tagging along and suddenly realizing the group's composition. Sure enough, it came up that one of them was the Dean of a southern university law school. Scott was listening to the conversation and thought that was fabulous. He commenced to compliment him on his being able to rise to such a level, given his race. Despite Raymond's best efforts to drag him away, Scott had to say his piece. Raymond was pissed!

Scott was totally confused as to why Raymond was upset since he was praising a black man for being able to overcome many obstacles and become the Dean of a southern law school. That is when Raymond explained that he was not the Dean of *a* southern law school, but of Southern University Law School. Southern University is a black university! Scott wasn't drinking nearly enough to take the sting out of that. That episode continues to haunt him.

Just a couple of years later, he arrived in DC It was really an experience to ride in a taxi with a black driver. He started to notice that the cab drivers were well-spoken and better informed about what was going on in the world than him, which at that time would have taken virtually nothing to exceed. The comparison was not intended to diminish the degree to which they were informed, but to highlight Scott's ignorance.

It was not long before his attitude really started to change for the better and he became very comfortable in Washington. That's not to say that he had left all of his history and prejudice behind, to be sure, but a major purpose of student foreign exchange programs is to expose young people to other cultures and races. And he was benefitting from the exposure. The primary difference was a domestic geographical "exchange" program.

All this history entered Scott's mind and memory as he waited to meet with his new client. Although he needed the money, he really did not want to take the case. Nevertheless, James convinced Scott that his friend was innocent. James, a southern white guy, knowing Timothy and his family, was very influential in Scott accepting his opinion.

By the time Scott got the case, Timothy had been arrested, placed in jail, posted bond, and released. He was represented by a court-appointed attorney, but as soon as he got out of jail, he went straight to James for a referral and that's how Scott ended up meeting him as a potential client. Thus, it was with this conflicting racial background, attitudes, and experiences that Scott embarked on what would be yet another uncomfortable, life-changing journey.

CHAPTER 9

During the first interview with Timothy in Scott's office, Timothy brought the Complaint, the Event Report, his Bond Release and Release Conditions. According to the Event Report, the offense occurred on May 7 at around 3:50 a.m. The complaining witness worked at a daycare center. Timothy was described as a black male, 28 years-old, 6' 2'', and 190 pounds.

Scott's first impression of Timothy was that he was a large man. He spoke softly and, as it turned out, he had three years of college. He was light-skinned, or what in the South was derogatorily referred to as "high yeller" or a "California nigger." What they were really referring to was uppity nigger with white blood and an education, commonly associated in their mind with California.

Scott's approach was to interview him with direct questions, which would lead to free-flowing responses. He scribbled a few notes, but also recorded the interview, each of which were later turned over to Scott's secretary Nikki for typing. Timothy was working at one of the network television stations, and it was his habit after work to go to one of the Capitol Hill bars. Even though he was married, he said he often briefly partied with women he met after work and went home, or so he said.

After finishing up his scheduled work about nine o'clock, and working on some other projects, he left the station between 10:30 and 11:00. Then, he headed home on Pennsylvania Avenue SE toward Maryland, but he decided to get something to drink, so he stopped at one of the bars on the Avenue called Jenkins Hill. "Oldies, But Goodies" were playing.

Around 12:30 a.m., a lady that he recognized from the Underground walked up and he started talking to her. She was white. At the mention of the Underground, Scott's attention perked up.

"Then, she started talking to some people in the bar. She walked away and people were dancing, so I finished my Rose wine and started walking outside through the crowd toward my car down the block."

"Duddingtons was down the street. It closed later at 3:00. I was walking down the street and was nearly to my car when I heard, *'Hey, Timothy!'* I turned around and there were the two ladies with a gentleman that was in the bar. I recognized one of the ladies."

"She walks up to me and puts her arm around me and says, *'I want to introduce you to a good friend of mine --- a good guy of mine --- a good friend of mine that I met in the bar. His name is Timothy.'*

"So, the other lady says, *'Oh yeah? How are you doing?'* I hadn't seen them until they approached me on the street," Timothy stated matter-of-factly. "After we chatted in the bar, she walked away. I didn't see the other woman the entire time I was in the bar. She put her arm around me. *'Come and go party with us!'*"

"I told her that I only had an hour left and that I had to go to work tomorrow. *'Well, come along with us.'* I had just come off vacation but thought I might stay out later. I would call my wife. So, I said OK. I showed them my car was right there, but they wanted me to leave my car. Then the other guy, an Indian I had seen in the bar, comes up. That's when she told the Indian what a great guy she met in the bar and the other girl puts her arm around me and says, *'We're high and let's go and party.'*"

"I said I only had an hour left and that I had to go to work the next morning. I told her in the bar that I had to work on Saturday and Sunday. I told them I had to go home."

Then they started walking down the street toward Roland's. As they were walking, a Vega pulled up with another guy in it. *'Let's get in this car here.'* The girl from the bar sat in the front seat, the Indian guy sat in the back, the other girl sat next to Timothy, and he sat in the right rear of the car. Trying to find their car, they began circling the block.

They didn't say what kind of car they were looking for and finally thought none looked like theirs. They were too high to even find their own car. After circling the block twice, they stopped. His legs were crunched up in the back. "I need to get out," Timothy said.

"I got out of the car and the Indian guy told us that his place was near Twelfth and Capitol. And then the girl in the front seat asked if he had any grass or beer there. He said, *'No but my place is close by.'* The lady in the back seat said she wanted to go with me, and I agreed."

Scott interjected. "Which one was 'she'?"

Timothy replied, "She's the one this incident supposedly happened with."

"Aren't you a bit confused? Earlier you said the lady who made the complaint was the one you met in the bar who was sitting in the front seat and this time you said she was in the back."

"I meant the lady in the bar was sitting in the back. The second lady I didn't know was in the front."

Timothy continued with his story.

"I got out of the car and was standing by the car when she asked the Indian guy again if he had grass at his place. He said no, but he lived close by. The second lady was still in the front. I was standing outside by the front seat and the lady was still sitting in the back. She got out of the car and was standing by it. Then she asked me if I had my car with me."

They started walking around the block from Duddingtons to where his car was parked.

They got in the car and he started the engine. She said, "*Wait a minute.*"

"I did not say anything about not going to the party, but I was thinking about not going."

He suggested she go with her friends because by this time, he couldn't handle them being high on the speed and beer. "I had to go to work."

He noticed that she paused about 10 seconds or so. They didn't go back to the others because she didn't want him to move. She wanted to get together.

"I told her to go back there with her friends because I was going home to my people in Suitland." He also had not told them he was married.

To Scott, it seemed strange how he was in the habit of describing his family as "his people," but he said he was in the habit.

"Why don't you refer to your wife and kids as your family?" Timothy didn't answer. It was as though he was in a tribe. "Are you in the habit of calling them 'your people' in singles bars?"

"I had my wedding ring on. I always wear it."

"What are you doing going to a singles bar?"

Timothy retorted, "I wasn't in a singles bar."

Scott snapped back. "Excuse me, but the Avenue being my old turf, there sure aren't any "married" bars there!"

Scott continued to press Timothy on why he was going to a party with some girls when he was a married man with three kids and one on the way. As he explained it, his wife knew that he met people and went to parties. "People on the Hill invite you to parties all the time. You meet people."

Timothy explained that he had been to several parties on the Hill that other people, like a bartender, told him about. Then, when he had an hour left, he could deal with the party and he would go out like he said twice a week and use the little time that he had out to have a good time. If he could, sometimes he would go and have a couple of drinks. And other times, he would go straight home, or he would do something else. "I've taken my wife to some of these parties," Timothy tried to explain rather abashedly.

"Does your wife trust you?"

"Of course she does!"

They apparently had the kind of relationship where she would tell him all the time to go out.

"She knows that I'm a responsible person who deals with all my financial obligations and we have an ongoing happy relationship."

Getting back to the events at hand, Scott continued to press. "Since she wouldn't get out of the car and you knew they were waiting for you around the corner, why didn't you drive around there?"

"Because she told me to take her with me because her cousin lives in a Suitland high rise."

Scott asked, "She thinks that they were coming around to you and you told her they weren't coming around there?"

"I told her that I was going home! But she said she'd go with me. I finally agreed but told her that I had to get some gas." So, I stopped at the Exxon Station next to Roland's and got three dollars' worth of gas. Then, I headed down the Avenue towards the Anacostia River and crossed the Pennsylvania Avenue Bridge SE toward RFK Stadium. I would have turned off at Branch Avenue to my house, but never got there. During the ride, there was general conversation about how she liked Philadelphia and had been there. She also shared that she had been in cars with strange men before."

As he recounted all of this, Scott listened intently. He did not want to interrupt Timothy's narrative too much because he wanted it to be free flowing, even if at times, it butted heads with reality and common sense. Bizarre might have been too strong of a word to describe the tale, but Scott couldn't help but internally scream, '*What the fuck were you thinking, or were you thinking? Couldn't you see this woman was an accident waiting to happen? If you wanted to dip your wick, couldn't you have found less of a nut case? Hello?*'

There was clearly no indication, however, that he had been thinking straight with either head! But his calm demeanor conveyed to Scott that he was, in fact, being truthful. Well, as he saw the truth. Or at least truthful with respect to the part he was telling Scott. Scott had come quite a way since he first started doing criminal defense work. He was not exactly cynical; however, he had become fairly analytical about his clients' "stories."

"When we got to the light at 27th and Pennsylvania Avenue SE, I stopped at the bottom of the hill, which is about four miles from my house. She said she had to take a leak right there. I was going to pass stations, but they were further down the street. I asked her why she didn't stop me at the Exxon station when I got gas or that we had passed to go to the bathroom and she said the speed and the beer were coming out of her and if I didn't let her take a leak right then and there, she'd take a leak in my car!"

Just to check his story Scott asked, "Did you offer to go to any other gas stations or the ones you passed?"

"No."

Then Scott asked him to draw a diagram of Pennsylvania Avenue SE and the stations where he could have stopped. He said, as he drew, "The second light is where we were when she needed to take a leak. It's a two-way street toward Pennsylvania Avenue and the Alexander Pope Funeral Home is there.

"We passed it and stopped near the corner. She told me to move up further across the street somewhat. After she got out of the car and closed the door, I turned the car lights out. She said, '*I feel kind of freaky going to the bathroom out here.*'"

She had on pants and asked for help getting up an embankment. The top of the embankment was wooded. After they got up there, she went to the bathroom.

Scott asked him why he was standing there, and he said, "To see that no people were coming. She's going to the bathroom. Squatting down, she fell over once. And she said, '*After I'm done, let's do something!*'"

"What did she mean let's do something?"

"I don't know. Maybe she meant let's go somewhere."

Scott was incredulous at his response but avoided any facial reaction as much as he could. "What did you think she meant? You've been around."

"I didn't think of doing anything in the woods, good gracious. I thought she meant let's go somewhere."

Following up on this thought, Scott calmly asked him, "It never occurred to you that she wanted to go somewhere and have some sex with you?"

"Not really. She told me that she was very funny, and I didn't think she wanted to do anything. She was ready to go party some more.

I had already looked for a way out of these woods. I told her I couldn't be in these woods like this because of my job, my people. So, I told her I was going to leave. If I wanted to do something, I had money, and I had credit cards. I told her I was leaving."

And that's when he saw the glare of lights come up the street from the opposite direction.

They were still up on the embankment. "I told her about the lights, and she was still going to the bathroom. I couldn't handle it and I told her that I was leaving because there are lights coming. Then she told me she'd holler rape if I left her."

"Why were you going to leave her? Why didn't you tell her to hurry up and take her home?"

"I couldn't be caught in the woods!"

"Why? Were you worried about your car lights being on or was it parked illegally?"

"No, it was on the side of the road with no lights on."

He told her he couldn't be caught in the woods like that. He was giving her an opportunity to come along, but when she said, *I'm going to holler rape if you leave me,* that's when he said, "I'm gone."

He was walking away from the car lights to go out on the street further down from his car and then come around to his car so no one could see him come right out of the woods where she was. He started walking towards the back of his car when he fell down in a gully. He got up and he walked to the left and out to the street. That is when he saw the police cruiser right there in the street, pulled to the side. Timothy walked straight up to the police officer.

The officer was just getting out of the cruiser and Timothy walked up on the passenger side. The officer couldn't have seen him, even though he wasn't far from the cruiser.

"Hey officer!" The officer was startled and quickly pivoted to face Timothy. "There is a girl in the woods on speed and beer and she said I raped her."

Scott presented his station identification and DC driver's license, even though the officer didn't ask for them. Then the officer said, "We'll see." He cuffed Timothy and put him in the car. Then he drove up around the other street and made a right instead of coming up the street where Timothy's car was. He circled around the block and came out between the funeral home and Timothy's car. Timothy didn't point out his car to the officer as he pulled up behind the three other cruisers. He didn't know what they were doing there.

Suddenly, he heard her yelling, *Rape! Rape! Rape!*

Without much fanfare, the officer drove Timothy down to the station. Timothy overheard the officer tell the other officers that Timothy ran from his car. Timothy didn't know why he said that. But he knew the officer was going to say something stupid because he heard him talking in the office at the station. Timothy called the officer back there to where he was sitting in a holding cell.

"Are you trying to say that I was running when I came up to you? How could I run from my car if you put me in your police cruiser and drove me to my car?" The officer did not respond.

On May 8th, Scott entered his appearance on Timothy's behalf in the Superior Court of the District of Columbia, Criminal Division. His next step, an obvious one, was to interview the employee at the Exxon station.

On May 19, Timothy picked Malcolm up in the District and brought him into Scott's office in Arlington. Malcolm was working the 11:00 to 7:00 graveyard shift the weekend before last, which was the weekend of May 5th. He sat nervously in his chair facing Scott.

"I remembered him pulling into the station between three and three thirty in the morning. I remembered him because he comes there all the time. I didn't know his name or anything but recognized his face and his car. I pay more attention to people's cars and he had mag wheels. I have been working there about eight years during the week on the day shift, but since they changed my shift to night, only on the weekends."

Timothy had not been coming regularly through the full year, but about twice a month.

Only reason Malcolm also recognized Timothy was because one night, Malcolm asked him if he had the correct change because they usually run correct change at night. He pumped the gas and Timothy gave him a twenty and he had to run around and find some change, so he remembered him. He also remembered how much gas Timothy bought that night: three dollars because he usually got only three dollars of gas.

Malcom also remembered Timothy had a lady with him that night, a white lady, and she had blonde hair. He knew exactly this because Timothy touched her on her head, just her hair. He didn't overhear any of their conversation while he was pumping gas because that's one thing he doesn't do, listen to people. He did notice that she was talking to him. He didn't notice anything to suggest she might be drinking or high on anything, however.

"She did not get out of the car and go to the bathroom. They stayed in the car. Timothy had never gotten out since I had been working there. The first time I had ever seen Timothy out of the car was when he picked me up to drive me to your office for this interview. Except for her being in the car, he came in just the way he always does, bought his gas, and left."

Nice, tight corroboration of Timothy's story.

While Timothy was telling his version, Scott was concentrating on how smooth Timothy told it and how well it all fit together, almost too well. Unbeknownst to Timothy, Scott did not frequent Jenkins Hill, but he did know the street area around where the events related to Duddingtons, Roland's, and the Exxon occurred. His story, at least that part of it, was very vivid to Scott.

Yet, an even more personal connection with Timothy's experience existed. Scott sometimes told the story that he had never picked up a woman in a bar, which was true. On the other hand, he had been picked up in a bar by a woman!

Bobby, his friend from college, was coming into National Airport for a few days visit and party time. He was due in around 7:30 that evening. Those were the days before cell phones, flight data, and *CNN*, or the *Weather Channel*. All anyone could do was go to the airport and find out real time flight status from the arrival board. There was a monster electrical storm all along the Eastern coast and huge delays that evening.

After one dry run, he decided to kill time at the Underground. There was a good looking dark-haired young woman with big, dark eyes and a body to kill for at the other end of the bar who was, at least he hoped, making eye contact, although, with his history, it was only wishful thinking. He made two more dry runs across the Potomac, each time returning to the Underground. During each return, she continued the eye contact routine, or at least that was his fantasy. After all, it was certainly more pleasant than multiple, dry run round trips to National. A combination of his history and focusing on meeting Bobby lent themselves to an appearance of detachment and/or aloofness, neither of which had ever worked even when he tried. Apparently, he wasn't any good at that either.

When he returned the fourth time, she was still there, only this time, she picked up her drink, walked over, and sat down beside him. *Wow! Be cool!*

She told him she had noticed his going and coming and was curious about what he was doing. Reversing the situation, had he used that line, the response would have ranged from: "None of your business," maybe a withering glare, a deflating, cold, stern, "Excuse me?", or "I am waiting on...." and "that stool is taken!"

However, he explained, and she didn't leave. When again it was time to go back to the airport, even he could tell she was interested. Only this time, he told her that they were coming back to the Underground to drink and catch up. She was welcomed to ride over and back, although this time, he was going to wait at the airport. She readily agreed. *Oh, happy days!*

Well, when Scott picked up Bobby, Bobby was clearly impressed and more interested in her than him! Scott knew Bobby extremely well. Bobby had two heads, but around a good-looking woman, one was always dominant. They went back to the Underground and it was exactly as represented: drinks and two college buddies catching up. That is, *when* Scott could get Bobby's attention!

Around three, Scott was ready to leave. They offered to give her a ride home. She lived on A Street NE. When they got there, although Scott didn't remember her asking them in, he parked, and they got out of the car. High intensity mercury vapor lights gave the street a yellowish glow almost as bright as daylight. She had only walked about fifteen feet from them, gradually moving toward the middle of their side of the street, when suddenly, she started waving her arms in the air and screaming at the top of her lungs, "I HATE MEN!!!"

Bobby always wanted to "rescue" damsels in distress and "comfort" them. So, he started to move toward her. As sternly as possible, without raising his voice, Scott said, "Get in the car," but Bobby ignored him.

Then Scott screamed, "Get in the fucking car! See all these lights. Don't get near her. People are already looking out their windows and the police have been called!"

They left immediately!

The next morning, around 10:30, they were still asleep when Scott's phone rang, and it was her. She wanted to apologize for her behavior. "I guess you're wondering how I got your number?"

Scott had a few drinks the night before, but he hadn't gotten drunk and certainly did not remember giving it to her. Turns out, his car had a vanity tag with his initials, and he had told her he lived in Arlington. No telling how many people she had called with his initials before she found him. Scott wished that Timothy had paid attention to the warning signs the woman had given him from the get-go. But once she was in his car, she really was in charge.

In Scott's case, his femme fatale didn't give any warning signs until she was in the middle of the street screaming and yelling! And despite those obvious warning signs and the somewhat more ominous warning signs when she called up the next morning, Scott failed to exercise good judgment, just like Timothy.

In the end, she was just too damn good-looking, too damn well-built, and too damn interested in Scott for Scott to damn resist. She was a student at the University of Maryland, and he used to go out northeast on the Beltway near Greenbelt, Maryland where she lived. She had a chess set that was a rug on the floor with eight-inch-high pieces. She was a most willing, although he was never sure, did not ask and did not care if it were true, "lousy" opponent at strip chess. It didn't matter to him if that was her version of the Yellow Brick Road!

So, not only was Timothy's description of the events and location full of vivid images for Scott, but he personally related to a night-time, playtime scenario, going extremely south, exercising poor hormonal judgment, and, more importantly, believe him!

Within 30 days from taking the case, before he could seriously get started and crank up a defense, the United States Attorney dismissed all charges. Dismissal, so quickly, said it all! It was certainly a relief for Timothy, for Scott, and it justified James's faith in Timothy. But, although Scott was relieved from a professional standpoint, nothing compared to his freedom from conflicting turmoil on multiple personal levels.

CHAPTER 10

In the following months, his office mates continued referring cases. There still were none of any note, however. Small collection cases were about it, but Scott would take pretty much anything to pay his share of the expenses. Some were misdemeanor cases. They paid better than court appointed work, but he still had to wait for referrals. On the other hand, with court appointed cases, he could go to court and get one to three per day. As his time in the office increased, however, he was able to obtain more referred civil and criminal cases, gradually phasing out of the court appointed cases in about four months.

James gave him the most. He used to work for the Company and sent a few referrals from people that he knew. He divided his time between his Arlington and DC office. Since James' practice concentrated on personal injury and divorce work, neither of which Scott did, there was no reason for him to refer any of those cases. Moreover, Scott didn't know enough about those types of cases to take them on anyway.

Around the second of week of November, James walked into Scott's office with a look that immediately caught Scott's attention. After a pause, James quietly spoke. "Timothy's been arrested again … for rape!"

Once again, Scott heard the very same speech. James knew him, Timothy was innocent, James knew his family, and James still believed him. By this time, Scott was aware of just how well James knew Timothy and Timothy's family. He preferred women of color and was dating Timothy's aunt! And Timothy, as well as James, given the outcome of the earlier rape charge, wanted him to take on the case.

Scott was both grateful and elated for the potential work but remained intensely averse to becoming involved again. Also, he was very mindful of his lack of substantive experience. He was equally cognizant that he hadn't orchestrated the result in the other case because it had simply self-imploded. Without a doubt, he had skated on his lack of experience and his deep emotional conflict issues.

Although he hadn't gained much more legal experience in six months, especially in the area of criminal law, what he did know he knew before he started practicing. Unknown to James, Scott brought a lot more to the table than appeared to the naked eye and significant experience in other areas. But he had never disclosed to James that he damned sure had the same personal emotional conflict issues that existed in the first rape case. Even more so now!

All the attendant circumstance triggered negative thoughts and set his head spinning. Once again, he needed the money, but he realized this case was definitely not one that would go away quietly. Two rape charges in seven months! The U.S. Attorney would be out for blood! It didn't matter that they had dismissed the first charge; their minds didn't work that way! Immediately, it flashed through Scott's mind that, notwithstanding the obvious problems that must've existed in the earlier case, there's always that lingering doubt he did not know what they were. In short, they may have believed that an offense had occurred, but given her drugged up condition, a decision may have been made that they could not convict because the victim would not be a credible witness, particularly considering she was the instigator of the circumstances under which they had ended up together. Nevertheless, despite his internal conflict for other personal reasons, Scott was unavoidably drawn to the case.

All his senses screamed: "*Is James fucking crazy to believe him and me to believe James? I don't know any of the facts or haven't even talked to Timothy and I already don't believe this bullshit*!"

Scott instantly sensed this case was going to be a moneymaker. Even more compelling, surely this was going to be an intriguing case and one that would give him a lot of experience. Those factors excited him! But they were not the clinchers. All his misgivings aside, the hook that grabbed his gut and drew him totally in on a personal level, where his deepest personal conflict existed, was the question *"What if he really is being falsely accused?"*

All indications were that Timothy had been telling the truth in the first case. Or was he just extremely lucky? After all, Timothy was adamant that he was telling the truth and it was trumped up. Even though nothing about it appeared in the police report, he had told Scott that the girl had performed oral sex on him. Obviously, she hadn't disclosed that to the police because it would been detrimental prosecuting the case. They didn't conduct any tests or take hair or blood samples from Timothy. Moreover, standard procedure would have included transporting her to a hospital ER, collecting hair and blood samples, in conjunction with her statement. If they had done so, even as a precaution, Scott was unaware of it. Under the circumstances, then, there was no need to pursue obtaining any police reports or medical examination results.

Even considering these factors, the first case failed to satisfy, at that stage, a bare minimum probable cause threshold necessary to proceed to an indictment. And it was dismissed in three weeks! Obviously, the U.S. Attorney had more information now than had previously been shared. While it wasn't important to know all the details of the first case, under the circumstances at that time, now these considerations made Scott nervous.

There was a delay between the incident and the arrest this time. The complaint was filed by a woman he knew, who he had had drinks with the night before and who had identified him by name, which led to his arrest. Once more, as in the May incident, there had been a delay in Scott becoming involved early on and doing some damage control. By the time he had come to Scott, Timothy had already given a statement.

The current incident occurred on the night of November 7-8, but Timothy was arrested and interviewed on November 13. And, once again, he had a court-appointed attorney. They were known as "6th Streeters" because the DC Superior Court was on 6th Street NW, and these were lawyers who hung out in the courthouse hallways waiting to pick up clients. They weren't ambulance chasers! Scott called them "Hall Chasers!" They were easily recognizable from their cheap, ill-fitting, worn out suits with shiny seats.

Scott felt there would be more of a sense of urgency the second time around. *Fuck! Why not wait to hire him at jury selection and save some money!* Timothy had a copy of his statement to the police. Scott began to read it. In Timothy's statement, sex squad officers asked questions, Timothy answered, all recorded. Both were transcribed and the statement signed by him and the arresting officers conducting the interrogation.

The questions and answers in the statement were not the best King's English, but the questions were in that cryptic arresting officer style designed to confuse an off-balance, disorganized, intimidated, defendant under arrest:

"Q. It was reported to this office on November 8 at approximately 0415 hrs. that you, armed with a knife, broke into an apartment, and raped a female. Please relate the events which you can recall on November 7, when you went to work, and on November 8, when you arrived at home.

A. I was scheduled into work at 12:30 P.M. for the election. I was there until around midnight to 12:30 AM. Then I got myself together and went to Duddingtons Underground. The bartender's name was James, a black guy. I sat and drank a Rose. [*Oops,* Scott thought to himself. *I've heard that before.*] I was there until the bar closed-2:00 AM or 2:30 AM. Then I walked a friend home who I have known for a while. I forget her name. James knows her. She lives across the street, the next street over. Then I came back, got in my car, and drove home. [*The phrase "my people" sprang back into Scott's memory as he read this portion.*]

Q. What car were you driving?

A. Grand Torino, gold, with bucket seats.

Q. How long did it take to walk this friend home?

A. 10 minutes.

Q. Was the friend male or female?

A. Female.

Q. How much did you drink that night?

A. Three Roses. Glasses.

Q. Did you go into the friend's apartment?

A. No. She lives in a house. You have to open an outside door to get to her apartment.

Q. Did you pick up anyone on the way home?

A. No.

Q. What time did you get home?

A. I guess 3:00 or 3:30 AM.

Q. Was anyone up at home who can verify your arrival?

A. No one was there. My roommate was not home. He stayed in town because of his car. [For the first time, Scott learned that, by this time, despite his "understanding" wife, Timothy was now separated.]

Q. Did you go back to this friend's apartment?

A. No. I went straight home.

Q. What is this friend's name?

A. I don't know her name. She hangs out at Duddingtons.

Q. Have you ever taken her out prior to this day?

A. No.

Q. Have you ever gone to her apartment – inside - prior to this date?

A. Never. That was the first time I walked her home that night.

Q. Have you ever had sex with her?

A. Never.

Q. What is your blood type?

A. Possibly "O." I forget.

Q. Did you kiss this friend that night?

A. Yes.

Q. Did you obtain her home phone number or work number?

A. No, nothing like that.

Q. How well do you know this friend you walked home? Isn't it strange you don't recall her name?

A. Not very well. I see her at Duddingtons, and she comes up and talks to me. We just have conversation. She works at a space thing in statistics.

Q. Did you rape her?

A. No, of course, not.

Q. Did you force a kiss on her?

A. No.

Q. How many times did you kiss her?

A. Twice.

Q. Did you go anywhere after you left her?

A. No, just straight home.

Q. Is there anything you wish to add to this statement?

A. That is the verbatim for that night."

In the Prosecution Report, the modus operandi of the suspect was cryptically described as "Picks up Caucasian women. Then rapes them. Hangs at bars in the 300 blk of Pa. Ave. SE, Rose wine."

In very matter of fact police language terminology, the Event Report described the incident as:

"On November 8, at 0415 hours, the complaining witness said the Defendant entered her apartment VIA a side window, placed a knife to her nose causing a laceration, ordered her to roll over, and then forced her to commit sexual intercourse against her will and in fear of her life.

On November 9, the complaining witness responded to the Sex Offense Branch for a statement which was taken by Detective Richards. In her statement, she positively identified the Defendant, Timothy Rogers, who is personally known to her, as the Subject who raped her at knife point and broke into her apartment.

On November 11, the Facts in this case were presented to a Judge of the Superior Court of the District of Columbia by an Affidavit. A warrant was issued for the Arrest of the Defendant Timothy Rogers.

On November 13, the Arrest Warrant was executed on the Defendant; advised him of his rights; transported to the Sex Offense Branch at 300 Independence. Ave. NW.

On November 15, an order was entered for him to give blood and saliva samples.

On November 15, another order was entered for him to appear in a lineup on December 5."

Scott later reached an agreement with the police and the Assistant United States Attorney that Timothy would appear at the lineup on December 5 and accept service of the two orders with the understanding that the preliminary hearing would be postponed so Scott could be better organized in view of all the charges.

CHAPTER 11

Before the lineup, they spoke in Scott's office. Timothy told him essentially the same information that was in his earlier recorded interview. The scenario reeked of Deja Vu on several levels! Scott could not get it out of his head that not only was Timothy in Scott's local bar, but it was the bar where a few years earlier, Scott had met Jennifer. The area was very popular with Hill staffers who frequented the Underground and the Avenue.

On December 5th, Timothy and Scott appeared at the police headquarters for Timothy's lineup for the charges of first-degree burglary while armed; rape while armed; assault with a dangerous weapon; and assault with intent to kill while armed.

Timothy went with the police officers somewhere else to get ready for the lineup. Scott went into the lineup room. It was his first time to ever attend a lineup! Anyone who'd ever seen a lineup on a television crime show or in a movie knew as much as he did about what was going to happen. If indeed, it really happened that way.

Scott was shown into a large room, approximately fifty-five feet by forty feet. To his right was a podium in front of a "bar" like the railing that separates people attending court proceedings from the lawyers and the audience, parallel to the wall to his right and running the length of the room. Beyond it was a large glass window and behind it was the platform for the people being viewed. It was just like in the movies! At least *that* part looked familiar.

To the left, were rows of darkened-wooden chairs with the backs, arm rests, and seats stained from years of sweaty backs, arms, palms and butts. Scott was happy he was wearing long sleeves. And then, he just waited to see what was going to happen, all the while hoping someone else went first.

Shortly, 11 people filed in behind the glass. By then, he had learned a lot and what he quickly noticed were lots of cops' eyes in the lineup. A couple of men in the lineup, plus Timothy, maybe, looked like defendants. An attractive young woman gave them instructions on how the lineup was going to proceed and that they were to read certain statements when prompted. Then, to Scott's surprise, the curtains were closed. He was momentarily confused, but then he realized it was to be a voice-only lineup.

Scott was surprised, again, when he heard her call him to the podium. "This is your case Mr. Carmichael. I am conducting the lineup. Stand next to me at the podium."

While focusing on what was going on in front of him, he had failed to take note as to whether any other attorneys had come into the room for the lineup. So much for watching and learning!

The first person she called in wasn't a woman, but a man. A white man! Never having done this before, it occurred to Scott then that the white man was there for one of the other people in the lineup and the police were bringing in the victims and witnesses for other cases. Then, he wondered, if that was how it worked, why was he up there and why not another lawyer? Scott's confusion intensified. Even so, his thinking accelerated and became focused. Since there wasn't another man present in the room the night of Timothy's offense, other than the intruder, he wasn't worried. That was because he still didn't really understand what was happening.

All 11 men in the lineup repeated the phase, "Don't move or I will cut you, hear? Ok? Hear?"

Then the witness said, "No. 11."

Holy fuck!! *That is Timothy's number*!

She then called in the next person who turned out to be a woman. Timothy had described the woman who identified him and accused him of rape as a short, attractive, slightly pudgy brunette with big hooters. This was not the brunette he was expecting, but an attractive, stringy-haired, strawberry blond. A white woman! The woman in charge instructed the men to read a different phrase:

"Don't make any noise or try to wake him. Now roll off the bed onto your knees."

"I recognize No. 11!" the victim then exclaimed.

Scott knew he had a very good poker face and prayed like hell it was holding up. Even though he had yet to see who he was expecting to see, it was obvious this case had just gone over the cliff and was in total free fall without a parachute. He felt betrayed and snookered! All the rationalizing to take the case, riding in on his white charger to save a wrongfully accused man, and his personal reasons for doing so, went right out the fucking window! He dismounted faster than you could spit! All he could think about was maintaining his poker face and deciding whom he was going to kill first when he got back to his office: James or Timothy.

Then, they called the next witness. Finally, a brunette appeared. But *not* the one he was expecting! She was thin and flat chested. *Holy shit! What is happening here?* By that time, the gravity of realizing that the lineup was only about his client was overwhelming!

His shock increased! Even more disturbing, the brunette had been badly beaten about the face. And her skin was at that stage where the bruising had blackened. Scott had never seen anyone beaten badly, let alone a woman. That visual alone distracted and disturbed him. Her incident occurred on December 4 after Timothy's arrest for the offense for which they were there in the first place! But Scott had no time to focus on this development. All his cerebral reserve was consumed in focusing on her reaction to the voices.

Everyone behind the curtain was instructed to repeat yet a different phrase. "Roll over and take off your panties. I have a knife."

"I think it is No. 11," she whispered.

By then, Scott didn't know what to expect next. This lineup was not to try and clear the books on different assailants. It was to show that Timothy was a serial rapist!

He was reeling in shock and desperately attempting to disguise it, although not feeling confident that he was successful, as they called in the next witness. Rather anticlimactically at this point, in came the short, attractive, slightly pudgy brunette with big hooters. His expectations were all down the toilet and mattered not at this point. Behind the curtain, each man was instructed to say, "Keep your hands on the pillow. If you move or scream, I will kill you. I'm going to be in here a while."

Again, Scott heard, "No. 11."

At that point, the lineup was finished. So was Scott! He had gone there expecting one case that might be a mistake, like the first one, and had been hammered with two more. Years later, a lawyer would tell him that a case never got any better than the day it walked in the door. At the very moment that lawyer conveyed his sage observation, it generated a flashback to this very experience.

He went back to his office and Timothy came as soon he was allowed to leave the police station. Needless to say, Scott was, among other emotions, still in shock. Soon, Timothy was also in shock when Scott told him of the results of the lineup and that, undoubtedly, he would be charged and arrested for two more counts of rape. Events took a stranger turn when Scott told him the names of two of the complaining witnesses.

The first white woman and the white man were married, and Timothy's friends! Scott had learned that their names were Nelson and Lynn Daniels. She was four months pregnant at the time of the rape in May and had given birth in October. "I have been to their home several times for parties and occasionally seen them at bars on the Avenue. Also, Nelson teaches communications at a local university. I have spoken to his class about the opportunities for blacks in the communications field." Timothy's familiarity with them and their house was not good.

"I don't know the brunette who had been beaten." The skinny brunette's name was Sharon Wood. His familiarity with the short, attractive, slightly, pudgy, brunette with big hooters, and the location of her apartment was not good either. Her name was Crystal Hawthorne. The prosecution was on a roll. Scott didn't comment to Timothy, however, Scott no longer believed him.

At that point, Timothy and Scott were confronted with some hard, negative facts. The facts were that Timothy had only recently been charged with rape in May, was arrested in November after again having been identified by a complaining witness, by name, and summarily re-arrested. Here they were in December and he had just been identified in a voice-only lineup by not only the original complaining witness expected at the lineup in the first place, but by three complaining witnesses from two new incidences!

Timothy was incredulous about his friends' accusations. Scott could understand, but he was neither a therapist nor was it his job to sympathize with Timothy's problems, or, at least not to the extent to allow it to interfere with his judgment. Again, Scott had his own baggage with this messy situation. What started out as what psychologists call an approach-avoidance conflict had unexpectedly and painfully evolved into an avoidance-avoidance conflict.

When he first started doing court appointed work, although he was somewhat book-wise about the criminal justice system and had lived at a prison for a month doing intern work with inmates when he was in law school, he was not anywhere near streetwise about how criminals played the system and lawyers in the criminal justice system, especially a young and inexperienced lawyer like him.

One of the first experiences he had was one he always referred to as his "fanny patting" case. The assault had taken place in a diner. The diner had no tables, and everyone ate at a counter with eight stools. Customers coming in for takeout stood behind the diners and ordered from a menu on the back wall as they looked over the diners' heads. Their orders were then handed to them over the seated patrons. Scott's client was standing behind the seated customers and waiting on his order when he was accused of patting a sitting female patron on the derriere.

He said it wasn't him, and that his buddy could vouch for him. But when Scott asked him his buddy's name and contact information, all he could tell Scott about him was his street name. That certainly wasn't any help.

Well, Scott wasn't experienced then either, but he knew his client was lying. He just couldn't figure out where in the story lay the lie. There appeared to be no contradictions in his story. When it came time for trial, Scott chose a bench trial, which is a trial with just the judge. When Scott mentioned this in the lawyer's lounge to the 6th Streeters, they emitted a simultaneous, unanimous, groan! Immediately, with this judge, it was obvious he had made a big mistake. Nevertheless, it would have been an even bigger mistake to take a jury trial. It was an impossibility, primarily because he didn't even know how to pick a jury.

Trial was assigned to a courtroom away from the main courthouse in the old Immigration Building. It was not a formal large courtroom like the regular courthouse. There was a huge center atrium area with doors all-around and walkways on each of six floors. He had no idea how many courtrooms there were, but his assigned courtroom was on the first floor. It was about fifteen by eighteen with a small judge's bench next to the wall directly across from the entrance. The clerk sat lower and directly in front of the judge. In the far-right corner to the judge's left was a door.

They took their seats. The prosecution made an opening statement and Scott made an opening statement. The prosecution called in the complaining witness. She was black and wearing the white pantsuit of a nurse. She was strikingly beautiful and appeared to have some Cherokee blood. Her eyes were filled with intense anger. If looks could kill, his client, as well as Scott, would have been burnt toast.

She was not afraid of eye contact. She glared at Scott's client with pure hatred and anger as she testified about sitting in the diner eating her lunch and suddenly feeling someone groping her butt. She turned around and there was his client.

When it was time to cross examine her, Scott asked, "How do you know it was my client and not his friend, since you had your back to them?" If possible, the anger in her eyes intensified even more.

"*What* friend? He was the *only* person there!"

Shit! In a split second, the unknown became the obvious!

Against Scott's advice, his client insisted on taking the stand, denying everything, and insisting it was his friend. On cross examination, the Assistant U. S. Attorney asked him the name of his friend. Inexplicably, he said, "William Smith."

"When was the last time you saw him?" asked the attorney.

"Oh! Thirty days ago."

"Where?"

"At the DC jail."

"Did you tell your lawyer about this?" At this point, Scott was cringing and thinking to himself, *Please God, tell the truth*!

"No ... I just thought about it while I was sitting here on the stand."

At that moment, Scott knew his client was going away for a good while, and everyone in the courtroom also knew he was going away. Not only because of his testimony, but, as he was doing his song and dance, Scott was distracted by the clerk in front of the judge's bench. He had his fingers interlocked with his hands behind his head, leaning back in his chair with his head against the bench, looking up to the ceiling as he rolled his eyes, smiling.

They were called up in front of the bench for the judge's rather obvious decision. Scott and his client stood side by side. Two U.S. Marshalls stood behind them and between them and the entrance door, just in case his client got rabbit blood. They were big like NFL defensive linemen. They did not have just one or two big guys in the U.S. Marshall's Office. They were all huge!

As they stood there and listened to the judge's reasoning, Scott heard two consecutive sets of clicking noises behind them. He didn't have the nerve to turn around, but suddenly realized that everyone in the courtroom, except maybe his dumb-ass client, knew he had been found guilty. The Marshalls not only knew it, but, with *that* judge, in *his* courtroom, they *could* go ahead and cuff his ass. And they did! He went out the door in the far corner to the judge's left to go downstairs to wait for the five o'clock bus to take him to the DC jail. Scott went to have lunch with Jennifer.

Even retained clients presented a challenge for Scott. He once represented a woman charged with embezzling government property. Someone had "dropped a dime on her." She had been under surveillance for six months and was arrested going into her boutique 15 miles from where she was supposed to be by two government security agents who had followed her. She was found to be in possession of the very type property she was suspected of stealing.

She had come to him as a referral from a congressional aide who was a friend of her friends. The congressional aide, in turn, was a friend of the client charged with embezzling from the House of Representatives Post Office. Scott knew the congressional aid had helped her pay her legal fees. She once came in with a handful of brand new $100 bills. She sat there for 45 minutes with them in her hand before turning them over to him. Scott was distracted, wondering how many she had in her hand. New bills don't take up much room. Anyway, that case had turned out well for her, so, through the friend connection, the woman had been referred to him.

Most of the details of her story are unimportant here. What is important about her story is that she was adamant about her innocence. And, despite the fact that she had been 15 miles away and headed in the wrong direction from where she was supposed to be headed and was caught red-handed with the more of the same type property she was charged with previously stealing, she insisted that it wasn't what it looked like. So she said!

She had been represented by two lawyers for about two months when she was referred to him. In all that time, they had not told her what she was charged with. Nor were they receptive to her pleas of innocence. They had also done no investigative work to corroborate her story.

Essentially, her story was that she had possession of the government property legally; she had made arrangements to turn it over to someone who worked for her to take it back to where it belonged, and when they did not show up, she had to carry it with her. The property had gotten dirty in the back of her station wagon and she was taking it into her store to clean it. Of course, anyone would believe that!

From the get-go, she said she berated the two lawyers to check out her story and they did nothing but take her money. Scott did not know about that, but not telling her what she was being charged with was inexcusable. A first-year law student in a criminal law class would know that she would be charged with theft, at the very least. Quite by accident, he later learned that the senior of the two had been found to have lied under oath to a congressional committee and, when given a chance to come clean in a later hearing, acknowledged his previous testimony was false. The committee chairman proceeded to address new questions to the lawyer. After the committee chairman challenged him, the lawyer acknowledged that he was lying ... again!

She wasted no time in telling Scott all the details of her day involving the arrest and what she said really had happened. She gave him names, places, and times, together with prior history of her work environment. Pieced together, her story was a beautiful mosaic.

From the first case, Scott created the concept of the "donut" defense and from the second case the "wagon wheel" defense.

The donut defense is like the hole in the donut in that, although a lawyer senses the client is lying, everything is in and remains inside the hole in the doughnut. There is nothing or anyone extrinsic to the client's story to confirm or contradict his or her version, and the lawyer can't get outside of the center of the doughnut. The lawyer becomes the hamster.

In the wagon wheel defense, the defendant is the hub of the wagon wheel and the spokes represent the possible multiple directions and extrinsic sources to confirm the client's version. Unlike the doughnut defendant who offers nothing that a lawyer can use to verify the defendant's version of the offense, the wagon wheel client pushes, pushes, and pushes the lawyer to check the sources out and talk to witnesses until, incrementally, the confirmation builds and most of the spokes and pieces of the rims of the wagon wheel are filled.

Generally, the lawyer begins to conclude that the client was guilty in the first place even when the story the defendant offered was a doughnut theory. And with the innocent client, they just keep building the wagon wheel!

Timothy's story wasn't exactly a donut and it wasn't exactly a wagon wheel, at least, according to him. Of course, either defense would have been better applied to one case, rather than both defenses overlapping and being used in multiple cases. In Timothy's case, he, of course, knew the short, busty brunette, but claimed that she asked him to walk her home and he never went in the door. "I am on my period," she told him. They played smacky mouth at the door and she told him that they would get together again. "I never start anything I don't finish." Donut! In the case involving his friends, he denied everything. Donut! Same thing in the thin brunette case. Donut!

Scott found himself confronted by three donuts. And, maybe, the beginning of one wagon wheel, only it was the wagon wheel of a child's wagon that is pulled along by the handle. But it wasn't even a very small, very bumpy wheel; rather, it was only the beginning of one with one tiny spoke and a tiny portion of the rim: James, the bartender.

There was no one else to talk to and when Scott considered that the persuasive weight of the testimony of four complaining witnesses, and the available evidence produced donuts for the prosecution, it was not looking good for the home team. But just when Scott thought it was as bad as you can imagine, it got worse!

On December 22, another rape occurred. The assailant broke into an apartment and attempted to rape a woman at knife point. She was asleep in bed with her boyfriend. Very quickly, they testified before a grand jury.

The Assistant U.S. Attorney conducting the grand jury asked: "Did there come a time that you learned that someone named Timothy Rogers had been charged with at least one other rape?"

She had looked at mug shots. "I know this man. But I do not know his name. I have danced with him several times during the last year." Where? Where else? Of course, on Nard's night at the Underground! Where else would Scott have expected? She said she could not remember his voice well enough from the Underground to know if he was the assailant. Later, she and her friend listened to a tape of the voice-only lineup. They each, independently, identified No. 11!

As a result, the grand jury returned an indictment called a "Grand Jury Original." Because there had been no prior arrest, the indictment was the charging document that resulted in Timothy's arrest ... for a third time. Again, the donut versus the wagon wheel, and the prosecution donut was the victor … again!

CHAPTER 12

After his arrests and the lineup, the first battle began. Women at his base television station were up in arms about having a serial rapist, *not* an accused serial rapist, but a serial rapist, in the building and "lurking" in the hallways. Obviously, their being in the news business, they quickly learned of the lineup identification results. Immediately, Timothy was notified that he was on administrative leave, *without* pay! It was catastrophic and meant, potentially, losing his house and car.

On January 4th, Scott wrote a letter to the AUSA assigned to the case to begin formal gathering of Rule 16 Disclosure information. It would include any and all information, which could constitute evidence favorable to Timothy, or which may lead to material exculpatory evidence within the meaning of *Brady v. Maryland*, a landmark United States Supreme Court case. *Brady* imposed a duty on the prosecution to turn over potentially exculpatory material to the defense, so called *"Brady"* material.

It might be information such as a confession by an accomplice or someone other than the defendant; eyewitness statements; identifications; misidentification; initial description of the assailant vs. a subsequent different description; initial description of offense vs. a subsequent different description; identification of a photograph of another individual (composite or photo array); or identification of voice of another individual; identification of another individual at a visual lineup, all of which are within the possession, custody, or control of the government, and which are material to the preparation of the defense, or intended for use by the government as evidence in chief at trial, or where obtained from or belonged to the defendant.

Despite the specificity of Rule 16 Disclosure criteria, the government played all kinds of games with this duty, all the way from not disclosing it on the pretense they did not think it was material; not disclosing everything, with the omitted part sometimes being the most significant; delaying disclosure; or to representing that they thought they had disclosed, although there was no paper trail to document it. In the end, it all depended on the alignment of the ethical compass of the particular AUSA assigned to the case, something Scott was all too familiar with from his experience in the Magistrate's Court.

Within a couple of months of the March meeting, a new AUSA was assigned to the case. Scott met with Jonathan Evans, the post-indictment newly assigned AUSA. Scott's butt had barely touched the seat when, right out of the blue, he asked Scott whether he believed his client was guilty or not. Scott was mildly shocked. Despite his inexperience, at least in a meeting on the government's home turf, he was very confident. Scott already knew about the significant exculpatory information.

In the Event Report in the May incident, the husband and wife, described a man as 35, short, and with a bush haircut; in the November 7-8 incident, no physical description was given of the assailant; and in the third, a man was described as being 30-40, 5'8"and medium weight around 165 pounds. It was not lost on Scott that these descriptions all generally described a man his size, not a man as tall and as heavy as Timothy.

"You know that is not the kind of question you're supposed to be asking a defense attorney and you also know it's not a question that any defense attorney would ever answer. However, at this point in time, all of the objective information excludes my client. If and when you get any objective evidence connecting him to the crimes, my answer may be different … if you ask me again," Scott replied confidently.

Right after he had given his response, the phone rang. Suddenly, Scott felt that he was having an out of body experience. He was behind himself viewing the two of them sitting in the room. In his vision, everything was black and white, and he was in the middle of a "Sam Spade" movie. Evans was talking on the phone, nodding his head, and saying, "Oh ... Uh huh ... Uh huh ...Uh huh ...," and then he hung up.

"I've got some good news for you. They found several different Negroid head hairs on Hawthorne's bedspread and none of them match your client. In fact, the lab said they are distinctive and don't even come close." All eloquence aside, Scott silently thought to himself: *That feels damn good! Guess he got his question answered ... for now.*

Very quickly, Scott set up a meeting with people at the TV station. Soon, it was readily apparent *they* were not the real decision makers and were on the defensive from female staff at the station. At that point, Scott was unclear who they were and why he was even meeting with *these* particular people. As the meeting progressed, he could not help but ask, with a bit of sarcasm, "Do the women think he is going to hide in a dark alcove or a broom closet waiting for someone to pass, grab them, and rape them?"

To his astonishment, they responded that was exactly what the women at the station were thinking. Hysteria was running amuck in the hallways and canning him was, in their view, the only solution. Scott's response was to recount to them that several samples of Negroid head hair from different men had been found on Hawthorne's bed, the one who had them arrested by name, and not only did none of them match Timothy's hair, but his wasn't even close. He did not share with them Timothy's input that she had a reputation for liking and sleeping with black men, and that Timothy knew one of them by name. He especially did not want to share this information with the prosecution, at least, not at this point in the case. He had learned in an earlier case that disclosing something adverse to the opposition early on can be disastrous and backfire. Timing is everything!

He recounted the descriptions in each of the Event Reports in the other cases, in particular, highlighting that not only were the descriptions dissimilar, but none of them were even close to Timothy's size, height, and weight. Next, because he assumed they all worked with him and were familiar with his physical size, height, and weight, which they confirmed they were, he asked them if they believed that people in three separate incidents would give dramatically similar descriptions that did not fit Timothy, but described a much smaller man, for example, like Scott himself. Even they agreed that was unlikely. Nevertheless, doubt was implicit in their responses. Perhaps, it was because the information was coming from his lawyer. Scott pointed out that it was objective information from the police files and invited them to check it out with the prosecution. They readily agreed to do that.

Hardly feeling he had carried the day, Scott decided to explore a sense he had developed from listening to them throughout the meeting. "Are you Union?" They confirmed they were union. In fact, they were the Union representatives! Now, he knew who they really were. Finally, he had something concrete he could use.

Scott was void of inexperience impediments in this environment. Suddenly, his experienced background was in play and he had leverage. The moment they responded they were "Union," the intensity in their faces faded and their jowls sagged. They knew what was coming. Scott's confidence swelled! He was in his element! Give him leverage and he became the stalking Tiger. Negotiation was his forte and the slightest sign of weakness triggered a short, slow, low-key transformation in his speech pattern. Not knowing Scott, they probably thought he was being polite and solicitous. Thus, they were oblivious to the lowering of his voice as a signal he was about to launch an attack to the juggler. At that moment, he had them by the balls!

"If you are Union, aren't you supposed to be protecting your members, not caving into management and hysterical women?"

Silence!

When Scott either became very angry or was in a real solid position and knew it, his demeanor was radically deceptive. In either case, it exuded exceptional calm. His voice was very calm, relaxed, and his speech methodical. All the while, his thought processes were razor-sharp and his delivery was deceptive, but extremely deliberate. They may have been ready, willing, and able to throw Timothy under the bus, but now Scott's scalpel was out, and he was ready to operate.

Years later, when he had teenage children, one of his children reported to Jennifer that his younger sister was trying beer. She told him: "Thanks, I'll take care of it." Although he was only 15, he told her: "No, let Deeda do it! He does that lawyer sneaking up thing really well!"

That "union" meeting was one of the earliest times that Scott recognized the beginning and development of his "sneaking up" approach. It has often been said that information is power. In retrospect, without even knowing it at the time, he was just damn good when he sensed vulnerability!

In a very low key, deliberate manner, he observed that such a decision would not play well with the membership or be viewed favorably in the press. To no one in particular, Scott opined, "Since the case is already getting coverage by the *Washington Post* because Timothy sometimes works at the White House, it would be easy for this "tidbit" to find its way into the *Post*!" He dangled that out there like fish bait. As he laid it out, their facial droop increased. They got it!

The meeting concluded with an understanding that they would talk to "higher ups" and get back to him. But he already knew he had won that argument. Shortly thereafter, Timothy was on administrative leave - *with* pay!

CHAPTER 13

Under the "speedy trial rule," the government was obligated to bring the case to trial quickly. As such, things were moving along rapidly. Before Scott knew it, the cases were set for trial for January 15, 1979. However, neither the government nor Scott were able to prepare for trial that quickly with all of these cases pending. So very quickly, the original trial date was moved forward from January to October of 1979.

On February 22, a notice was mailed by the Clerk of the Criminal Division setting Monday, February 26 as the date Timothy was to be arraigned for First Degree Burglary While Armed; Rape While Armed; Assault with a Deadly Weapon; and Assault with Intent to Kill While Armed.

After the voice-only lineup, Scott quickly collected himself and began to get organized. The very first thing he did was to look for an investigator. Not only did he need some logistical help, but he also needed an independent source of information for documentary evidence and witness testimony. In particular, with four cases, there were significant amounts of details that needed to be examined, not the least of which were interviews with various complaining witnesses. Even though he didn't really expect these interviews to reveal any new information, he had to make the effort.

Under the law, witnesses do not belong to either the prosecution or the defense. Also, it was ethically improper for either side to tell a witness not to talk to the other side. Scott learned early on that this is another area where the government played games. While they would not tell a witness not to talk to the other side, the question invariably came up in conversation with the prosecutor because witnesses would ask the prosecutor what they might expect. Naturally, prosecutors tell them that they can expect to be questioned by the defense side. Equally obvious, the question coming from the complaining witnesses and others to the prosecutor's, was. "Do I have to talk to them?" or, "What should I do?" Obviously, the prosecution would explain to them that they cannot tell them not to talk to the defense representatives, but, with a wink and a nod, the prosecution would always "share" the observation that while they cannot tell a witness not to talk to the defense representatives, they would say: "You're not obligated to do so!" The complaining witnesses always got the message.

Notwithstanding this real-world impediment to investigating the factual background and developing a defense, the effort had to be made. Scott needed an independent investigator to interview witnesses so that, if necessary, their statements could be presented as evidence in the ultimate trial. Through some contacts, an investigator for the public defender service in DC was referred to Scott. Her name was Cindy Hill. She was taking a year off after college prior to entering law school.

On April 5th, Jonathan and Scott had a telephone conversation to discuss the known evidence at that time. On April 7, Scott wrote to Jonathan to summarize the contents of the conversation. By then, there was even more objective evidence available than when Scott met with Jonathan and later with the TV station "representatives."

The letter wasn't intended to be all-inclusive of what they discussed or what was known at the time but was intended to outline the matters that they had discussed in reference to the four cases. Scott addressed the cases in chronological order and didn't attempt to cover all of those matters which might arise in each case, such as confessions, physical evidence, etc., except to note they either didn't exist or that they had discussed the results of physical or scientific tests, etc., which Jonathan provided him under *Brady*.

****

"I want to confirm my understanding that Timothy had made statements to government agents and you indicated, likewise, you were aware of said statements. As of March 29, our most recent meeting, Timothy had no criminal record and no arrest other than the one in in May 1978.

You indicated that the Daniels were present at a visual lineup conducted on September 21, 1978, at which time each of them indicated they did not recognize any of the individuals composing the lineup. However, subsequent to leaving the lineup room, Nelson Daniels indicated that the individual wearing identifying tag #2 'Looks like he might be the man.'

I requested that you provide the exact statement for my records. You also told me that #2 and #5 had since confessed to 15 rapes and entered guilty pleas to three rapes while armed, each of which occurred on Capitol Hill where the victims lived.

You confirmed there were no blood samples present in that case, and according to the medical records available to the government, Lynn Daniels was examined for the presence of sperm at George Washington University Medical Center and the results were the presence of a few poorly preserved sperms. In addition, the results of the medical examination indicated that the examining physician was unable to determine whether there has been any intercourse or sodomy in this case.

Pubic hair samples were taken from Timothy for comparison purposes, but, according to the government's records, no hair samples were examined of either of the Daniels.

Lynn Daniels was combed out in the pubic area and the examination revealed no hairs of Negroid origin. The only physical objects examined in this case were a black comb and a light blue shirt, which were later identified as belonging to the complainant or her husband. The shirt contained no blood stains but did contain seminal stains which were being examined.

The initial description of the assailant by Lynn Daniels was that he had the voice of an educated man. Nelson Daniels' identification indicated that the assailant never swore and had just of an edge of a "Washington" accent. I also wanted to confirm my understanding that neither of the witnesses have ever seen a photo array or attended any other visual lineup, other than the one of September 21, 1978, and have attended only one voice lineup, December 5, 1978, when they identified Timothy's voice.

Finally, according to the police report, the description of the assailant given by Lynn Daniels was that he was a Negro male, aged 35, short, with a bush haircut.

In Hawthorne's case, on November 13, he provided a written statement to the police. There were no physical samples of evidence other than several head hairs of Negroid origin, which were found on Hawthorne's bedspread, sheets, and pillowcase. Prior to your revealing this information to me, arrangements were made for Timothy to voluntarily go to the Mobile Crime

Unit of the Metropolitan Police Department and provide a sample of his scalp hair. During the meeting on March 29, you advised me that the lab technician who examined Timothy's hair for comparison purposes with the sample stated that Timothy's hair sample was dissimilar, 'not even close,' and that if asked to testify, the lab technician would have to say that it was definitely not Timothy's hair in Hawthorne's apartment.

Timothy also provided saliva and blood samples to the Mobile Crime Unit for comparison, but as of our meeting, the results are not yet available. According to the medical report, the examining physician at George Washington University Hospital was unable to determine whether there had been intercourse or sodomy. Tests for the presence of sperm were performed, but the results were not indicated on the medical report.

My recollection was that there was no sperm found in this case. My notes indicate that pubic hairs were taken from both the complaining witness and Timothy, however, the results were at the Mobile Crime Lab and I presumed that the results either were not available at the time of the phone conversation, or were negative, since you reported that only a sole-type scalp hair sample was found in the apartment. The police report only indicated the assailant was a Negro male. Under the age category appeared the letters NFD (No Fixed

Description?) and listed no other identifying characteristics.

Finally, you indicated that Hawthorne had also only attended the voice lineup on December 5 at which time, she identified Timothy's voice. And she has attended no visual lineups or has not been shown any photo arrays as of this report.

In the Wood case, you and I agree that Timothy had provided no written or oral statement to any government agents. There was a preliminary report of the presence of blood in the apartment, and while there is no written record in his file, you have verbally confirmed Timothy's version in that at the time of his arrest on this charge, officers in the sex squad did physically examine his hands and arms for any cuts and the results were negative. Wood has been shown one photo array of nine photographs from which she selected Timothy's photograph and she subsequently appeared at a visual lineup on December 13 at which she identified Timothy as the assailant.

The blood sample previously referred to as being found inside Wood's apartment was insufficient for the laboratory to type. Blood found in the hallway outside of the apartment is type O, which is the same blood type as her blood type. No hair of Negroid origin was found on her, and when Timothy was arrested on December 5th, the morning after the alleged offense, no hairs of Caucasian origin were found on his person. Intact sperm was found upon examination and blood typing tests are still being conducted to see if a blood type can be determined.

The description given by Wood of the assailant listed in the police report is that the suspect was a Negro male, 30-40 years of age, height is 5'8" and of medium weight. The description you gave me was that the assailant spoke softly, but firmly, had a round face and seemed educated. He wore a knit hat, a jacket with a belt, probably some kind of cloth. He was described physically as being 5'8" to 5'10", medium build, weighed 150-165 pounds, and was around 30 years old. You further related the complaining witness gave the estimated weight based upon the weight of the assailant when he was lying on top of her. She indicated that he was light, not too heavy.

Under the point of entry, a bandage was found, which appeared to have been on a finger, but no blood was found on the bandage. No fingerprints were found that was of any value for comparison purposes.

The Cooper-Lockhart case was a grand jury original. There are no statements made of any kind by Timothy and there are no physical objects or items which are susceptible to scientific examination. I do not have a copy of the PD251 in this case, but the description you gave to me, as related by Mr. Cooper, was that the assailant was stocky, had a beard, and wore a white stocking mask with red trim. Cynthia

Lockhart heard a recording of Timothy's voice from the lineup conducted on December 5th and indicated that #11 sounded more like him (the assailant) than any other the night the man was in her apartment. Mr. Cooper heard the same tape and stated that #11 sounded like the man and then indicated 'there was no doubt.'"

****

In concluding the letter, Scott reemphasized that "the information in this letter is not intended to be a complete listing of everything you told me. I have tried to be as precise as possible in items that were listed and feel certain that you will add your own qualifications where you feel it is necessary and fill in information which you have provided me, but I have not listed."

As a result of this report and his letter in response, Scott was challenged to prepare multiple motions. On April 20, he filed a Motion to Sever to Obtain Separate Trials for Each Offense. On the same date, he also filed a Motion to Suppress the identification made by Wood.

Physical and mental visceral revulsion is unavoidable for the average person when they are exposed to the trauma suffered by rape victims. A courtroom is no longer just *a* courtroom. It is transformed into a gladiatorial arena with the hyper-charged atmosphere of a trial laying out the gruesome details inherent in a rape scenario. While it is common knowledge that the law requires proof beyond a reasonable doubt in a criminal trial, only complete naïveté would lead one to conclude that in the minds of the public and potential jurors, that someone charged *must* be guilty, as charged, or, at least guilty of something or, they wouldn't have been arrested and charged! This being so for one case, an individual charged with multiple rapes raises the bar considerably. For multiple offenses, it is a daunting burden!

In seeking separate trials, Scott argued that, under the Superior Court Criminal Rules relating to joinder of offenses, the counts were misjoined. The government was allowed to join offenses when two or more offenses were charged in the same indictment "... if the offenses charged ... are of the same or similar character or are based on the same act or transaction or on two or more acts or transactions connected together or constituting parts of a common scheme or plan."

The defense's argument was that the offenses charged in Counts 1 through 7 were not of the same or similar character in that they contained no unique characteristics such as to qualify them as "signature crime." They were not part of the same act or transaction, or part of a common scheme or plan. The acts occurred over a period of nine months and, therefore, there was neither simple proximity in time to establish "a specific or unitary goal toward which all the acts alleged in the indictment were directed," nor was there a "logical development" between the offenses, so that one "necessarily led to or caused" the other; and there is "no substantial overlap of proof" of the counts.

In addition, even if joinder were proper, the counts should nonetheless be severed because it would be unfairly prejudicial to require Timothy to stand trial before the same jury, on these ten counts, and there were no substantial interests, either of the Government or the Court, to be served by a single trial involving all 10 counts. Evidence of multiple offenses is nearly always prejudicial, since it involved the risk that the jury will cumulate the evidence or convict because of a general "criminal propensity." This is especially true when a number of the offenses involve the highly sensitized crime of rape. In addition, there would be only a small overlap in proof between the ten counts and that would be principally directed at the identity of the assailant.

Scott pointed out to the court that information provided to defense counsel during discovery conferences with government counsel indicated that the assailant involved in one offense had a beard. Consequently, there was a strong indication that the identity of the assailant in that offense was not the same person alleged to have committed the three other offenses because none of the other Complaints or Event

Reports disclosed in discovery conferences suggested that the assailants in those three offenses had any facial hair. Any minimal savings in judicial time or governmental convenience could not justify the prejudice to Timothy if he were forced to defend against ten counts at a single trial.

On March 3, the government filed a Motion for Continuance to file motions to respond to Scott's motions. On May 3, Scott received the Government's Motion for Expansion of Time to Respond to The Motion to Sever and The Motion to Suppress Identification. They also filed a Motion for Leave to File Their Opposition to the Motions because the time for responding had expired. They filed their Opposition to The Motion to Sever Counts. Scott's Motion to Suppress Identification Testimony only addressed the Wood incident.

The Government argued that the defendant now contended that the voice and photographic identifications were impermissibly suggestive and, thus, violated his right to due process. It argued that his contention was not meritorious. The test for excluding pretrial identification procedures due to suggestivity involved a determination of whether the procedure utilized was so impermissibly suggestive as to give rise to a very substantial likelihood of misidentification. In the present case, the government argued that none of the three procedures was tainted by suggestivity. In the voice lineup, all 11 men were instructed to say the same words and each of the voices were sufficiently similar to negate the possibility of suggestivity. Likewise, in both the photo array and the visual lineup, the physical characteristics of the men used were sufficiently alike to preclude the possibility of suggestivity.

But even assuming *arguendo* that defendant's suggestivity claim has some merit, the government argued that the more significant inquiry is "whether under the 'totality of circumstances' the identification was reliable, even though the confrontation procedure was suggestive." The factors to be considered in evaluating that reliability included: the opportunity of the witness to view the criminal at the time of the crime; the witness' degree of attention; the accuracy of the witness' prior description of the criminal; the level of certainty demonstrated by the witness at the confrontation; and the length of time between the crime and the confrontation.

In the present case, the government submitted that a hearing would establish the reliability of Hawthorne's identification. She had a significant opportunity to view the defendant at the time of the crime. For a period of thirty seconds, the defendant was virtually within arm's reach of the victim and bathed in the light from outside streetlamps, which came through white Venetian blinds. In that light, she was able to pick out significant characteristics of the defendant's appearance. She also had a good opportunity to hear the defendant's voice. The intruder spoke almost continuously during the entire incident, which lasted about five minutes. For most of that time, the defendant was literally on top of the victim on the bed. She paid strict attention to the defendant during the entire incident. She was able to describe his physical appearance as well as the quality of his voice. Her respective identifications of the voice and the photo of the defendant on the day after the crime as well as her lineup identification about one week later were all made with a significant degree of certainty. Finally, even if the Court were to deem the identifications as unduly suggestive, the government, naturally, argued that there was a sufficient independent source for an in-court identification by the witness.

On May 7, Cindy wrote a separate memorandum to Scott.

"I feel a need to convey to you my efforts in this case and to ensure you that I've tried to handle and will continue to handle the case with all the professional skills and talent that I can muster. But in very few cases with four witnesses, I would say none, have I had zero work product in the form of statements or at least interviews. You have no knowledge of my prior work; therefore, it cannot defend me. Please be assured and assure Timothy that I have, and I am trying to do my best for this case."

Scott was surprised and puzzled by her memorandum. Quite the contrary to her opinion, he thought she was doing an excellent job. In particular, one thing that really impressed him was that she was absolutely fearless and tenacious. She would go into some of the less savory areas of DC late at night or very early in the morning trying to catch officers going on or coming off their shift so that she could interview them, rather than leaving a message at the station and waiting for them to get back to her, if at all. At the same time, however, Scott realized that because she was so intent on the case and had high standards, she didn't think she was doing a good job. As quickly as possible, he was in contact and disabused her of any thoughts to the contrary regarding the quality of her investigative efforts.

On May 10, Cindy made another effort to speak with Roberta Wood. She was very firm, but nice about refusing to discuss the case. Cindy had been tracking down Sheila but discovered that she had moved and left no forwarding address with the post office. So, she took two approaches to locate her. One was going back through the townhouse apartments and finding out where they paid the rent. Some management offices would give out addresses, but many would not.

Her other source was Larry, another bartender at Duddingtons. On May 23, she spoke very briefly with Larry and found out that he didn't know where Hawthorne had moved. Cindy continued to try to talk to him about the incident. The problem here was that Larry was very busy every minute and he was not shy about saying so.

On May 21, she went to Rosie Daniel's address again only to discover that they had moved to "somewhere on Kentucky Avenue." Cindy requested a forwarding address from the post office. On June 4, she tried to track down Cynthia Lockhart. She noticed when she went to the apartments where she had lived that the name on the mailbox was different and that her boyfriend's name wasn't on there either.

She went to the rental office on June 7, and the receptionist, though she wanted to, would not give her the forwarding address. They had also moved. The receptionist said, "If you can't find it, call me and I'll try to help you."

On the same day, Scott received an additional memorandum from Cindy summarizing her investigative efforts up to date regarding the composition of the voice-only lineup. One of the things that she had been asked to do was to check on some of the people in the lineup. There wasn't much there, but it was helpful to know that they were not police officers. So much for seeing hard eyes and thinking about policemen. It was just another tidbit of information that went into Scott's memory bank for future reference.

On June 8, there was a hearing on the Motion to Sever.

On June 18, the government filed Supplements to Its Opposition to The Motion to Sever Counts.

On June 20, when Scott returned from lunch, he was in for a big surprise. Nikki was on vacation and they had hired a temporary secretary. Ironically, she had the same initials as his ex-wife. That was a bit unsettling. Even more so when he found out that her first and middle names were identical as well. She was an interesting person, and he could see why she did not have a full-time job. She had a bit of an attitude. However, on this day, she could have written her own ticket. She told him that she had received an anonymous phone call and she had written up a memo on it.

"An anonymous caller called this afternoon about 3 PM asking if you were the attorney in the Rogers' case. I asked him if he would give his name. He said under no circumstances would he do that. 'You should talk with the original investigators,' he said, 'not the officers who made the arrest. The original investigators know the story completely, and if put to the test, would tell the story truthfully,' he continued. 'There is bad ID here. The witnesses talked to each other before the lineup; there's collusion here. This is a bad case' and then he hung up."

"What did he sound like?" asked Scott.

"Mr. Anonymous spoke with a slight broken accent, smacking of a Latin American accent, maybe Asian. That is all I can report."

"Thank you."

On June 25, Scott arranged for a luncheon meeting with Jonathan to discuss the anonymous phone call. Returning to his office after lunch, Scott dictated a memorandum to the file:

"Today, I had a luncheon meeting with Jonathan Evans regarding an anonymous phone call, which was transmitted to my office (see memo in file) regarding contacting the original investigators in this case to question the validity of the identification with Timothy Rogers as the defendant. My initial position was to request Jonathan Evans to assist me, if necessary, in establishing contact with Internal Affairs Division of the Metropolitan Police Department to determine if the police officers involved in preparing this case, specifically the Sex Squad officers, were attempting to substantiate their belief in their case with tainted identification testimony (notwithstanding that appearing in this memo, I have not abandoned this position, as yet). I informed Jonathan that I wanted this meeting to be on the record and requested that he prepare whatever memorandum to the file or whatever was necessary in accordance with the operating procedure of his office to make it official.

On that basis, I informed him of the anonymous phone call and the information repeated therein. He indicated that he felt that it was not a matter for the Internal Affairs Division. He raised the point that he felt that he had previously brought this information to Scott's attention; that is, that the witnesses had the opportunity to talk amongst themselves prior to their identifying the voice of Timothy Rogers. This is not the case, as I pointed out to him.

Rather, I had raised the question subsequent to the voice lineup identification as to whether or not the witnesses had the opportunity, or had actually communicated between or among themselves before any of them attended the identification lineup, or after some had gone in to attempt to make an identification and while others were waiting to go in. At that point, he related to me the fact that Sheila Hawthorne and the Daniels had discussed the identification of the person who raped Sheila Hawthorne. Sheila Hawthorne had, in fact, related to the Daniels, apparently not knowing that they knew Timothy Rogers, his name as the person who raped her.

I further indicated that the Daniels knew Roberta Wood because in her part-time position as a real estate agent, she had sold the Daniels their home. I pointed out to Jonathan that all of this was new information to me. He was surprised, however, in view of the numerous conversations and telephone conversations we have had on these cases, he had no doubt that he truly believed that he had related this information to me on some prior occasion. In any event, he did not hesitate to discuss the information with me and, in fact, discussed it initially on the belief that I already knew the information. He does not know to what extent the conversation, if any, continued beyond identification by name of the alleged rapist.

He proposed that he and the new assistant assigned to the case call the witnesses in individually and under the guise of making a smooth transition from one prosecutor to another, the witnesses be questioned in depth as to the conversations that occurred outside of the lineup room. We plan to keep in close touch on this matter and, hopefully, he will have some information to relate to me prior to my leaving town on July 11."

Shortly before the end of summer, Jonathan called Scott. "Would your client take a polygraph test?"

After little consideration, Scott replied, "Yes."

At that point, objectively, the government's case was extremely weak, if nonexistent!

The police reports, the complaints, the interviews, and the statements of the complaining witnesses were void of objective facts or physical evidence of any kind connecting Timothy to any of the cases. There were only the statements of the witnesses expressing what they believed or thought they believed. Undermining any credibility or reliability of their statements was the simple fact that the physical descriptions, standing alone, came nowhere close to describing Timothy. Additionally, even though Timothy's alibi witnesses testifying before the grand jury were disregarded, Scott anticipated that at trial, the jury could determine for themselves the alibi witnesses' credibility without the isolated influence the grand jury had been under when it was only hearing from the prosecutor.

Probably the weakest link in the government's case was additional information that Jonathan had shared with Scott subsequent to the "Sam Spade" meeting. Jonathan disclosed that the Sex Squad detectives were having "problems" with the Hawthorne case! Although Jonathan didn't elaborate or provide any details, Scott strongly suspected a connection between the Sex Squad detectives having a problem with her case and the anonymous phone call from somebody with a Spanish accent. He also learned through another source that the U.S. Attorney's Office quickly connected the dots on this issue and had focused considerable attention on the officers in her case.

Scott recalled during the "Sam Spade" meeting Jonathan asking him whether he believed his client was guilty. He remembered telling Jonathan that if he came up with any physical evidence connecting Timothy to the offenses, that "I may change my mind on that issue."

Here they were some months away from that conversation, more than 15 months from the first offense, about nine months from the last offense, and the government had been unable to come up with any hard evidence against Timothy.

Now, Scott was ready to answer that question. Because there were so many objective facts in the record, coupled with the government's lack of any other significant hard evidence to connect Timothy to the cases, it seemed logical to accept Jonathan's proposal. In addition, after nine months of continuous intensive review of the record, updated interviews with Timothy, Cindy's investigative results, and having never caught Timothy in a lie or a contradiction, Scott had become a believer in his innocence!

Notwithstanding all of his objective analysis, Scott was well aware of the dangers of being too close to the case to spot the obvious. Of equal concern to him was his awareness of his difficulty with simple and obvious things, notwithstanding his intellect. In fact, he was of the opinion that his intellect got in the way of seeing things that were right in front of him. Fortunately, he had an in-house backup that he trusted implicitly. Jennifer!

Even though she was not a lawyer, she was extremely intelligent and very good with details. Moreover, because of his long experience with her and his nervousness in this case, he had "discussed" it with her, perhaps from her viewpoint, *ad nausea*. Nevertheless, there was no one else that knew the case as well as she did, and he relied on her to spot obvious contradictions or omissions that escaped his attention.

It certainly wasn't the first time that he raised the question: "Despite all of the objective evidence that not only failed to connect Timothy to the crimes, but objectively described another individual, why was the government continuing to pursue this case?"

The case had been highly publicized because Timothy had worked at the White House. Was the government so fixated on a victory that it would pursue this case despite the lack of support of any objective evidence that they had the right person? That was the more obvious consideration that kept bouncing around in Scott's head. But the real questions giving him heartburn, stress, and interfering with his sleep was: *They must have something significant that I don't know about. What is it that they have that I have overlooked?*

Going over the facts of each case time after time failed to suggest or reveal any missing material facts to conclude that he was guilty, let alone, to go to trial and necessary to obtain a conviction. The case had already produced enough surprises to fill a book. But in going over each case in detail, there just didn't seem to be anything that was missing. Also, he couldn't escape wondering why, if they had something that conclusive, they didn't confront him with it and try to do a plea bargain just to get Timothy to plead guilty to at least one count of rape?

Although he discussed these considerations with Jennifer on multiple occasions as the case matured, he didn't know whether to be comforted or nervous about the fact that she couldn't see any contradictions in his conclusion. Ultimately, his dilemma was not predicated on doubting her analysis; he simply wanted relief from his anxiety and would've been satisfied if she could point out something, a contradiction, *anything*, he was missing so that he could fully understand what was happening. It was that nagging feeling in his gut that came from not having an answer to the problem. More accurately, it was not so much from not knowing the answer, but that he couldn't identify the problem, which there certainly was one!

Apparently, to break the deadlock, Jonathan brought up the subject of Timothy taking a polygraph. A polygraph was inadmissible in evidence but could be crucial to bringing everything to a favorable conclusion. "If we agree to do it, do you give me your word that the government will drop the cases if Timothy passes the polygraph?"

"Yes."

Since the District of Columbia is a Federal enclave and all the prosecutors are Assistant U.S. Attorneys, the resources of the Department of Justice are at their disposal, which includes the FBI laboratory. Their proposal was that the FBI conduct the polygraph. At that time, Scott still had faith in the FBI as well as in the system itself. But he had *more* faith in Jonathan's word, so he agreed.

Jonathan set up a meeting between Scott and the FBI polygraph examiner to explain to Scott how the test would be conducted. Before the test, the examiner would conduct a pre-test interview. Scott would receive an advanced copy of the questions. The examiner indicated he may change the phraseology of the questions. There would be a post-test interview to clear up any unclear responses.

In 1977, the FBI began occupying a new building in Anacostia at a site known as Buzzard's Point. Scott couldn't help but appreciate the allegory. Nothing could more symbolically convey the government's view of Timothy. It was bleak, isolated, and on the Anacostia River, not in the best part of town. Several government agencies had refused to move there. The FBI did so without any struggle. The reasons were linked with the law enforcement agency's tradition of pride and discipline and with the plain fact that there wasn't much choice anyway.

The old post office building at 12th and
Pennsylvania Avenue NW, where the field
office had been located for more than 26 years,
had become filthy and squalid, infested by
roaches, bats, and rats, and was a leaky fire trap.
Some called it the worst space in government.

Not knowing anything, once again, at all
about a polygraph test except what he saw in the
movies, Scott needed to hire his own polygraph
examiner to explain things to him and cover his
back. Through some resources from Company
friends, he found a former Army CID polygraph
examiner.

Scott was feeling very positive and
viewed this as the last step in a long road to
dismissal of the indictment. They drove to
Buzzard's Point on a Friday morning for a 10
o'clock appointment. He was unable to go with
Timothy into the examination room, of course,
but he had no problem with that and was quite
relaxed. In Scott's mind, this was the end of it!

About 20 minutes later, one of the Sex
Squad detectives who had appeared for the
polygraph came out into the waiting room in a
very highly agitated state. Literally, he was
almost foaming at the mouth! He said, "Your
client is a dirty, filthy, sick animal and needs to
be taken off the street and put away for the rest
of his life!" Although Scott doubted if he looked
as though nothing was going on, he did keep it
together pretty well, despite his shock. He didn't

engage in any conversation or even respond to the detective.

Before he collected Timothy, he asked for a copy of the questions that the FBI polygraph examiner had used for each case. They read as follows:

ROBERTA WOOD RAPE
DECEMBER 4, 1978
Washington, DC
1. Is your last name Rogers?
1a. Were you born in Y?
2. Is today Monday?
3. Were you ever inside ROBERTA WOOD's bedroom?
4. Have you ever been to the movies?
5. Did you put your penis in that woman?
6. Before June 1978, did you ever try to force sex on a female?
7. Are you now wearing shoes?

LYNN DANIELS RAPE
June 8, 1978
Washington, DC
1. Is your first name Timothy?
1a. Do you drive a car?
2. Are you employed by NBC?
3. Were you in the Daniels' bedroom on June 8, 1978?
4. Were you in the Marine Corps?
5. Did you put your penis in Lynn Daniels?

6. Before this incident, did you ever force anyone to have sex with you?

7. Did you go to high school?

8. Did you put a pillow over Lynn Daniels' head?

9. Did you climb through that window at the Daniels' house?

10. Before June 1978, have you ever attempted to force anyone to have sex with you?

SHEILA HAWTHORNE RAPE
November 7, 1978
Washington, DC

1. Are you now in DC?

2. Regarding that rape, do you intend to tell me the complete truth here today?

3. Are you convinced I won't ask you a surprise question on this test?

4. Before June 1978, did you ever attempt to force your sexual desires on anyone?

5. Did you put your penis in that girl?

6. While in the Marine Corps, did you ever deliberately assault anyone?

8. Did you force that girl to have sex with you by putting your penis in her?

9. Is there something else you are afraid I will ask you a question about on this test?

10. Have you ever thought about having sex with a relative?

11. Did you climb through that window in that girl's house?

PETER COOPER and CYNTHIA LOCKHART
ASSAULT & BURGLARY
December 22, 1978
A. Did you go to high school?
B. Were you born in NY?
1. Do you intend to tell me the truth on this exam?
2. Were you ever in the Cooper/Lockhart apartment?
3. Are you now in DC?
4. Did you stab that man?
5. Before 1978, did you ever deliberately assault anyone with intent to do harm?
6. Were you born in Y?
7. Did you touch CYNTHIA LOCKHART that night?
8. Did you illegally enter that apartment?
9. Do you sometimes drink water?

As quickly as possible, Scott hauled ass to his office across the Potomac, contacted his polygraph expert, and met with her to give her a copy of the examination questions. All he wanted to know was what the hell happened!

She looked at the questions and very quickly told him. "They tricked you!"

"They changed the questions as well as the standard format of the questions. Remember I told you that relevant questions would to be interspersed with neutral questions not associated with the case? In changing the questions and the order, they corrupted the test.

They also had inserted inappropriate questions," she said.

"It was very clear that they did it so that Timothy would poorly perform, and they could let both of you know so as to scare you." They combined the FBI's acting with telling Scott that Timothy had done poorly on the test, which was true. "They just wanted to see which way you would jump!"

It hadn't gone unnoticed by then that, given the revelation, they couldn't even be sure the lists of questions given Scott were valid.

Becoming aware of the ruse really pissed Scott off! Promptly thereafter, he met with Jonathan and expressed his strong displeasure and disappointment at the way the polygraph had been conducted. Scott made it clear in no uncertain terms he knew he had been sandbagged! In the intervening months since entering the case, his strong background had served him well and experience with this case had accelerated exponentially his learning curve, confidence, and natural aggressiveness.

Aside from the fact that he knew Jonathan did not give the test, unbeknownst to Scott, there were heavy hands on the scales of justice. That is, a new AUSA had been assigned to the case. Although Scott knew that there was to be a change in the guard, he was not put on notice that Jonathan was no longer calling the shots. Obviously, the deal to drop the case was no longer on the table.

It was quite clear from his silence that Jonathan expected Scott to inquire about a deal or ask if the prosecution had an offer he could take to his client. Scott was reminded of the old adage in negotiations, "He who speaks first, loses!"

"What do you want to do?" asked Johnathan sheepishly after a few moments of silence.

"I will see *you* at trial!"

CHAPTER 14

On August 30, the government filed a Motion to Continue the Trial Date since a new AUSA was taking over the case. Until then, Scott was also unaware that Jonathan was also leaving the Office of the United States Attorney. As it turned out, the post-polygraph meeting was to be Jonathan's last involvement in the case....and their last contact.

Slowly, Scott sensed what was going on behind the scenes and how everything had really unfolded. He was unable to determine whether Jonathan knew in advance about the deception. However, he wanted to continue to believe that Jonathan had offered the polygraph deal in good faith but was pushed aside by other developments within the office.

Upon his departure, enter Stephanie Kincaid. Scott's first impression when he heard her name was that it was a sexy, rich kid, prep school name! But his first impression when he saw her was the opposite! Even though she was good-looking and sexy, her demeanor and movement conveyed an entirely different image in Scott's mind.

The first impression he had upon interacting with her demeanor was of a commissar's unattractive fat wife! Well, maybe not all that fat. Rather, one that was built like a chunky high school running back. Belying her good looks, she wore the standard black dress outfit and black high-heeled shoes with thick, *chunky* heels. He knew that those thick, *chunky* heels had a name that only women knew, but he was just a guy and, to him, even if he knew the name, they were still just thick, *chunky* heels! Reinforcing the impression, whenever she walked down the hall, you could hear her coming from a long way off because those thick, *chunky* heels were always "clogging" the floor. It was as if she was stomping her feet for emphasis.

To this day, neither his initial impression, nor his feelings about her, has changed. All his experiences before with Jonathan were that of dealing with a lawyer who understood and implemented the letter and spirit of *Brady*. Because it was such a natural, accepted manner in dealing with him, Scott never foresaw the dramatic changes headed his way.

His first meeting with "Broom Hilda", as he would come to reference her, was to discuss the anonymous phone call that his office had received regarding the hallway collusion of the witnesses before the December lineup. Also, he intended to bring up the earlier conversation with Jonathan regarding the Sex Squad officers having a "problem" with the Hawthorne case. Jonathan had never elaborated, but Scott's impression continued unchanged that they did not believe her. That was great news for his team and really bad for the prosecution. Much as there cannot be a conspiracy case without more than one defendant, a serial rapist case disintegrates if one of the cases falls by the wayside.

Even more damaging was the fact that hers was the principal case and instrumental in putting Timothy in the spotlight by name as a suspect for the other cases. More significantly, she was the one initiating the pre-lineup hallway collusion and identifying him by name to the other complaining witnesses.

When Scott entered Broom Hilda's office, standing beside her was a Sex Squad detective assigned to one of the cases. They presented an amusing image with him standing to her right beside her non-government issued, high wing-backed chair with his left arm over the top as though he was guarding her as she sat on her "throne!"

All Scott could think about was the image of Bette Davis and Errol Flynn in *The Private Lives of Elizabeth and Essex*. At the time, it occurred to him that if they could see themselves as he saw them, they would not have set the scene in that fashion. Perhaps it was mutual reinforcement orchestrated to intimidate, but for Scott, it was pure comic relief. It was so theatrically contrived that it was impossible for Scott to take them too seriously despite the gravity of the situation.

After learning about the anonymous phone call, they were both obviously very upset. She let him know in no uncertain terms, her opinion being reinforced by the sneer on her "major domo's" face, that she was very upset that Jonathan had also shared new information concerning the other identifications by the Daniels at other lineups. "He should never have disclosed that information!"

She also took issue with him sharing information regarding the Daniels being unable to sleep at night until it was daylight, driving down the street and repeatedly pointing out different black men as the rapist. And Jonathan also shared that when Nelson Daniels saw a black man going down the alley behind their Capitol Hill townhouse, he routinely bolted out of the back door in broad daylight and chased them with a hand ax!

The most unsettling news for them was that Jonathan had shared that the Sex Squad detectives were having a "problem" with the Hawthorne case. That revelation caught them completely off guard! The expressions on their face confirmed their composure had suffered a serious hit! Scott sensed they wanted to bolt out of the room screaming for someone's scalp. He kept a straight face, but inside, he was laughing.

Expecting to take some hits of his own, Scott's self-confidence ramped up a few notches during the meeting. Obviously, their purpose for the meeting and the posturing had been to intimidate Scott, but once their composure weakened, it was a total failure. The Tiger was loose again!

It was also from this meeting that Scott formed the opinion that Broom Hilda had no intention of strict adherence to *Brady* and was ready, willing, and able to cut corners whenever necessary. Everything Jonathan had shared, except the Daniels' sleeping habits, was clearly *Brady* material. At that moment, more than at any other, he formed the opinion that she wanted the scalp of an accused serial rapist working at the White House and she didn't care what she had to do to get it! Who knew what other *Brady* material existed that he would never see because it wasn't deemed "material" by her standards! There was no question about it. She wanted Scott to know there was a new gunslinger in town! And she wasn't going to follow gunfighter protocol!

From then on, their "relationship" went down the toilet at avalanche speed. Early in his practice, he had heard the phrase that some prosecutors love to "take the real and imagined sins of the defendant, vest them on the lawyer, and treat them accordingly." And that's exactly how she treated Scott the rest of the case. Like pond scum! Communications were nonexistent and professional courtesy a phantom.

Throughout law school, Scott was always told that it was more important to know the questions than the answers. Recounting this admonition to friends, as well as many lawyers, always generated puzzled expressions. Scott knew what laypeople were thinking. "You think lawyers know all the answers?"

"Yes. Why do you think we have all the law books? The thing is, knowing the question is equivalent to knowing you have a problem. Then you focus on finding the solution. If you don't know the question, you can rest assured that your opposition will let you know about it at the most inappropriate time, typically right in the middle of trial. And they will include the answer!"

For years, the United States Code Annotated, containing Federal Statutes, ran an ad showing a young preppie-type lawyer in court wearing horn-rimmed glasses. He was wearing a suit, standing in front of the jury in his boxer shorts and his pants were down around his ankles. The obvious purpose was to illustrate lack of preparation, which Scott equated with not knowing the question.

Thus, the Tiger may have been loose again; however, the Tiger was still wrestling with an inescapable nagging feeling regarding the most obvious question. Notwithstanding all the objective facts and circumstances that failed to incriminate Timothy, *what* did they know that he didn't know? Scott certainly knew the question! It just would *not* go away. It had become his unavoidable, daily, compulsive thought. However, he was equally, agonizingly, aware that repeated analysis had not offered any insight or solution.

The only relevant answer he had to this dilemma was that he knew that whatever it was, *Brady* notwithstanding, "Broom Hilda" would never give it to him! What bothered him even more was the conclusion he had reached that he couldn't figure out if there were any pieces of missing material evidence. Logic provided no relief from the tension. As far as he could tell, he had explored every element of every case. Despite the almost nonexistent objective factual basis undermining the government's case against Timothy, Scott didn't find it comforting. His acute awareness of his weakness for missing the obvious continued to gnaw at him.

But Scott had drawn one intellectual conclusion that he found very reassuring, even if it did not entirely eliminate his anxiety. One thing was obvious; unwittingly, they had revealed their "tell." If they *really* had something, they wouldn't have rigged the polygraph!

In September, Scott filed a Motion to Dismiss the Indictment for Abuse of the Grand Jury Process and To Compel Production of Minutes of Grand Jury Proceedings. In response, the government filed a motion for more time to respond to his motion. More time! It was always the government's response.

In his opinion, the grand jury should have been made aware of the dissimilarities of the physical descriptions contained in the various police reports; the fact that prior to the Daniels attending the voice lineup where they identified Timothy, both had previously attended a visual lineup in September 1978 where they had identified another man; later in October, Nelson Daniels attended a visual lineup by himself and identified even a different person (this information was not disclosed during the "Sam Spade" meeting, but later); and the information regarding their multiple identifications together on the same day and on many different days, when they were just driving down the street, of any black man they happened to see as the rapist. In addition, Scott argued that the grand jury should have been made aware of the multiple incidences of Nelson Daniels barging out of the back of his townhouse on Capitol Hill in broad daylight with an ax and chasing different black men down the alley.

In Scott's mind, there was a material difference between presenting inculpatory facts to a grand jury to secure an indictment in a circumstance where there's really little, if anything, materially exculpatory to present to the grand jury, which is the norm, and presenting *in*culpatory information to the grand jury that is significantly, objectively, and materially contradicted by *ex*culpatory information known to the prosecution, i.e., *Brady* material.

The government opposed the motion, of course, and said they were at a "loss" to understand exactly where Scott obtained the facts as to what occurred in the grand jury, but firmly believed that the abuse of due process was speculation on his part. Of course, Scott didn't know what happened in the grand jury room. But it didn't take a rocket scientist to read the objective facts and seriously question how a grand jury could indict in the face of all of the objective contradictory information contained in *just* the event reports.

AUSAs were fond of the word "disingenuous," a polite way of calling you a liar and not risking the court imposing sanctions for making improper comments about opposing counsel; the allegations amounted to a very serious allegation against the government based, not on good faith, but on pure speculation.

He still remembered the first time he heard the word "disingenuous" used by an AUSA. He was distracted first, by her good looks, and second, hearing the words *fuck, shit, motherfucker, damn, suck my dick, fuck me like a whore you bitch,* and *hell* coming out of her mouth! He had never heard a woman talk like that at all, let alone in public, and certainly not in court. Viewing her matter-of-fact demeanor, she may as well have been Betty Crocker reciting a recipe on television! It was his first lesson to the real world of the courtroom. That is, no paraphrasing 'son-of-a-bitch' with 'SOB.' After all, the prosecutor is confronting an accused rapist with the language used during the offense. It would be totally incorrect to include paraphrases when questioning whether something was said or what the victim heard.

Nevertheless, he got over his shock and was very impressed about the sophistication of the language until he realized what she was really saying when she used the word "disingenuous." Eventually, he came to understand that it was a favorite term around the United States Attorney's Office, and, in fact, their vocabulary was quite limited and predictably staccato.

They relied on the fact that the grand jury had heard live testimony, not only from the complaining witnesses, but from two of Timothy's witnesses. Further, they argued that the government had endeavored to present all "relevant information" to the grand jury and the defendant had been afforded an opportunity to present any evidence.

Present all "relevant information?" There they go again! It's a variation of their interpretation of what is material and relevant in the *Brady* context implemented in the grand jury context. Same principle: just different venues and a different catchphrase. The "opportunity" to present any evidence completely slipped by Scott and he had no recollection of ever being offered the opportunity to present any evidence. Of course, it is incredibly rare for a defendant to appear before a grand jury to present a defense, which they could, and, at the same time, subject themselves to cross examination by the members of the grand jury and the prosecutor, all without their attorney present to advise them. However, "Broom Hilda" had implied the opportunity had been presented and declined. No overt misstatement or misrepresentation *per se*, just a little sleight-of-hand to throw the thought in the mix to make the government look good.

As usual, they put all the usual bullshit explanations that you could not really get your teeth into to prove that they lied or withheld relevant material information from the grand jury. Naturally, under the circumstances and in this context, Scott was much more sensitive to the concept of lying by silence. The issue was not whether complaining witnesses or even defense alibi witnesses had appeared before the grand jury, but, rather, was the grand jury presented with any of the significantly contradictory objective *Brady* material, which Scott believed was essential to form an independent opinion as to the likelihood that Timothy was, or was not, the assailant. After all, Scott neither authored the objective descriptions given by the victims in the four separate cases, nor authored Timothy's height and weight factors, which differed distinctly and significantly from the various descriptions of the assailant contained in the police reports.

Since grand jury minutes *are* secret, obviously, he had *no* inside information on what had been presented to the grand jury in either testimonial or documentary form. However, given the significant factual inconsistencies in the case to date, he was incredulous that the grand jury would indict Timothy if they were aware of the inconsistencies. At this stage of the proceedings, the necessary level of probable cause is not very high to obtain an indictment. But it is common knowledge that the government only presents derogatory information to the grand jury in order to obtain an indictment and Scott knew that was exactly what had happened. While he had no direct confirmation about what had been presented, Scott was smart enough to have a pretty clear picture of what had not been presented in order to make a reasonably intelligent and plausible argument to support his motion.

One of Scott's strongest points was the fundamental argument that the government had violated its own guidelines regarding a defendant's due process rights. A major threshold point of the government's case was that, according to Hawthorne, Timothy had initiated the idea of walking her to her apartment on the evening of November 7. Timothy's version was that James, the bartender, suggested that Timothy walk her home. By that time, based on Cindy's investigation and interview of James, there were two versions of what had happened, just from James.

At first, James said that he might have suggested that Timothy walk her home and after that he wasn't too sure. He made a comment about how everybody was not too "sane" that night, meaning they were drinking a lot. He even offered the opinion that *she* may even have asked Timothy to walk her home.

At that point, it was immaterial what James ended up testifying about because Scott had independent corroboration that either recollection clearly supported and contradicted either Timothy's or Hawthorne's version of what happened. In short, she was not a very credible witness and, if anything, impeached her testimony on this point, which was extremely damaging to the prosecution's case. Best of all, it reinforced Cindy's expected testimony and eliminated the dilemma and ineffectiveness inherent in the "he said, she said," argument the prosecution would no doubt pursue. Further supporting Scott's reasoning was knowing that the Sex Squad officers were having a "problem" with her case.

Cindy interviewed James again on November 23 and 24. He had told Cindy that he had been subpoenaed by the government to testify. Timothy also needed him as a witness. Despite the frustration, it wasn't all that bad. Since James had been subpoenaed by the government, Scott fully expected him to appear.

James left out, at least Timothy believed it to be so, that he had slept with Hawthorne. There was another witness they were interested in subpoenaing. Arthur also was a former employee of the Underground. Timothy believed that he had slept with Hawthorne. When Cindy tracked him down and told him that Scott wanted him to testify, he told her that Scott really didn't want him to testify. She asked him why and he said that he had been convicted of a felony. She tried to get him to tell her what the felony was, but he refused. Working for the Public Defender Service, she had access to their computer resources. Despite this advantage, she could not find out any information about him or a felony conviction.

Almost immediately after the interview, Arthur quit his job and literally dropped off the map. It was very unfortunate because his testimony, contradictions aside, significantly benefitted Timothy. The issue was whether Cindy would be able to interview him again before trial.

A short time after he disappeared, Cindy told Scott that she had heard that there was going to be a gathering of former employees of the Underground at 10:30 that Friday night. She asked Scott what he wanted to do about it.

"I want you to go and park your pretty butt on a bar stool at the Underground, drink beer on our client, and see if Arthur comes in for the reunion."

"What should I do if he shows up?"

"*If* he shows up, smile *really* big, and *serve* the subpoena!"

Cindy arrived at The Underground a little after 10 o'clock, parked her pretty butt on a bar stool, and ordered a beer on Timothy. Arthur showed up precisely at 10:30. And, a few minutes thereafter, she made herself known to him. He must have forgotten who she was or why she had been talking to him. Or maybe he was influenced by her speaking to him and, because she was very good-looking with a soft feminine and sexy voice, thought she was coming on to him. In any event, he was very happy to see her right up to the point that she served him the subpoena! As she relayed the events to Scott, he visualized all of it. "I would have loved to have been a fly on the wall!" he exclaimed.

The government's Motion for A New Trial date had been granted and the trial was set to start on Monday, November 26.

CHAPTER 15

The trial was to begin Monday at 10 a.m. Still pending were the defense motions to dismiss the indictment and to suppress Timothy's identification. The Judge in the case was Harriet Carrington. She had a reputation as being a fine jurist and was highly respected. Scott had never seen her before, but she had her hair pulled back in a bun so tight, it clearly delivered a message about the way she ran her courtroom.

Needless to say, he was very familiar with his motions and he was ready to roll. More importantly, as opposed to being awkward when dealing with procedural matters, he was good on his feet and supremely confident in addressing the court and advancing his arguments.

First up was his Motion to Suppress the Identification.

Scott was asking the Court to suppress testimony concerning voice identifications, photographic identifications, lineup identifications as well as prospective in-court identifications made by Wood.

"On December 4, shortly after the incident, Wood was shown a photographic array, which contained a picture of Timothy and 10 others. She selected his photograph as that of the assailant. On December 13, she identified Timothy in the voice-only lineup as the assailant.

The circumstances surrounding the voice and photographic identifications were so unnecessarily suggestive as to create a substantial likelihood of irreparable mistaken identification and violation of due process. Three of the complaining witnesses knew him or had been associated with him and were familiar with his voice. Moreover, given the circumstances in the hallway, they knew in advance that he, in particular, was in the lineup.

The lineup identifications had no source independent of the tainted voice and photographic identifications; moreover, the prospective in-court identifications likewise had no source independent of the tainted voice, photographic and lineup identifications."

Scott relied heavily on the anonymous phone caller episode to undermine any credible basis for later action by the government. He could not believe the police had literally sat in the hallway outside the lineup room and allowed a conversation among the victims to compromise the threshold evidence of the witnesses' identifications and the premise of a common offender.

Another basis for suppressing the identification was more critical and at the heart of Scott's efforts to suppress identification testimony of all the complaining witnesses. It was all hands-on-deck for the Hawthorne case.

First, he called Detective Stevens to the stand.

"Your notes show that you reported at the scene of the Hawthorne incident at 06:58 hours to investigate the rape charges. They contain identifying information including the address, phone number, and her place of employment."

Detective Stevens, your field notes indicated that at approximately 4:15 AM on the morning of November 7, she was asleep, and she was awakened by the suspect, who had a knife to her nose. Suspect number one stated, 'Don't move, or I'll kill you.' Suspect # 1 ordered the complaining witness to roll over on her side, then on her stomach, placed a pillow over complaining witness' head. Suspect pulled down pants and got on top of complaining witness and stated 'put it in.' In fear of her life, complaining witness complied. The suspect got off and requested money. The complaining witness told him she had just paid her rent and had none. Suspect told the complaining witness to 'not move or he would kill her.' Complaining witness lay still until she believed suspect had gone. This is what your notes state, correct, Detective?"

"Yes."

"Your field notes even contain a diagram of the apartment. Is that correct?"

"Yes."

What his field notes did not show, however, but was later revealed in his testimony, was that immediately after the suspect left her apartment, she did not call the police, but her aunt and uncle who lived nearby. They came and picked her up. She did not call the police until after she had arrived at her aunt and uncle's place. In discussions with them, she had indicated her certainty as to who was in the room that night and raped her. She told them she was "absolutely positive" that it was Timothy.

Unbeknownst to Detective Stevens when he appeared as his shift started and assigned to this case, and when he had first arrived on the scene, was that she had identified the assailant by name. No one actually told him that she had done this, but he picked it up in the conversations he overheard after he arrived.

"Your notes show that you explained to her that in order to obtain an arrest warrant, you needed probable cause. She reiterated what she told her aunt and uncle and told you that she was absolutely positive of the identification of the suspect in the room that night that raped her. Isn't that correct?"

"Yes."

"Detective, please read for the Court this passage I've marked here." Detective Stevens shifted uncomfortably in his seat.

"Was the voice the same?"

"I'm next to positive."

"On a scale of 0 to 10 (10 being positive), how would you rate Mr. Rogers?"

"8 ½."

By the time Detective Stevens had finished questioning her, it was 11:28 a. m. Only in response to Detective Stevens' questions about her certainty did she answer that she was only positive to the extent of 8 ½ on a scale of 10! She never voiced any doubt prior to being questioned.

Scott's 22-page Motion to Dismiss was seeking to dismiss the indictment on the grounds of abuse of the grand jury process. Specifically, the United States Attorney, in obtaining this indictment, withheld, or failed to present to the grand jury substantial exculpatory information in the possession of the government, or live testimony. His Memorandum of Law supporting this motion was very detailed in outlining the exculpatory information from the police reports and the officer's field notes, together with the hallway conversation.

Scott turned to the judge. "Your Honor, the contents of the Memorandum highlighted the void of physical evidence of any kind that connected Timothy with any of the offenses charged in the indictment; the physical descriptions of the assailant, as provided by the complaining witnesses and others present during the offenses, varied substantially from Timothy's; identification of Timothy by four witnesses consisted of voice identifications, which are known to have occurred after the witnesses discussed the cases and prior to identifying Timothy's voice. Identification of Timothy's photograph by Wood was only after the hallway discussion, an ability that had not been previously conveyed to any law enforcement official."

In Scott's mind, there was a good faith belief that some or all of the complaining witnesses or witnesses present during the incidences did not appear before the grand jury, but rather their statements were presented through hearsay testimony of various police officers involved with the cases because the United States Attorney refused Scott's request to confirm whether this had occurred. This was yet another example of lack of actual knowledge on Scott's part of what occurred before the grand jury, but the result of deductive reasoning.

He continued: "The prosecutor's withholding or failing to present substantial exculpatory information, which was in the possession of the government or live testimony of the various witnesses to the grand jury effectively prevented it from exercising its constitutionally mandated duty to act as an informed and independent body charged with the dual purpose of investigating crime *and* protecting citizens against unfounded charges. Furthermore, the absence of the live testimony of various witnesses was critical in the case because of the availability of exculpatory testimony and the need for the grand jury to be able to judge the demeanor of the various witnesses in evaluating this conflicting information."

"All these omissions deprived Timothy of his right to a fair indictment on these felony charges and his right to due process of law under the Fifth Amendment. The prosecutor's manner of presenting the government's case to the grand jury rendered the grand jury unable to make an independent determination as to the existence of probable cause, and thus, deprived defendant of his constitutional right to indictment by grand jury."

"The Fifth Amendment to the United States Constitution provides that 'No person shall be held to answer for a capital, or otherwise infamous crime, unless on a presentment or indictment of a Grand Jury.'" Scott's memorandum focused on the very purpose for the establishment of the grand jury process."

"While it is not common knowledge among laypeople, enshrinement of the Grand Jury as a constitutional guarantee was done to provide a fundamental protection to those accused of serious crimes by police or prosecutors. A body of lay citizens was to pass upon the sufficiency of the government's case against an accused to determine whether the government could be permitted to subject that person to a criminal prosecution."

"The grand jury, then, was not intended to be an arm of the prosecution, but an independent institution to protect citizens accused of crime from overreaching by prosecutors or courts. The working relationship between the prosecutor's office and the grand jury is extremely close. Except for a few formal occasions in court, and aside from the witnesses whose testimony they hear, grand jurors, during their tour of duty, have contact only with members of the prosecutor's office. In fact, the essence of the relationship is dependency. The grand jurors in performing their constitutional function are completely dependent upon the tools given them by the prosecution."

"Almost without exception, the grand jury in the District of Columbia does not initiate cases but instead awaits the presentation of cases by the prosecution. grand jurors, in the ordinary course, are citizens without broad experience with the legal system who serve but a brief tour of duty as jurors. Prosecutors, of course, are trained professionals. Under these circumstances, it is unreasonable to expect jurors to play anything but a passive role in terms of the procedures employed in the grand jury process and the methods of presenting evidence."

"Given this relationship, the risk is great that the grand jury can lose its independent identity and become little more than an arm of the prosecutor's office. The integrity of the grand jury process must, then, depend upon the care taken by the prosecution to assure that the grand jury has a basis for exercising its independent judgment. To rest the integrity of the process upon the expectation that the jurors will react to incursions by the prosecution upon their prerogatives would, given the realities, empty the institution of the grand jury of all content."

"Scott brought to the court's attention a situation where a New Jersey court dismissed an indictment based solely on the hearsay testimony of a police officer. "The New Jersey court noted several defects in that case. One, the testimony presented to the grand jury had the characteristic of smoothness. Two, a grand jury presented with such 'evidence' is unable to perform its proper function. It is unable to determine whether a crime has in fact been committed and whether there is sufficient evidence to justify a charge against the accused without relying completely upon the testimony of the investigative officer."

"In this country, from the popular character of our institutions, there has seldom been any contest between the government and the citizen which required the existence of the grand jury as a protection against oppressive action of the government. Yet, the institution was adopted in this country, and is continued from considerations similar to those which give to its chief value in England, and is designed as a means, not only of bringing to trial persons accused of public offenses upon just grounds, but also as a means of protecting the citizen against unfounded accusation, whether it comes from government, or be prompted by partisan passion or private enmity. No person shall be required according to the fundamental law of the country except in the certain types of cases to answer for any of the higher crimes unless a body, consisting of not less than 16 nor more than 23 good and lawful men, selected from the body of the district, shall declare, upon careful deliberation, under the solemnity of an oath, that there is good reason for his accusation and trial."

The judge watched Scott intensely as he argued his case. He could feel the heated glare of the prosecution on his back as he stood firmly in front of the judge.

"Historically, the grand jury has been regarded a primary security of the innocent against hasty, malicious, and oppressive prosecution; it serves the invaluable function in our society of standing between the accuser and the accused."

In light both of these fundamental considerations and of the facts in this case, Scott emphasized that the question for decision was not whether incompetent or inadequate evidence was presented to the grand jury, which indicted Timothy. Rather, the issue was far more basic: "Whether the actions of the prosecutor in presenting the case to the grand jury served to deprive the grand jury of the ability to make an independent determination as to the existence of probable cause, and thus, to deprive Timothy of his constitutional right to indictment by a grand jury.

"Furthermore, Your Honor, the government not only failed in its duty to bring substantial exculpatory information to the grand jury for consideration in its deliberations but violated its own standards for presenting cases to the grand jury. Given these basic principles, a substantial and growing body of Federal and state case law had concluded that where the government has in its possession substantial exculpatory information or tainting its own evidence, it must present it to the grand jury considering the case and that failure to do so necessitates the dismissal of an indictment returned in its absence."

Scott argued vigorously that the duty of the prosecution to present the exculpatory evidence was clear and no countervailing policies existed which should have prevented its consideration by the grand jury.

"First of all, the existence of the exculpatory evidence and its substantial weight was of necessity clearly apparent to the government. In none of the four separate offenses considered in returning the indictment was there any physical evidence of any kind that connected Timothy with the offenses."

"Secondly, no one was in a better position at that time than the government to know that its case rested solely on the identification testimony of the various witnesses."

"Thirdly, the government was aware that prior to entering the voice-only lineup of

December 5, the Daniels, Hawthorne, and Wood all discussed their experiences and, more importantly, in the Wood case, Timothy Rogers's name and description. Totally avoiding and not addressing the substantial factual contradictions, the prosecution pressed onward and argued the point very strongly that all the witnesses were positive of their independent identification of Timothy's voice at the voice-only lineup and Ms. Wood's later identification of his photograph."

"Some 36 hours had elapsed since Roberta Wood was raped and she had yet to indicate to the police that she could identify the assailant or that he had facial hair. This information became all the more critical in the Wood case because two witnesses testified before the grand jury on Timothy's behalf and placed him at his home in Suitland, Maryland, some 45 minutes distance away at the exact time."

Scott was advised of this information by Jonathan, who was not the Assistant who presented the case to the grand jury, prior to his leaving the United States Attorney's Office.

"Tests have shown Timothy has type "A" blood, to be a "secretor"; that is, blood indicators are present on all of the cells in his body that will also be found in his semen. FBI analysis of semen samples in the Hawthorne and Wood cases "did not disclose the presence of the A or B blood group factor indicating the rapist is a non-secretor. Scalp hair samples of a Negroid origin were found on the Hawthorne bedspread and FBI analysis concluded that they were "dissimilar to the head hairs of Rogers and could not be associated with Rogers." Results of the above tests were not available at the time of the indictment, but, with due diligence of the government, could have been. Certainly, it was available before the hearing and should have changed the government's view of their case."

Not surprisingly, the government did not bring this to the Court's attention in its response to Scott's motion. In his mind, the government's not bringing it to the Court's attention was a breach of its duty to disclose exculpatory information and equivalent to not disclosing *Brady* material to the defense because it wasn't material. At the time of each of the offenses, Timothy had a very distinctive and prominent mustache.

Scott kept hammering.

"The demands of the grand jury provisions of the Fifth Amendment and the due process clause, plus the *Brady* duty to disclose exculpatory information to the defense, mandated that if the grand jury was to exist as anything other than the mere tool of the prosecutor, the available exculpatory information available must be presented for its consideration. This factor was all the more critical when there are multiple offenses being considered by a grand jury and there is substantial danger of cumulative injury to an accused. Accordingly, the prosecutor has no right to selectively present only that evidence which will support guilt. That is neither his duty nor his prerogative."

Attempting to leave no stone unturned, Scott pointed to another body of case law that he felt would likewise compel dismissal of the indictment. Those cases established the doctrine that, when an agency of the government violated rules, regulations, or procedures, which it had established, its action cannot stand, and the courts will strike it down.

"Indeed, according to the internal policy standards of the United States Attorney's Office itself, the prosecutor presenting the case to the grand jury is *explicitly* directed to present to the grand jury substantial evidence of which he is aware, which would directly negate guilt.

This should be especially so when, as here, the internal guidelines of the United States Attorney's Office are an obvious extension of all the protections afforded by the Constitution. They represent an attempt at self-regulation and this case represents the arbitrariness, which is inherently characteristic of an agency's violations of its own procedures and the very evil the regulations are designed to prevent," stated Scott triumphantly! Or, at least, he thought so.

He then posed the question that: "If this case had already been tried and this were an appeal, under existing case law, the verdict would have to be reversed, even if a new trial would produce the same result?"

"By a logical extension, the absence of total "live" testimony and substantial exculpatory information before the grand jury taints the indictment and leads to the same conclusion: a new trial before the grand jury."

Finally, he argued that the grand jury was denied its inherent right and duty to act as an independent source of a finding probably because some or all of the complaining witnesses, or witnesses present during the incidences did not appear before the grand jury, but rather their testimony was presented through hearsay testimony of various police officers involved in the cases. This was based on a good faith belief because the United States Attorney refused his request to confirm whether this occurred.

"Such action, Your Honor, which will not, in and of itself, invalidate an indictment, but has all the characteristics of smoothness condemned in many cases, especially when live witnesses are available. Moreover, when the grand jury is denied the opportunity to observe the demeanor and the ability to test the credibility of witnesses the very process itself is turned into a farce."

"This is especially true when, as here, there is substantial exculpatory information contradicting the charges. This case presents an even stronger case for dismissal of the indictment because Timothy merely stands accused of a crime; there is no conviction which could be said to have vitiated any error before the grand jury."

As he continued, Scott pressed the argument that Timothy was entitled to disclosure of the transcripts requested because he had a particularized need for it and there no longer existed a need to maintain the secrecy of those transcripts.

"If the Court determines that it needs further information before ruling upon defendant's motion, it should order the government to produce the minutes of the grand jury proceeding so that the Court and counsel for the defendant may determine exactly what occurred in that proceeding."

Scott urged the Court to consider that it couldn't treat this consideration in a vacuum. In other words, it had to consider the real-world aspects of what was actually occurring in the case. He urged the Court to take recognition first of the fact that whether such a "need" exists is a matter designedly left initially to the discretion of the trial judge. In the absence of an absolute prohibition against disclosure, an exercise of judicial discretion is manifestly required. Secondly, "it must 'be kept in mind that, in making a determination of when to permit a disclosure of grand jury proceedings, the court must examine not only the need of the party seeking disclosure, but also the policy considerations for grand jury secrecy as they apply to the request for disclosure then under consideration. In other words, "if the 'reasons for maintaining secrecy do not apply at all in a given situation or apply only to an' insignificant degree, the party seeking disclosure should not be required to demonstrate a large compelling need," stated Scott.

In deciding this motion, Scott urged the Court that it could and should consider Timothy's need for disclosure and the need for secrecy. Timothy had a compelling need for the transcripts; without them, he would be severely prejudiced by a denial of the motion. Indeed, disclosure and inspection should be required whenever it appears that the grand jury has heard only hearsay testimony.

In conclusion, Scott emphasized that the interest in preserving grand jury secrecy simply did not exist. On the other hand, the defendant's need was compelling.

"Do you have anything to add?"

"No, Your Honor."

"Your motions are denied."

CHAPTER 16

Before this case, Scott had been involved in only one jury trial in the fall of 1978, which was in the United States Federal District Court in Alexandria, Virginia. He had drawn a senior judge, that is, a retired judge from the Virginia Beach area in the Eastern District of Virginia. He was tall, dignified, very courtly, and exuded old upper crust Virginia money.

From the outset, it was patently clear Scott did not know what he was doing. The only person in the court room besides the jury, the court personnel, the judge, and he and his client, was Jennifer. At times, the judge would practically yell at him, "Mr. Carmichael, we have been over this! Can we move on?" At other times, he would say, "Mr. Carmichael, can we speed this up?"

As Scott faced the judge, the jury box was to his right and parallel to his line of sight. It was easy to tell when Jennifer could not take any more of Scott's humiliation and rose to leave the courtroom. En masse, the jurors' eyes shifted slightly to their left because she was behind him. And that made it obvious to him that she was leaving the courtroom. By the same token, when she returned, en masse, their eyes again shifted slightly to their left. And he knew they knew she had gotten up enough nerve to come back into the courtroom. However, he didn't have the nerve himself to turn around and look. Lucky her; she could get up and escape the overwhelming humiliation.

Because that trial had been such a traumatizing experience for him, he knew he could not handle this trial without learning how to *actually* try a case! So, he arranged to take a training course from the National Institute for Trial Advocacy scheduled to be in the Washington and Lee University Law School in Lexington, Virginia. It was referred to by the acronym "NITA."

He knew there was no way that he would be able to try a case like this that was so complicated. Out of the 10 most common errors committed by an inexperienced trial attorney, he was guilty of 13! He had enough experience and could do well on his feet because he knew his material. As much as a disaster the trial in Alexandria had been, when it came to the closing argument, even he knew he was as smooth as a seasoned professional! He was comfortable doing the substance of presenting his motions. But this case was not about knowing the material. Rather, it was about the evidentiary and procedural requirements necessary to present evidence, cross-examine adverse, if not hostile, witnesses and police officers, and, ultimately, present a complicated case to a jury. He needed help with everything and, most importantly, he knew it!

The course was limited to 25 attorneys and consisted of a faculty of six instructors. They were composed of professors who taught trial practice, experienced trial lawyers, and a judge. The course was designed for attorneys who had been admitted to practice five years or less. Scott had been admitted to practice for eight years at the time but had only been in private practice for three years. As a result, they made an exception and allowed him to take the course.

The curriculum consisted of daily classes based on six different paperback books dealing with both civil and criminal cases. They did not tell the "students" which of the cases they would be using during the course, so they had to prepare for all of them before the course began. The course was scheduled for 10 days, with one evening off.

The class format was to take a portion of a faculty-selected case in the morning, for example, cross examination, and each of the "students" were expected to get up and cross-examine one of their fellow classmates who acted as witnesses. Each person had a videotape that they carried around all the time because their individual session was videotaped. In some ways, this made Scott feel like an old-time college freshman wearing a beanie with a propeller on top.

The class was organized in a fashion so that there was an "all object rule," meaning that each of his classmates, as well as faculty, could and would object to any of multiple transgressions. Naturally, the objections from students had to be legitimate objections because faculty wouldn't tolerate people being cute or obstructive. Candidly, the course was serious; the tuition was $600, and students were too damned nervous to be doing something like that anyway. Besides, they weren't experienced enough to be making many meaningful objections.

There was one aspect of the course that was especially disconcerting. It was not a sit, drink coffee, and listen to a lecture course, but was an obstacle course that had you constantly dodging bullets from all directions. There was no such thing as a "front line" with the enemy in front of you and your comrades to your side and rear; rather, you were surrounded and there was plenty of "friendly fire."

Within two days, everybody moved beyond having been thoroughly embarrassed and humiliated. More in retrospect than at the time, it was obvious how inexperienced and inept they all really were, so the results could not have been any different. After all, that's why they had enrolled in the course.

What they were required to do was ingest the six casebooks and pick out facts that were beneficial to develop, for example, cross-examination questions. The cases were real world cases that had been slightly, factually modified by the faculty to give something to either side. In other words, it was up to the student to pick out things that could be used most successfully and create their questions.

The exercise was still very challenging, even if they had had some trial experience, because it required the students to get themselves into an unusual mindset. For example, when cross examining, you had to go after the witness on cross-examination, even though he was one of your fellow classmates and had not given any direct testimony. In other words, there was no previous testimony from which to frame questions and to launch the cross-examination. The springboard was simply the scenario you created in your own mind based on your reading of the "facts" that you found would be adverse to that witness's "previous" testimony. The ground rules provided that the "witness" had to testify truthfully according to the facts in the case book. They were prohibited from being obstructive but were not required to be helpful. They merely were required to answer the question truthfully, as they saw it.

Combined, the classroom activities and the evening viewing of videotapes on evidence consumed 10 and a half hours *every* day. After a very long day, and the two-hour evening session looking at videos on evidence, they were expected to return to the dormitory and prepare for the next day's challenge. The dormitories were across the street from the law school and most of them cooked their meals rather than take the time to go out to eat. After the third day, they forgot that they had a life, a law practice, friends, a wife, or family. It was an all-consuming, extremely educational experience, which intimidated the living hell out of them.

One member of the class was significantly older than most students and had gray hair. They never did find out what happened to him, but he must have packed up in the middle of the night and snuck out of the dormitory because after the third day, they never saw him again. They had concluded that the intimidation must have been too much for him.

Another aspect of the structure of the class was that, although individual videotaped sessions lasted five to seven minutes, if a student wasn't going anywhere at all in three minutes or so, the instructors just stopped him. That was a horrific thing to endure!

One day, when Scott was "doing his thing," he wasn't doing very well at all. In fact, he was failing miserably!

One instructor, a former Assistant United States Attorney, to his everlasting credit, tried every way in the world to help Scott get through a particular ordeal. Scott was trying to refresh a witness's recollection. This procedure is accomplished by either a verbal stimulation referencing previous testimony or refreshing their recollection by having them read a document from which they could testify without further relying on the document. Scott had absolutely no idea of the concept the instructor was trying to "spoon feed" him. He did everything but hand Scott a "cheat sheet."

And try as he may, he could not possibly refresh Scott's memory or recollection of the process. Of course, the instructor had no way of knowing Scott's light was not going to come on because of Scott's unfamiliarity with the procedure. Scott had, of course, studied the concepts in law school, but most law schools at that time did not teach trial procedures and tactics, so he had no real-world experience with utilizing those tools with a witness who had memory issues. All he could think about was he was standing there in front of the group feeling totally humiliated! His stomach felt like it was the size of a peanut!

After everyone did their little standup routine in the moot court room of the law school, each would take their little tape, march their little selves back behind the judge's bench to the judge's chamber, wearing their little "beanie with a helicopter blade on top," and another member of the faculty would critique them one-on-one. Good God! It was bad enough to have to endure that humiliation in front of the group, but now they had to go back and do it again! On the plus side, at least, it was a private humiliation.

All his life, for reasons that he never really understood, Scott had always been able to find the good in a bad situation. Life had consistently shown him that even bad situations had silver linings. Perhaps learning from a bad situation is, itself, the silver lining! In this instance, as bad as it was to have to look at that tape again and listen to the instructor critiquing his performance, he accidentally and privately learned one of the most valuable lessons ever in his professional career. And it would continue to serve him well throughout his career.

While looking at the tape, it was obvious he didn't have a clue what he was doing. But for reasons Scott did not understand, the instructor asked him what he thought he was doing.

"What are you doing there, Scott?"

"I have no idea," replied Scott honestly.

Duh! Of course, he couldn't answer the instructor's critique inquiry any better than he could figure out what he was supposed to be doing in the courtroom! To him, it still involved an unfamiliar and unmanageable procedure. But, again, the instructor had no way of knowing about his ignorance. He just asked a logical question to obtain Scott's thoughts to try to help him improve.

But, as Scott looked at the tape, reliving the moment, extreme humiliation swept over him again and his stomach reverted to peanut mode. As he observed himself on that tape, it was as vivid and gut-wrenching as though he was still standing out in the courtroom! Suddenly, something he noticed overwhelmed him. As he suffered through the repeat of the experience, his attention was drawn to his face.

Despite his physical and agonizingly emotional reaction, his mental reaction was so intense that it allowed him to emotionally detach and observe as though he was looking at someone else.

Observing his face, he would've thought that person was sitting at one of Paris's Latin Quarter sidewalk cafés eating ice cream and people watching, except he wasn't smiling. At that moment, Scott realized that he had a great poker face! Recognizing that if he could experience that degree of humiliation and not express the pain, then he could survive any experience!

CHAPTER 17

Upon his return for the NITA course,
Scott's Motion to Suppress Roberta Wood's
identification was scheduled for hearing.
Related to the motion, a stipulation between the
government and Scott was filed with the Court.
The purpose was to not only narrow the issues in
the trial but, at that stage, inform the judge of
very pertinent facts related to the motion itself.
The stipulation related that all of the latent
fingerprints listed at Sheila Hawthorne's
apartment and some fingerprints found in
Wood's house were of no value for comparison
purposes; they lacked clear and sufficient ridge
characteristics to be identified as any one
individual's fingerprints. The stipulation also
advised the court that the remainder of the latent
fingerprints found at Wood's house and those
lifted at the Daniels' house were determined not
to belong to Timothy. Finally, they'd agreed to
stipulate that the police were unable to lift any
latent fingerprints at the Lockhart-Cooper
apartment.

Central to the motion was the argument
that Hawthorne had never provided a physical
description of the assailant. In her statement to
the police, she merely identified Timothy's
voice. With respect to Wood's testimony
regarding identification, she had selected his
photographs from a photo array and then seen

him in a visual lineup. Most telling, however, was Hawthorne's statements in the hallway preceding the voice-only lineup. It didn't take a rocket scientist to appreciate the influence on all of the witnesses to have a person identify him by name and discover that three of the four in the hallway knew one person was accused of the crime and he was in the lineup!

Detective Stevens' testimony was the central theme of the government's opposition to the motion. He testified in the usual professional staccato voice of an experienced Sex Squad officer accustomed to giving testimony in court. He referred to and testified based on the contents of his initial interview notes and conversations that he had with Hawthorne regarding her certainty as to the identity of the voice in her room the night of the incident.

Well, Scott was loaded for bear and eager to argue. At that point, having survived the ordeal of the NITA course and knowing the material in intimate detail, he was full of piss and vinegar!

Judge Carrington asked him, "Mr. Carmichael, are you ready to proceed?"

"Yes, Your Honor."

"Is the government ready to proceed?"

"Yes, Your Honor."

"Mr. Carmichael, I have read your motions and memorandum. Do you have anything to add to your motions or your memorandum?"

Scott's stomach knotted up. "No, Your Honor."

"Your motions are denied!"

Scott was stunned by the judge's ruling. Needless to say, he was biased, but his motions and memorandum were predicated on objective underpinnings to the legal theories advanced to suppress the identification and dismiss the indictment. He knew it was an uphill fight to prevail on the motions, but he expected more than a summary dismissal. In fact, it was the last thing that he would've expected.

Thus, at that moment, he knew they were going to go to trial. He was defending an individual who was arrested shortly before all of these incidences started happening and accused of a rape, and now he was on trial as an accused serial rapist whose voice had been identified by six individuals as that of the assailant and one victim had identified his photograph from a photo array of 11 individuals. Notwithstanding that he had attended the NITA course, this was still his *second* case with a jury! The first was one day. This probably would last a week!

The judge continued as these thoughts raced through Scott's mind. "We shall now proceed to impanel a jury. The clerk will inform the jury room to send some potential jurors for voir dire."

As all of this sunk in, Scott began to realize that now they were going to have to wait on potential jurors to come in to conduct a voir dire. It was a time for reflection and recovery. The worst part about that was that, here he was getting ready to try a serial rapist case, and because the people who had been called for jury duty had already been sent to other trials, all he was going to have for his potential panel were the rejects. Not that he knew exactly what that meant, if anything, but it sure as hell didn't seem like a very good way to start off picking a jury.

They waited the better part of an hour before potential jurors started to trickle in from other jury panels where they had been rejected. The first few potential jurors that came in sent chills down his spine. All he was getting were all these little old black ladies who probably had a bible in their purse. It was bad enough to try a case like this, but all he could think about was his client is going away to jail for life!

He had come a long way in the short time that he had been in DC. Specifically, his racial attitudes had changed a lot. At first blush, it would seem that his thought about all the little old black ladies with bibles was racial. Nothing could have been further from the truth! When he first went back home after arriving in DC, some friends had asked how he liked living in DC. He told him that he really liked it a lot. Invariably, someone would bring up the racial issue. Usually, it was a question along the lines of either, "They're mostly all black there, aren't they?" or, more likely, "Isn't DC full of niggers?"

Not only had he come a long way in his thinking, but he had developed a dislike and discomfort with that view and those expressions of opinions. Typically, his answer was something along the lines of, "The blacks in the District of Columbia are not like the blacks you and I grew up with. They are well-educated, many better than a lot of white people we know, and, it has been my experience that most of them would qualify as WASPs, except, they can't qualify for some of the initials." Or stated another way: "They are as law-abiding as anybody you've ever met and will send you to jail faster than you can spit. You have to understand something; in the District of Columbia, since almost everybody *is* black, it is primarily the blacks against whom the crimes are being committed. And they don't like it, they won't tolerate it, and they will send your ass to jail in a heartbeat!"

During the next 30 or 45 minutes, they began to get a real mix of people coming in the door. There were men and women, mostly younger than the first group that came in, and more of them were white. That wasn't very reassuring either since all of the victims were white. It seemed that neither fork in the road offered a smooth ride.

Before long, there were enough people to begin the voir dire. Questioning the jurors during the voir dire is the process of questioning the jurors about their prior history, prejudices, and so forth regarding sitting on a rape case. The most fundamental thing Scott needed to remember was that any challenges to the jury regarding their partiality had to be memorialized with either a request or an actual question regarding their impartiality. In lawyer terms, it's called making a record; that is, stating explicitly, with the court reporter taking down your statements, and the particular questions and objections you wish to make regarding whether a member of the jury panel should be seated on the jury. This is called challenging for cause.

There is no limit to the number of jurors that may be challenged for cause. Each side is given 10 pre-emptory challenges, which can be used to exclude a member of the jury panel from the jury for any reason, without the necessity to provide any reason. Because they are limited, they must be used with great care. At the judge's discretion, they could receive more.

Some of the fundamental areas of inquiry were whether that had any previous experience with police officers and would accord undue credibility to a police officer's testimony; whether a potential juror had experience similar to the evidence that was going to be introduced in the case; whether they were acquainted with the witnesses or counsel; and/or, whether they been a victim of a crime or witness or defendant related to crime. They would also be questions about whether they had attitudes toward the defense, cases involving an alibi or no alibi; and whether they understood reasonable doubt, burden of proof, and so forth.

It was important to frame the questions in a manner so as to elicit an individual response, not one which can be answered by silence or a "yes" or "no." Some individual questioning might occur at the bench regarding whether the juror had experience as a witness, had been the victim or suspect in a crime, whether they had prior experiences, either personal, or as the members of a jury, with the type of case on which they are now being asked to serve as a juror. They are also asked if they had been victims of crime or have friends or close relatives who had been victims of crime, in particular, of course, a rape case.

As it turned out, most of the jurors were acceptable. Interestingly enough, there were about a half-dozen of the potential panel who were directly related to or had family members married to police officers. Opinions vary among attorneys, but personally, Scott had a lot of confidence in police officers and their families. One of his closest friends from his Army paratrooper days in the 101st Airborne Division, Wayne, and the best man at his wedding to Jennifer, was a career police officer. Scott wouldn't say police officers were perfect or that they didn't bend the rules, but most of them were very honest and, most importantly to him, he felt that their families held the same values as the officer.

In particular, he was very interested in what he believed to be a particular character of law enforcement families. Specifically, they heard a lot of war stories from their relatives and no doubt heard the good, the bad, and the ugly of being a law enforcement officer. Nevertheless, he was especially confident in his belief that, having heard both sides of many situations, they would pay particular attention to the facts that were presented in a case.

He knew from his own experience of telling people more details, how to get someone's attention, and, at the same time, be certain that they paid attention to the important facts. After hearing many tales, he believed police officers' relatives became very adept at understanding what was really important in a case and what you should be looking for in a story. Certainly, he had much more confidence in their attention span and focus on the facts than the average layperson. In addition, he felt that their approach to examining the completeness and relevancy of facts, together with the presence or absence of important information, would influence them individually and, ultimately, have some positive influence on the jury regarding the contradictory facts in this case.

Scott didn't want to give the members of the jury pool the impression that he was challenging them for cause or using peremptory challenges to eliminate any potential juror from the jury panel because of any connection with the police. As a matter fact, even if he had wanted to use peremptory challenges to get rid of the people who had connection with law enforcement, there were too many to eliminate and still have peremptory challenges left for other potential jurors.

They used the rest of the morning to finish the voir dire and impanel the jury. After going through all the questions, Scott ended up with a jury of five men and seven women. The two alternatives were both women. Unlike the original jury pool members that walked into the room, this jury ultimately was composed of men, women, black and white, ranging in age from early 30s to approximately 60, three of which were relatives of police officers.

Ironically, two women members of the jury pool had children involved in a rape scenario. One's daughter was raped, and the other's son was accused of rape, but was acquitted. It came as no surprise that Scott used a peremptory challenge to strike the mother whose daughter was raped, and the government followed suit with the mother whose son was charged and acquitted.

The judge decided to take a break for lunch and then they would begin the trial.

CHAPTER 18

Reconvening after lunch, the judge instructed the jury about the nature of the case. She asked both parties to have all the witnesses that were going to testify to come into the courtroom so she could put them under oath. After putting them under oath, she advised that they should not discuss the case at all before they testified and afterwards not to discuss their testimony with other witnesses. Of course, this is something the court has to do, but it seemed a little pointless considering all the prosecution witnesses had already talked to each other extensively and had been coached by the prosecution. She then asked counsel if they were ready to proceed. Each responded in the affirmative.

The prosecution starts off as the good guys and the defendant is already behind the eight ball. Even though it is often erroneously and, in amazing ignorance, called the "opening argument" by experienced newscasters who cover trials, it is the opening statement. Why? Because there's no such thing as an opening argument! At least, not officially! But that's not to say that shots are not taken and given by each side. In fact, the prosecution, understandably, will take every opportunity to influence the jury by telling them every negative piece of evidence they intend to introduce.

"Ladies and gentlemen of the jury, this is what we expect the evidence to show."

One of the things Scott knew to be on the lookout for was the prosecution presenting an improper opening statement. It is a delicate tightrope to walk for both sides, but the defense has to be on the lookout for statements that are designed to arouse undue sympathy for the victims and appeal to the passions and prejudices of the jury. It was important for Scott to pay particular attention to the evidence that the prosecution said that it was going to introduce and what they actually introduced at trial.

Not only was it a preview of what was to come, but he needed to track it for the purposes of seeing that they *actually* introduced it. The prosecution telling the jury what it expected the evidence to be, but not actually introducing it, was a way to influence the jury by representing that influential evidence would be presented, when, in fact, they either didn't have the evidence or had no intention whatsoever of introducing it. Perhaps, now, his anxiety about what he didn't know would be revealed.

In the defense's opening statements, Scott would take advantage of the opportunity to explain the defense's theory. Unquestionably, while Scott was denying that Timothy was guilty of any of the crimes for which he was charged, the reality was that he was charged for separate offenses, which resulted in an indictment for burglary while armed, rape while armed assault,

assault with a dangerous weapon, and assault with intent to kill, altogether resulting in a 10-count felony indictment.

As with any criminal case, the defense attempts to provide an alternative interpretive matrix within which the jury can evaluate the evidence. An essential goal is to focus the jury's attention on the weaknesses of the government's case. Scott was aware that it is better to conduct a general versus a specific opening statement so as not to overwhelm the jury with details and lock himself into an absolute defense. Another reason, for each side of the case, as the evidence and testimony develop in the case, the methodology may change.

The prosecution generally provides a very detailed opening statement. Scott knew it would be better to make a general statement and acquaint the jury with the defense's theory, other interpretations, and focus on the weaknesses and elements of the government's cases, which were conflicting, possibly suggested in their opening statement by what they did not say. That's exactly what any defense attorney would and should do. Ideally, defense counsel would introduce himself to the jury and refer to his client by his first name to humanize each of them, and, hopefully, establish some rapport. This was not an easy thing to do in a serial rape case.

If things weren't bad enough already, exasperating the situation was the reality that

Timothy was black, and all of the victims were white. The cases were reeking with racial undercurrents. The tension in the courtroom was intense.

Scott was steeped in notes for each witness; he had outlined every single aspect of the evidence, the areas of direct and cross-examination that he wanted to cover, and all of the anticipated evidence that he expected the government to introduce. He was feeling very confident for someone who was only in his second jury trial.

Broom Hilda rose and went to the podium in front of the jury with her legal pad in response to the court's instructions that she begin making her opening statement.

At that point, Scott felt as though he was going to have a heart attack! Notwithstanding all that he had learned in the NITA course, which was disjointed in its presentation - that is, it was non-sequential, not as a real trial - an opening statement was never even mentioned or practiced, and it never entered his mind to prepare one! He knew about it, knew how, could have been prepared with an outline for it, but he was so focused on all the minutia of organizing his defense that he blew it! Embarrassment was overwhelmed by sheer terror!

Fortunately, he was the only person in the world who was aware of his vision of being on a precipice feeling someone eagerly waiting to push him over it. Not even the concept of the necessity for an opening statement had actually entered his mind. He had been overwhelmed and consumed by the complexity and interdependent interaction of the cases and trying to prepare for every conceivable thrust and parry of the prosecution.

Immediately, he remembered the old joke about a trial lawyer in court experiencing a humiliating moment, or an extreme irreparable reversal in his case, and praying that there was a lever beside him so he could pull it, releasing a trapdoor under his chair so he would immediately disappear from the courtroom! But there he was, in his panic, without a lever and left hoping that his poker face was holding up.

It was apparent that Broom Hilda had prepared a long and detailed opening statement. The pages of her yellow legal pad were dog-eared from obviously having been flipped over many, many times and contained a lot of detailed notes. Exacerbating his panic, if it were possible, was knowing that now he was going to learn why the government was so adamant and willing to go to trial in the face of overwhelming objective evidence undermining their case. Without a doubt, there was no way that Scott could counter her detailed opening statement, and he knew it.

It was also apparent Broom Hilda was going to go on for quite a long time. It is normal for the prosecution to give a lot of details of the evidence that it intended to introduce in its case. Generally, throughout each opening statement, besides referencing portions with the standard phrase "we expect the evidence to show" to avoid any objections that they are being argumentative, the prosecution proceeds to shovel as much crap on the defendant as they have, excepting any surprises they are holding back for direct examination or rebuttal. So, there was no guarantee that she would give up her secrets in her opening statement rather than reserve them for rebuttal. She went on for 45 minutes!

Without a doubt, there was no way Scott could offset the broadsides she was leveling at Timothy. Having recovered somewhat from his panic during her 45-minute soliloquy, he was comforted by knowing how well he knew the facts and he did not need a long list of details written down on a legal pad to slice and dice the case 10 different ways. As it happened, for example, he could cite, cross check, and cross compare in his head all the details of the various PD251s, Complaints, and Event Reports. And it gave him some confidence in knowing at least on that point, the jury would note the contrast between her having to refer to notes and his being able to recite everything from memory. Increasingly, he knew he could give a strong opening statement.

Gradually, the Tiger reappeared! He recovered and paid close attention to Broom Hilda's presentation, all the while making mental notes about significant objective facts in

Timothy's favor that she wasn't sharing with the jury. Thus, even before it was the time to make his "opening statement," he had regained his composure and was ready to go!

Wayne and Scott had many lively "discussions" over the years about the criminal justice system, given they were on opposite sides of the question. The way Scott calmly analogized it for him, which really pissed him off, was Scott telling Wayne that Scott was like a gunfighter going into a gunfight with an empty six gun. Each time the police made a mistake, Scott got a bullet. The more mistakes the police made, the more bullets he got. If he had only one or two bullets before trial, he would plea bargain. Once he went beyond three bullets, the odds started to favor him to win because of the prosecution's burden to win their case beyond a reasonable doubt. If he got four or five, he would go to trial. Scott kept telling him, "If you want to win the gunfight, quit making mistakes and giving me bullets!"

Broom Hilda's opening statement hadn't filled up Scott's six shooter, but she had left gaps in some important areas that gave him a couple of bullets to fire over the jury's head just to get their attention, which at that point was all he wanted to do. Specifically, he pointed out that, despite what the prosecution had done and what they're supposed to do, that is, tell the jury a lot of negative facts about the case and Timothy to make him look like a very bad person and guilty, there were objective facts that she had left out that were favorable to him.

"You will see when the prosecution introduces evidence about the various offenses that each of the police reports containing the description of the victims all describe a perpetrator about my height and my weight, that is 5'8" and weighing 155 to 165 pounds. You will also see from the documentation that the prosecution will provide you, and, if they do not, we will, that Timothy is 6'2" and weighs 190 pounds. So, objectively, Timothy is much larger than the person described as assaulting the victims. I think it's fair to say, that, under the circumstances, the victims would've described someone as much larger than they really are, due to the fear factor, not smaller!

I appreciate your time and attention during both the prosecution's and my opening statement. I will also appreciate your time and attention during the trial because trials can be long and detailed, and I urge you to focus on the testimony and evidence presented by *both* sides! Yes, both sides! Because Timothy is charged with very serious offenses. He is not guilty, and we fully expect that after you have heard all of the testimony and examine the evidence, you will agree."

Scott was very encouraged by some of the jurors' facial expressions and, in particular, the raised eyebrows and backward jerking head movement of one black female juror. He had awakened them from their soliloquy slumber.

In conclusion, Scott reiterated a few significant exculpatory facts that the prosecution had omitted in their opening statement, such as his alibi witnesses, the weight and height discrepancies between Timothy and the assailants, and the victim's discussion in the hallway before the lineup of Timothy being in the lineup.

"Even more omitted details would be revealed as the trial proceeds." Several additional jurors reacted to that statement. "Especially, I want you to pay close attention to the promises that the prosecution made to you; that is, that the prosecution will put on certain kinds of evidence and to be sure that the prosecution keeps those promises."

Then, he sat down and was very satisfied having dodged that broadside and safely walked away. He finished in four minutes!

CHAPTER 19

Unlike the voice lineup in December, Scott didn't have to wait for the short, attractive, slightly pudgy brunette with big hooters to appear or be surprised by other complaining witnesses. He had no idea who they would call first but would've thought they would save her anticipated strong, damaging testimony as the "cleanup batter" to emphasize their case and reiterate and reinforce earlier witness's testimony. After all, she was the one that had direct contact with him prior to the incident leading to his arrest and within hours of the incident where he was identified by name to the police, which led to his subsequent arrest in the later cases. Nevertheless, they decided to open with Hawthorne as a leadoff power hitter.

The prosecution began asking her to describe the events of October 7, 1978 leading up to the rape. Normally, a defense lawyer would object to such an open-ended question giving the witness an opportunity to provide a narrative response. Allowing a witness to testify in a narrative fashion deprives a defense attorney of the opportunity to object to improper and/or inadmissible testimony. It's a prime example of that happening and trying to "unring the bell!" Nevertheless, Scott elected to let her do it because, being intimately familiar with all the details, in written form, any omissions, misstatements, or embellishments to her story would expose her to credibility issues, if not outright impeachment!

He was also keenly aware that it was equally dangerous for the prosecution to let a witness testify narratively because the prosecution cannot be sure their testimony will track the evidence and their previous statements, which it typically does not. And, if the witness deviates from their expected testimony and the evidence and the prosecution attempts to stop them, defense counsel will undoubtedly successfully object. Should this circumstance develop, the prosecution interrupting their own witness to "correct" their testimony sends a very negative message to the jury and suggests that the prosecution is coaching the witnesses' testimony.

"On October 7, 1978, around 11:00 or 11:30 in the evening, I was in my apartment. I walked across the street to a restaurant called the Underground in Duddingtons. It's in the 300 block of Pennsylvania Avenue SE. I walked inside and saw that there were about six people in the bar. All my friends go to Duddingtons. I like to go there to play the pinball machines. I started talking to James, the manager, and ordered a beer. I played a couple of pinball games with some people I knew. About midnight, a man came that I knew as Timothy. I finished playing pinball and went to the bar where my drink was. Timothy was next to me. I said hello. He started talking to me about my job, the election, and what he did on his job. He told me that he worked for a local television station as a cameraman. We talked about our family and he said that he lived on the Hill at one time. I've had conversations with him before inside Duddingtons. I think it was about four other times. We would have long conversations and just talk about nothing."

"I got up and walked to the jukebox and was playing some records when he came over and started telling me that he thinks that I would be a good lover and that he wanted to get to know me that way. I told him no and that I don't just sleep with anyone. He said he was an honest person and just wanted to let me know how he felt. We talked for a minute and then walked back to the bar. I started playing pinball with some friends of mine. He was sitting at the bar watching us play."

"About 1 a.m., a woman by the name of Suzanne came into the bar along with a guy. I started talking with her and her boyfriend. We were sitting at the bar and I introduced her to Timothy. Suzanne said that she knew him from before. She said that one night she was in Duddingtons and he got really pushy about wanting to drive her home. He stated that he wouldn't take no for an answer. He stated that he never saw Suzanne before and that it wasn't him. The bar was closing. I was looking for James, the manager. He or Steve, who also works at

Duddingtons, would walk me home most of the time. Timothy was leaving also."

"I walked outside to go home when he said that he would walk across the street with me. I said okay. As we were walking across the street to my house by the bank parking lot, he stated that he may get a kiss after all. I told him that if he got a kiss, it would be all that he got. We got to my apartment house and we walked up the stairs. I opened the door and I turned and thanked him for walking me home. He then kissed me. He wanted to come into my apartment, and I told him no. He told me that he wanted to make love to me and that it would be good. I told him no and I made it clear back at Duddingtons. I said good night and turned to unlock the door."

"He grabbed me and turned me around. He kissed me and I was pulling away from him the whole time. He was hurting my face and back where he was holding me with his hands. I finally pushed him away and told him that he hurt me. He got this crazy look on his face. I just started crying and turned and went into the hallway and closed the door behind me. I didn't turn around to see if he was still standing there. I walked to my apartment and went inside and locked the door. I was very upset because he hurt me. About an hour later, I closed the front room window and blinds, and got ready to go to bed. Sometime around 3:00 or 3:30 I fell asleep."

"Sometime later, I woke up after I felt someone cutting my nose with a knife. The next thing I heard was a man saying to me, 'This is a knife and if you move or say a word, I will kill you.' As soon as this man started talking and stated those words, I knew that it was Timothy. I didn't tell the man I knew who he was because I was afraid that he would kill me with the knife. I didn't say a word. The man, said,' Turn over on your side facing the wall.' He took the pillow and put it on my face. He then told me to turn on my back. I still had the pillow over my face. He told me to put my hands on the pillow and hold it against my face. He told me not to move and pulled the sheets and blanket off of me. I was nude; he told me to spread my legs. He got between my legs and I told him that I was on my period and that I had a Tampax on. I asked him what I should do with it. He told me to get rid of it. I put it on the floor next to the bed."

"He had the knife touching my neck and he told me to put him inside of me. I put his penis in my vagina, and he told me to put my legs around him. He then raped me. While he was raping me, he told me to fuck him like he was my old man. I don't know how long he was inside of me, but he climaxed as he was coming out. He got up and told me not to move. He pulled up his pants. I didn't hear any sounds like a buckle. Timothy did not have a belt on while he was at Duddingtons. The man walked across the room by the desk and asked me if I had any money. I told him no. I told him that I had just paid the rent. He told me that he was going to look around and for me not to move. He said, 'Don't move your hands or the pillow.' I told him that I wasn't moving. He said again that he was going to be in my apartment for a while and for me not to move. He said, 'If you move or say anything, I am going to shoot you.' I just stayed in bed without moving for a long time."

"I finally moved the pillow off my face and looked around the apartment. I saw that the blinds and window were up next to the desk. I very slowly looked outside because I thought he may have still been outside. I went to close the window, but I remembered that is where fingerprints may be. I closed it using the curtain and locked it. Then, I pulled the blinds down. I telephoned my aunt and told her that I'd been raped. She stated that she would be right over. We hung up the phone. She called back and said that she and her husband would be right over."

"A short time later, my uncle came over and got me. He took me back to his house. I didn't tell him that I knew who raped me. Once we got to his house, he called the police. While he was on the telephone with the police, I told my aunt who the man was that raped me. I know that Timothy was the one who raped me because I knew that it was his voice when the man was raping me, before and after."

Naturally, her testimony was expected to track what Scott already knew about the case, except that he had learned some things that were not in the police reports. First, he learned from Timothy that she had a reputation for liking black guys. Although he had no basis to prove it and certainly would not have alleged it without proof, or bring up specific names in the trial, there was always a hint of suspicion that he could raise that the assailant might have been one of the other black men that had been in her apartment or that she had met in a bar just like Timothy. The strategy was reinforced because the Negroid head hairs from different men found on her bedspread not only did not match Timothy's but weren't even a close match to him. Obviously, they came from *other* black men, not potentially from *only* the rapist!

Although he had no basis to suspect James of the rape, it was not beyond question that James may have been one of the men from whom one of the hair samples might have been left in her apartment. In any event, it was a foundation to ask questions and suggest that other men, black men, had been in her apartment with her permission and knew where she lived. What he was going to try and do was delicately get the information into evidence regarding the other samples of Negroid head hair found on her bed, specifically, that they did not match Timothy's, and leave it open to the "WASP" lady juror members to take it from there.

In raising the subject about the Negroid head hairs in her bed, Scott was laying a landmine for future use against the prosecution. Certainly, it would become part of his closing argument that the government purposely left out the exculpatory information from their own laboratories. Moreover, even then he was aware that there was strong animosity among black women against black men who dated white, blonde women. And although she was not blond, Scott felt that, in this scenario, brunette would do just as well.

It seemed to follow, at least in his mind, that some black men may well have the same animosity, or, perhaps, even jealousy. His primary strategy didn't even take into account the views the white jurors might have of her social life or of the other black men dating a white woman, or her favoring black men, but then Scott's focus was to generate as much prejudice against her as possible and counteract her damaging testimony as well as discounting the expected animosity against Timothy as an accused serial rapist. His subtle references to Negroid head hairs found on her bed were totally in keeping with his kid gloves approach to the witnesses. Certainly, it was one of those times that, for many reasons, less *was* more!

Not contained in the police reports, naturally, was a complete version, at least from Timothy's telling, of all that happened at the apartment when he walked her home. Her version included his forcefully making her kiss him. His version was that they were getting along great at the Underground. When they got to the door of her apartment, he did make moves to get a kiss from her and received kisses in exchange. However, there was no force involved and, according to him, things were hot and heavy, and he wanted to come in and have sex.

To his friends, Scott described it as, "They got to the door and they were playing 'smacky mouth!'" She told him that she couldn't because she was on her period. He pursued the subject and said that didn't matter to him. However, it did matter to her, but she told him that they would get together later. "I don't start anything I don't finish." Hearing her testimony in the courtroom, was dramatically different from the sterile, unemotional Complaint, Event Reports, and the PD251.

On cross-examination, there really wasn't a whole lot to cross-examine her about. One of the things that he learned in the NITA course from hours and hours and hours of listening to a renowned authority on evidence, Irving Younger, was that one of the failings of American trial attorneys, as observed by his British Barrister counterpart, was that they were in too big a hurry to get an answer out of a witness and, oftentimes, would not allow the witness to finish their statement before they asked the next question. One serious fault in this methodology is, clearly, the American attorney is not really listening to the answer. Everyone whoever watched a television crime drama has seen this scenario. Its dramatic purpose is to badger the witness and create tension. Or, sometimes, hurrying onto the next question instead of patiently waiting through an extended pause, suggesting to the jury that the witnesses are manufacturing a non-prejudicial response.

Another point that Younger made, in his uniquely brief and concise manner, was that on cross-examination, there aren't really very many important questions a lawyer *should* be asking. The last thing he or she should be doing is repeating all the direct testimony, most of which in a criminal case is damaging to his client and should be left alone, not reinforcing it by repetition! What he should be doing, and what Younger emphatically recommended is, "Ask a few important, necessary questions, listen to the answer, shut the hell up, and sit the hell down!"

Of course, Scott wanted to get into evidence the results of the lab report information that several Negroid head hairs had been found on her bed. Needless to say, the government did not introduce any evidence on that point, but since it was *Brady* material, that information was released. Procedurally, it didn't matter that the government had not introduced any evidence on this point. Procedurally, it didn't matter either that Scott never intended to call the lab technicians to testify about this point. What mattered was that he could, by posing the questions correctly.

"Are you aware that Negroid head hairs from several men had been found on your bedspread?"

"Yes."

Naturally, she was aware of it and the jury heard it. That was all he wanted to accomplish. It was helpful, but legally immaterial whether she knew that the lab had determined that they were not Timothy's head hairs, so he didn't ask any questions on this point. Obviously, the jury understood if any of the head hairs were Timothy's, the prosecution would have told them in the opening statement and introduced the lab results. Moreover, it was Scott's intent to ensure that the jury became aware of the prosecution's omission of this information. Certainly, he would also be highlighting it during his closing argument.

Scott asked a few questions, listened to the answers, shut the hell up, and sat the hell down! The exchange put lead in Broom Hilda's panties and she never got out of her chair to redirect!

Even if the government had objected, which Scott was certain would have been overruled, the jury would have already heard the information. Besides, it was true and materially exculpatory evidence. Among trial lawyers, it is recognized that, while the opposing party may object to a question, even if it is sustained and the judge admonishes the jury to disregard the testimony, the jury has already heard the question and many times the witness had already answered if the objection is too slow.

The appropriate procedure is for the objecting party to move to strike the question-and-answer from the record. What trial lawyers are fond of saying is, "You can't unring a bell!" Once a jury hears something of this nature, no matter the procedural maneuvering of the attorneys and the ruling by the court, they don't forget it! In fact, under the circumstances, it would be extremely imprudent for the prosecution to object, move to strike it from the record, have their objection overruled, and then conduct redirect questioning on that very subject in order to "clarify" the witnesses' testimony. Doing so would only underscore the significance of the testimony they attempted to strike from the record.

There were several topics Scott was particularly interested in asking her about. "What is your recollection of your conversation with your aunt and uncle?"

"Basically, I told them the same thing I testified to earlier today."

"Who arrived first? The uniformed police officers?"

"Uniformed officers."

Next, he wanted to focus on her later conversations with Detective Stevens when he arrived around 7 a.m. The prosecution did not want to give Scott a shot at her in the pretrial suppression hearing, so they did not offer her testimony. They relied on Stevens. It wasn't that important because, at the pretrial suppression hearing, Detective Stevens had already given testimony regarding the kind of information he needed from her to support probable cause before a magistrate for an arrest warrant. It was uncontroverted from his field notes as well as her aunt and uncle's testimony at the pre-trial suppression hearing that when she first talked to her aunt and uncle, she was "absolutely positive" that the voice in the room that night was Timothy's. She still maintained when Detective Stevens appeared and started interviewing her that she was "absolutely positive" that the voice in that room that night was Timothy's voice.

But when Detective Stevens started to focus in on the particulars of her recollection and statements, he outlined the necessary criteria in order for him to obtain the arrest warrant based on probable cause. He needed to be certain of how 'absolutely positive' she was. Again, she confirmed that she was "absolutely positive."

"On a scale of 0 to 10, with 10 being the most positive, how 'absolutely positive' are you?"

"8 ½."

Scott went over this portion of her testimony with her on cross-examination and her testimony item by item because he was already certain of the facts from the police reports and Stevens' testimony, along with her aunt and uncle. He was not arguing with her or trying to embarrass her. He could have but he reminded himself that he had determined pretrial he was not going to be hostile to the complaining witnesses. In fact, his being gentle as possible with all the complaining witnesses was producing results. Moreover, unless she changed her testimony, he already knew the answers to all the questions he was asking her, and he knew that Detective Stevens' notes supported the contradiction in her testimony.

Rape is a very sensitive and emotionally charged issue. The last thing in the world he wanted to do was piss the jury off because he was jumping on all the witnesses. Being in a trial is not like television. In fact, television takes such extreme license for dramatic effect that it misleads the audience as to how trials really proceed.

Consequently, the jury probably expected television drama; that is, Scott jumping all over the complaining witnesses. Together, with his total preparation, except for the opening statement snafu, the positive feedback he was getting from his delicate treatment of the witnesses had a calming effect on him and increased his confidence.

In posing his next question, Scott highlighted the distinction between her earlier version of who was in the room that night and her statement about her certainty as being "absolutely positive," when only a few hours later, her degree of certainty had dropped to a "8 ½."

"My statements regarding being "absolutely positive" as to the identity of the person in that room being Timothy have not changed at all. What I meant when I responded "8 ½" to Detective Stevens' question, was that it did not relate to my certainty about the voice in my room being Timothy's; rather, it related to my confidence in my ability to pick out his voice in a voice-only lineup."

She wouldn't budge on that point! Having clarified the distinction, Scott didn't pressure her anymore. She had a chance to change or correct her testimony and didn't. She was now locked into the contradiction. Scott was very happy!

The government very wisely decided not to ask any questions on redirect. They knew as much about her pretrial testimony as he did, and it was an obvious evidentiary conflict and credibility problem. It presented an opportunity for him to impeach her and he had laid the foundation, without making it so obvious to her. But the prosecution understood what had happened. To the jury, it had the appearance of her simply being firm in her testimony. However, they didn't know what the attorneys knew; that is, her testimony was directly contradicted by Detective Stevens' pretrial testimony and she was impeachable! From there on, it was just a matter of which strategy to follow to complete the impeachment.

Next, the government called in Roberta Wood. Although it had been almost a year since the voice-only lineup, Scott still had vivid, disturbing images in his mind of what she looked like after having been badly beaten. She was an attractive woman and looked much better now. Although Scott and the AUSA had also entered into a stipulation affecting all the cases, which the judge had learned in the pretrial hearings, it was now time for the judge to inform the jury of the stipulation and its contents.

She stated, "It is stipulated between the prosecution and the defense that: All the latent fingerprints lifted at Hawthorne's apartment and some of the fingerprints found in Roberta Wood's house were of no value for comparison purposes; that is, that they lacked clear and sufficient ridge characteristics to be identified as anyone individual's fingerprints. It is further stipulated that the remainder of the latent fingerprints found at Roberta Wood's house and those lifted at the Daniels' house were determined not to belong to the defendant. Finally, it is stipulated and agreed between the parties that the police were unable to lift any latent fingerprints at the Lockhart-Cooper's apartment."

Wood took the stand. Broom Hilda began to take her back over her earlier statements and recounted the information in the police reports. It was still very disturbing and unsettling for Scott to actually listen to her recount the details, which was much more extensive than at the pretrial suppression hearing.

"In the early morning hours of December 4, 1978, I was asleep in the second-floor bedroom of my home in the Capitol Hill section of the District of Columbia. At about 2:00 AM, I was awakened by the presence of a man in my bedroom."

"When I first saw him, he was standing in the archway about four feet from my bed. I sat up and looked at him. Though the only light that was on inside the room at that time was the pilot light on the electric blanket switch, the room was somewhat illuminated by light from outside streetlamps shining through the white Venetian blinds. I observed that the man wore a knit hat that was puffed up and a hip-length winter coat made of some kind of cloth. The man spoke to me as I sat up. In a soft, articulate voice, he ordered me to lie down and rollover.

He repeated his orders firmly several times and advanced toward the bed coming right up to where I sat looking at him. When I failed to comply with his orders, he hit me in the face with his fist and knocked me back on the bed. He then placed a pillow over my face, told me he had a knife, and let me feel the blade.

A period of about 30 seconds passed from the time I first observed the intruder to the time the pillow was placed over my face. The man continued to speak to me as he prepared to rape me. He ordered me to pull down my panties and sought my help in putting his penis into my vagina. When his first attempt proved futile, he left the bed for 15-20 seconds and then returned. He entered me, climaxed quickly, rose and fled the scene."

The police were summoned, and an investigation was initiated. She described her assailant to the officers on the scene and described the suspect as a "Negro male, 30-40 years old, 5'8" in height, of medium weight, and wearing a dark jacket." Her statement was recorded in the PD251. In a written statement the next day, she described the rapist as a "Negro male around 30 years old, 5'8" to 5'10" in height with a medium build." To her testimony she added that "his weight on me didn't feel that heavy, maybe 150-165 pounds. His face was round, his voice was soft, and firm. He sounded educated in his speech."

On December 5, 1978, Wood attended a voice-only lineup and identified Timothy's voice. Subsequently, on the evening of December 5th, she was shown an 11-photo array, which contained Timothy's picture. She identified his photograph as that of the assailant.

The police then arranged for another lineup on December 13th. This time, it was a visual lineup. Timothy was identified by Wood as the assailant. Of particular interest to Scott when he saw the photograph of the lineup was that every individual had facial hair! All the way from a full beard, chin, or jawbone hair, to only a mustache. At the time, he simply couldn't connect the dots to understand why.

The impact of her testimony was even more troubling than that for each of the other victims. By this time, it was the third day of trial. Because Scott was a sole practitioner, he was the chief cook and bottle washer for the entire trial. Between getting ready for trial, being at trial all day, assessing what happened at trial that day, and then preparing for the next day, he was putting in 18-hour days.

Little did he know then, but very few lawyers really do any trial work. Moreover, most lawyers who do some trial work generally don't have a trial last more than one day, if that, and even fewer of those are jury trials.

Even though he had outlines for every phase of the trial and was on top of everything going on, he still wrote prodigious notes during all the testimony, even though he had heard most of the testimony at the pretrial suppression hearing. Scott was taking notes as quickly as possible so that he would be aware of anything that was materially different from what he knew and would give him some basis, if possible, to cross-examine any of the witnesses. This was important because, although he had information from the Complaint, Event Reports, detective notes, Timothy's version, and medical reports, he had become aware of information that was in none of the documents and he was on high alert for new facts.

Plus, a witness' testimonial version *never* tracks the reports and sometimes either contradicts or adds new facts. Even on minor variations from previous testimony, he could not allow his attention to waiver, despite his fatigue. Even the smallest material factual deviation can have a major impact on the preparation of a case, trial strategy, or the outcome of the trial.

Even more frightening to Scott, always looming over his shoulder was the reoccurring fear of the ominous possibility that at any moment, the prosecution would unload the "hidden" devastating information propelling them to go to trial in face of all of the countervailing materially objective, exculpatory, evidence. Ever on Scott's mind was the unknown, again, becoming the obvious! *What did they know that he hadn't been as yet able to see?* After all, just because Broom Hilda had not alluded to anything new during her opening statement, it did not mean she didn't have an ace up her sleeve. Everything about the circumstances of the case and the prosecution going ahead with the case, despite serious defects in the evidence, screamed that there was an extremely unpleasant surprise around the corner.

Wood's testimony was riveting, as was the testimony of the other witnesses. At times, the testimony was so vivid that Scott imagined himself in the room with his wife or girlfriend and wondering how he would react. Their description of the trauma was palpitating, and it was a challenge at times to ignore their terror and focus on his job. While he had no first-person knowledge of the crime scenes, he had first-hand knowledge of the Underground where all the victims were connected to Timothy. For all he knew, Jennifer and he had sat on the very bar stools where it all began.

Soon, Wood came to the part where she was describing what she could see of the assailant. At the pretrial suppression hearing, she testified that it was so dark in the room that night that all she could see was a black outline of his head and it was so dark she could see absolutely no facial features except the outline of his ears and a round type head.

When Scott questioned her about this, he spoke in such a manner as to use words that the court reporter could take down to accomplish what lawyers call "making a record" of the testimony. What this means is that he described his interpretation of her verbal testimony and her physical mannerisms to manifest the parts of the silhouette in such a way that if the case were to be appealed, in the very likely event of a very adverse decision against Timothy, that the Appellate Court could read the record and visualize what she was describing. What he needed to do was describe her testimony regarding her perception of the assailant's head features and how she had moved her hands around her own face to illustrate the visual image she herself had of the assailant.

In making the record, he repeated her pretrial testimony on this point as accurately as possible and described her physical movements with her hand to illustrate her testimony. "During your testimony, would it be accurate in describing the use of your hands to say that you used the ends of your fingers, which you placed on the side of your face approximately at the middle of your ear, and moved them down to the bend of your jawbone?"

"Yes, that is accurate. That is the area of the face that I could see in the silhouette and there was no facial hair."

By now Scott had been able to figure out why all of the individuals in the visual lineup had facial hair. The composition of the lineup was not based on her testimony that she could see no facial features, but the effort of the police to influence her toward identifying Timothy as the assailant. In order to do this, the composition of the lineup had to include individuals who had facial hair so the composition of the lineup would be "fair" and survive a later defense suppression challenge.

Scott had learned earlier on that she was a part-time real estate agent and a part-time actress. He wasn't afraid to ask questions, even though Cindy had been unable to interview her because he had a high degree of confidence that these areas were so unrelated to the details of offense itself that they would not produce any damaging testimony.

After going over all her testimony, he inquired about her being a part-time real estate agent. "Do you know the Daniels'?"

"No."

He got her! She lied! She sold them their house, and she and Nelson have the same broker, and they share a desk!

What he was really counting on for making some mileage with the jury was revealing her to be a part-time actress. In particular, he was hoping that she did drama. Obviously, he thought it would help with the jury to note that she was a dramatic actress. Even though she was testifying against Timothy, she came across with a lot of credibility. She reminded Scott a lot of a deer in the spotlight who was very nervous and totally oblivious to where the questioning was going, except that she exuded calmness. Also, asking her about her real estate and acting experience were non-threatening areas and no doubt questions she was not expecting. But, being non-threatening subjects, she really got into them.

Again, he was trying to make some mileage on the drama side, but it turned out that she liked doing comedy more. She really enjoyed talking about it and he just let her go on. Certainly, it wasn't hurting the prosecution's case or his, but, perhaps, it was a light moment for everyone. It wasn't exactly what he was after, but it was clear to the jury that she was in her element talking about acting. Also, Scott knew that he was asking questions the answer to which he did not know. An extremely dangerous thing to do in a trial! However, none of her answers hurt and they might even help, he thought.

All the while he was questioning her, he was smiling a little bit inside thinking that the prosecution as well as some of the members of the jury, were paying very close attention. And he couldn't help but feel that the prosecution was nervous and wondering just where the hell he was going with this line of questioning. But they didn't object. Now, *they* were waiting for the other shoe to drop!

In going over her testimony once the trial started, the prosecution again covered all of the circumstances of her incident in detail. Being intimately familiar with all the documentation on her case and having heard her pretrial testimony, nothing new was going on, but Scott was still furiously taking notes. Late in the afternoon at about 3:30, the trial was dragging on, he was fatigued, and his hand was very tired. He alternated between taking notes and keeping an eye on the witnesses while they testified.

Then it happened! He didn't know if it were luck, or divine intervention, but he just happened to look up as Wood testified about what she could see of the assailant. What Scott saw struck him like a lightning bolt!

Simultaneously, he was elated and terrified because he almost missed it! She continued testifying about her incident.

Even when he was nervous, all his life he had dry palms. But, during this trial, so far, his palms were wet and clammy. He was reminded of a character in the "Lil Abner" comic strip with a perpetual black cloud over his head raining on him. The character's name was Joe Black, a.k.a. Black Cloud. Eventually, she came to the part of her testimony where she was describing being in the room that night and what she could see and hear.

It was a stroke of absolute fortune that he looked up while she was testifying about the pure black silhouette in her room that night. Just listening to her testimony, it seemed to be the same as it was in the pretrial hearing. But one of the things that he had learned from the pretrial hearing was that the prosecutor and the police had lied to him about her picking Timothy's photo out of an 11-photo array. They told him that she had identified Timothy's photo. Unfortunately, Scott had assumed that she had an actual visible image and recall of the person's face that was in her room that night and, when shown a photo array, picked out his photograph and said, "That is the man who was in my room that night." Lesson learned. Don't assume the obvious!

He had been lulled into a false sense of believing the police and the prosecution. He never imagined they would be dishonest! She *never* identified Timothy's *face* in the photo array! The pretrial suppression testimony revealed that the police were well aware that she could not see any facial features of the assailant. So, they put together a photo array and when she was unable to identify any of the photographs visually, they asked her if any of the men in the pictures had a head shaped like the head of the man that was in her room that night. She narrowed it down to two.

"Of the two, which head is shaped most like the head of the man who was in your room that night?"

This represented yet another egregious example of the total disregard by the prosecution and the police of adherence to the rules and the truth to tilt the scales of justice!

Scott didn't think any experienced attorney would have interpreted the prosecutor or the police having related that one of the victims had identified a defendant's photo from an 11-photo array in any way other than in the normal understanding as that term is used. Of course, a big advantage to the prosecution was that it meant that at pretrial, Scott had to deal with *two* people having "visually" identified him.

Even though he became aware of this helpful information during the pretrial phase, during the trial phase, it gave him a big advantage. Now he had a most important additional element of Wood's identification that occurred by sheer luck to create a hastily revised defense strategy. All because Scott just happened to look up from his notetaking as she was going over her testimony regarding the pure black silhouette and she was, again, using her hand and her fingertips to physically demonstrate the areas of the assailant's face that she could see.

To this day, he does not know whether he was the only person in the room who noticed the difference between her pretrial testimony and the testimony she was giving at that moment. But he was extremely elated with what he saw!

When the time came for him to recross-examine her, he went over again her cross-examination testimony regarding her real estate and acting experience to intentionally relax her. The prosecution hadn't brought that up on redirect, so procedurally, he wasn't able to re-cross on those areas. He could only surmise, since it seemed hey were immaterial and harmless areas of inquiry, they decided to just let it pass and not object.

In addition to treating the witnesses with a lot of respect and being low-key, he continued in his efforts to be non-confrontational, non-argumentative, and non-threatening. So far, it appeared to be working well. The prosecution had not objected to any cross or recross-examination up to this point.

She continued to be at ease, especially talking about her acting. While he didn't get any mileage out of it as he originally thought he might, it did have the benefit of establishing some rapport with her and she certainly wasn't the least bit intimidated.

Then it came time to get down to the nitty-gritty.

He remembered before taking the NITA course that he had joked about the 10 most common mistakes an inexperienced trial lawyer makes and his making 13, which, of course, is an unlucky number. But in this instance, he knew exactly where he was going and was hoping that his heart would not start racing so much that he would appear nervous. But he wasn't actually nervous except to the extent that he was worried whether he could get her to articulate and confirm his description of her previous direct testimony about the physical gestures she used to demonstrate what she had seen. For all intents and purposes, she had given the same testimony at trial that she had given at pretrial.

Except for one portion, it was virtually identical testimony. The difference was that in her trial testimony, instead of rubbing her fingertips from the middle of her ear about where a man's sideburn would end to the corner of her jawbone, this time, she rubbed her fingertips all the way down from her ear to the corner of her jawbone *and* continued all the way down along her jawbone to the middle of her chin, all the while indicating that she could see the *entire* side view of the assailant's face and there was no facial hair!

Words cannot express how much he would have liked to look over at Broom Hilda and stick his tongue out and say something on the order of like, "How about them apples?" Or give her a raspberry. Or, in his fantasy world, ask for the court's indulgence, walk slowly over to Broom Hilda's table where she and three of her assistants were seated, and in a low key, inaudible voice the jury could not hear, ask her, "Can you read lips?"

You see, Timothy had, as he sat there at trial and had for many, many years, a Fu Manchu mustache! Obviously, when he was arrested, photographed, and was in the visual lineups, he had his mustache.

Even though Scott wanted to do cartwheels across the courtroom, or sail paper airplanes at Broom Hilda, he understood that the best reaction was somewhat along the lines of the old adage, "never let them see you sweat," except, in this circumstance, the best reaction was "don't gloat!" Besides, as tempting as it was, the last thing he wanted to do was call their attention to a contradiction in her pretrial and trial testimony and allow them to possibly recover. And, if indeed, no one but him saw what was going on, then he was burying another landmine!

Oddly, the FBI lab analysis on the semen samples for the Wood case revealed a very surprising connection. This information was another landmine that Scott was laying for the prosecution.

282

CHAPTER 20

Out of nowhere, for their next witness, they called Timothy's supervisor from work. Scott was very surprised by this and totally in the dark about the nature of his testimony.

Suddenly, he was testifying that on the day after each and every one of the offenses, Timothy called in sick and had taken the day off. The jury is always watching your mood and your facial expressions. Scott tried to look cool as he leaned over and whispered to Timothy, "Don't show any emotion. But is this true?"

Timothy slightly shook his head in a negative way and Scott knew the jury would see it. He denied his supervisor's testimony. At that moment, there was no way to refute the testimony. Scott looked at his watch; it was about 10:30. His first thought was that at noon, he would call the television station and get a copy of Timothy's work records.

At the noon recess, he called and was informed that the police had already picked them up! It was no surprise that he was already at an extreme disadvantage being a sole practitioner, but this only highlighted the disparity between his resources and the resources available to the United States Attorney's Office. Undoubtedly, it had not even come to his attention that all Broom Hilda had to do was lean over to an assistant and have one of them call the office on the phone they had on their table and tell them to have the police go get the work records. It was unnerving and it pissed Scott off!

After the noon recess, it was Scott's time to cross-examine his supervisor. Scott wasn't exactly sure what he was going to ask him. Scott repeated his direct testimony and asked him if that was correct just to get more detail than what he had revealed in his direct examination. Again, Scott was painfully aware this procedure was one of the elementary things that in an inexperienced lawyer will do; that is, ask a question to which you did not know the answer. And it is a dangerous procedure!

Now that he was a graduate of the NITA course and was no longer truly "inexperienced," that was one mistake that he would never make again. But under the circumstances, he had no choice, he felt. He couldn't just sit there bleeding and not respond to counter the damage. Besides, the testimony was so damaging, there wasn't much danger in being hurt any more than they had been already. He saw no other alternatives. He had to take a calculated risk and go for it!

As Scott reviewed the supervisor's testimony, he incorporated into his questioning the fact that he now had the work records from the station, which turned out to be handwritten notes on a legal pad. It never occurred to him to challenge his earlier testimony on the basis that his testimony was hearsay because it was based on work records.

On the other hand, he was testifying as Timothy's supervisor from his own personal recollection that Timothy had called in the day after each and every one of the incidents and asked for the day off. His referring to the work records now, purportedly his own notes, was appropriate. Moreover, Scott was at such a disadvantage from having been surprised at this testimony and not having seen his notes, he was simply trying to recover.

Rather than attacking his earlier testimony or his credibility, Scott proceeded to ask him about the work records. "What do your notes show regarding the purported phone calls made by Timothy in relation to each of the incidences?" To Scott's shock, the supervisor talked about how after one of the rapes, Timothy called in saying that he had a flat tire, and he would be late.

"Late?"

What the hell does that mean? Scott screamed in his head. "Do your notes show how late he was that day?"

"Yes."

"How late was he?"

He looked at his notes and then he looked up and said, "45 minutes." Scott wasn't sure if he had heard him correctly, so he asked him to repeat it. Again, he said, "45 minutes."

"So, on that day he was 45 minutes late, but he did show up for work?"

"Yes."

Scott continued asking about the work records. "How about Timothy calling in for a day off after the other incidences?" As Scott went over each of the other dates, one by one, nothing in the notes supported his earlier testimony. None of his testimony was true! Timothy never missed a single day of work on the days after the incidences!

Scott never once looked at Broom Hilda, despite the temptation; but figuratively speaking, he instead was scratching his head and wondering just what the hell they thought they were doing! He thought it very damaging to their case to put on a witness who impeached himself by his own testimony on cross-examination. And not only did Scott not have to work for it, but he had also stumbled into it!

To him, the prosecution seriously dropped the ball by never obtaining any supporting documentation for his testimony before they put him on the stand. Moreover, it was obvious they didn't even have his notes prior to his testifying. They relied on his representations and he clearly had lied to them. This revelation alone destroyed his credibility and seriously damaged the government's common scheme argument. It had the same effect on their theory that Timothy was the rapist as the weakness in the Hawthorne case had on the existence of there even being a serial rapist.

After the supervisor finished his testimony, there was a witness that the prosecution wanted to call, but Scott objected, so the jury was excused and there was a hearing without the jury present. It was Timothy's wife! After the first rape charge, they had separated. So much for the good relationship! Timothy had never disclose this information to Scott.

They were trying to put on her testimony to show that, according to her, Timothy had called and asked her to provide him an alibi. Naturally, Scott objected to her testifying based on the privilege accorded married couples. The fact that they were separated would not negate the privilege and allow her to testify. Significantly limited in her ability to testify, the court confined her testimony to their being separated. Scott could not understand why they did this. It was, in his opinion, extreme overreaching!

After her testimony, the government began to put on some lab evidence. Part of the lab evidence the government wanted to put on were semen samples that had been gathered at two of the locations. The two samples had been examined by the FBI laboratory and shown to be from a secretor.

Turns out this concept has been around since the early 40s. Most people are familiar with blood types and may even know their own, but it is doubtful whether they ever heard of a secretor or a non-secretor. Most people have no idea that this blood typing sub-system even exists. Scott certainly had never heard of it prior to this case.

Whether someone is a secretor, or a non-secretor is completely independent of their blood type. Simply put, a secretor is a person whose body secretes its blood type antigens into its fluids, saliva, mucus, etc. In a non-secretor, body fluids and secretions like the mucus in the digestive tract and saliva do not contain antigens of their blood group.

In Scott's earlier discussions with the lab technician and the FBI agent, they confirmed that the two semen samples were from a secretor and that Timothy had been determined to be a non-secretor. Good, hard evidence like that was a big plus in his favor. With the Negroid head hairs, one could not include a suspect with certainty, but one *could* exclude a suspect with certainty. That was another big point in their favor. Now Scott was ready to score another big point by showing the objective difference between a secretor and a non-secretor and that the FBI's own lab test had excluded Timothy.

When the lab technician, Agent David, took the stand, they went over the preliminary matters to establish the substance of his testimony with respect to the blood samples and the secretor versus non-secretor issue. Now it came to a time that Scott was to learn yet another hard lesson about the ethics and moral views of some prosecutors and now, some FBI agents, even beyond the polygraph lesson.

When it got down to the critical part of his testimony, rather than testifying hard and fast about the indicated exclusions that would apply to Timothy, he testified that "the samples could have been old or compromised, therefore, the results were not finite and reliable!"

Agent David totally fucked Scott and there was nothing he could do about it! Scott was confident that even bringing up the earlier conversation in which the distinctions were made that he would explain that everything they talked about was accurate and was true as far as it went, however, Scott had never asked him if there were any issues that could compromise the results, or something to that effect. In other words, the lab technician could very easily weasel out of it and there wasn't anything Scott could do to pin him down.   Scott   simply would've looked incompetent for failing to ask the proper questions when he interviewed him. Scott knew he didn't want to go there! He knew it was time to shut the hell up and sit the hell down!

Sometimes, Scott felt like a confident boxer who was blind to a left hook. Wading through and surviving the negative testimony of Timothy's supervisor only to the hammered by the "updated" lab results had made for a long day!

CHAPTER 21

Next up were the Daniels.

First, they brought in Nelson Daniels who recounted his recollection of the night in question. Again, he went into detail and described the events.

"Around 2 AM, I was in bed asleep and the next thing I remember rolling over. I raised up a little bit and felt a hand on my chest pushing me back down. It was a left hand. My eyes opened and I heard a voice say, 'Don't you move, you hear, or I'll cut you.' Then he said that twice. Simultaneously, I saw the blade of a knife sticking out of his hand and it appeared to be pear-shaped. It looked like it was a box cutter knife. It was dark. Also, I remember seeing a round head and it was larger than a face. So, I was lying there, and I stopped for a split second. Now, I felt the bedspread come up over my head. It felt like it was pulled up over my head with two hands. My arms were up over my head and I paused. And then I pushed the blanket up as hard as I could and I said, 'Now you wait a minute.' This all happened in five seconds.

After I pushed the blanket up and I started to roll out on my right side, I heard my wife scream. So, I started to roll back over and as I recall, I saw her body coming around and there was another arm lunging up at the same time. Then I don't recall the figure leaving, but I recall moving towards her and she leaned down and was screaming and said, 'Get him, Nelson; be careful. He's got a knife.' I stayed for a split second and asked her if she was alright. Then I jumped out of bed and got my darts and ran downstairs. And that is all."

"You kept referring to a shadow. What type of lighting was in the room? Can you describe the subject to the jury?"

"No. In the conversations and words that he spoke, he never swore during any command he made. He did not use the street language but had just the edge of a Washington accent."

What the hell is a Washington accent? I've never heard of such a thing.

"How did the subject get into your house?"

"A 12-foot ladder was out in the alley behind the house. The house is being restored. It was brought into our yard in the back and put against the wall and the window on the second level was pried open. The next morning, I checked the back alley. I noticed a fresh tennis shoe print that was a couple of inches larger than mine. The sole was like it was boxes and squared, and the toe impression had been worn off. There was just a slight ridge in the footprint."

"While you were asleep, you could not hear the subject talking and you could not feel the movement in the bed?"

"I heard nothing. I was in a deep sleep."

"Why did you have the instinct to pick up and use the darts?"

"Those were the only things that was available at the time."

Since about January 1977, both the Daniels had known Timothy socially and confirmed having drinks with him three or four times between the incident on June 8 and their identifying his voice on December 5 as that of the person who raped Mrs. Daniels. Each was very familiar with his physical features and his voice.

On September 21, both Mr. and Mrs. Daniels attended a visual lineup at Metropolitan Police Department (MPD) at which neither indicated that they were able to identify anyone in the lineup as the assailant. A short time later, outside the lineup room, and also a few days later on the telephone, Mr. Daniels related to Detective Thomas Richards of the MPD Sex Branch that one of the people in the lineup "looked like" the assailant.

That man was Richard Snyder, and another person in the lineup, a Steve Cornelius, who were suspected of numerous armed rapes which had occurred on "Capitol Hill" in the District of Columbia, the same area where the offenses charged in this indictment occurred. Scott was aware of this development and that they were presently in jail for those offenses.

Notwithstanding that he thought Snyder look like the man and the contradiction and inherent discrediting of his earlier statements, Nelson Daniels felt that he would recognize the assailant if he were to see him again and was asked to attend another visual lineup on October 24. The MPD and/or the United States Attorney had reason to believe some other persons fit the description of the assailant and/or had some basis for believing that someone else other than Timothy was the assailant. No photograph of the lineups or that of December 5 was presented to the grand jury for comparison.

Mr. Daniels did not identify anyone in that lineup as the assailant and neither Mr. Daniels nor Mrs. Daniels had up to that time, some four and one-half months after the incident, given any indication to MPD that either of them: (a) knew the assailant; (b) knew whose voice they heard that night; or (c) that Timothy was or sounded like the assailant.

At some point early in June, certainly prior to November 7, Mr. and Mrs. Daniels had drinks with Timothy, a fact confirmed by the Daniels. Mrs. Daniels was pregnant at the time of the rape and had since had a boy on October 20. Timothy commented on that fact.

On December 5, Rosie and Nelson Daniels were called to MPD Headquarters to attend a voice-only lineup in an attempt to identify a voice in the lineup that they believed to be that of the man who assaulted Mrs. Daniels. Insofar as Scott was aware, this was the only voice-only lineup attended by either of the

Daniels. At that lineup, they identified Timothy's voice as that of the assailant.

At this point, Scott reminded himself of all of the information that he had learned about the hallway conversation.

Prior to the December 5 voice lineup, there was a conversation in the hallway of MPD, outside the lineup room, between Sheila Hawthorne and the Daniels. The substance of the conversation was that both Hawthorne and the Daniels were there in an attempt to identify a voice that might be that of the assailant in their respective cases and each learned the other's case involved rape. They discussed the details of their cases and the assailant. At some point, Sheila Hawthorne stated that she felt she knew the identity of her rapist and had identified a suspected assailant to MPD and was there to see if she could identify his voice. She then stated to the Daniels that his name was "Timothy Rogers." Both the Daniels knew before they entered a lineup room that Timothy Rogers was a suspect in another case and that he was present in the lineup. Also present, of course, was Wood.

Because Scott was now, as far as he knew, fully aware of the history of their various "identifications" of the assailant, it was important to lay them out for the jury in chronological fashion.

Their incident had occurred in May 1978. Another critical piece of information also had been shared by Jonathan, which Scott had then shared with Broom Hilda and her *Major Domo*, was that barely a month after the incident occurred, they ran into Timothy at the Underground.

Upon hearing his voice, Lynn Daniels whispered to her husband, "That's the voice! That's the voice! It's Timothy!"

Nelson responded, "No it's not. We're just very nervous."

On the stand, he readily confirmed this incident. "Neither of us ever again talked about it or even thought about the possibility that Timothy was the assailant. We never reported the incident at the Underground to the Sex Squad detectives assigned to our case." His testimony was remarkably calm, and he was not hesitant in answering Scott's questions.

"We attended previous lineups before Timothy's voice-only lineup. We attended a visual lineup in September 1978 and identified a potential assailant. We were made aware that that particular individual and another person were suspected of 75 rapes on Capitol Hill around where we lived and, thereafter, had confessed to 15 rapes."

"I attended another visual lineup in October 1978 and selected a different individual. Yes, I saw black men in broad daylight walking down the alley behind our townhouse, grabbed a hand ax, raced out of the back door, and chased them down the alley. Yes, we would be driving down the street and changing our identification of the assailant to each black man we saw on the street."

One of the aspects about their particular case that cut both ways was that Timothy was known to them, had been to their house for parties, and had even spoken at Nelson's class at a local university on the advantages to blacks in the communication industry. This familiarity, not only with the Daniels, but with the location frequented by other victims, and some of the victims themselves, worked against Timothy.

On the other hand, it worked in his favor because, despite the fact that Scott had not been successful in getting his pretrial motions granted or the cases severed for trial, it was a sound basis for arguing before the same jury the cumulative suggestive factor in everyone's identification of Timothy as the assailant.

Even though Jonathan made Scott aware of the prior "identification episodes," there was a long delay in providing that information. Broom Hilda certainly would not have told him! After all, the incidences had occurred in 1978, well over a year before trial. In fact, all the lineups had occurred before the December incident.

Nelson also confirmed having a real estate license. All the while, he had claimed he did not know Roberta Wood. It befuddled Scott that they would be testifying in an untruthful matter about something that was basically meaningless in the case. Since it was already known that the witnesses were discussing Timothy out in the hallway, it served no purpose that Scott could see to deny that they knew each other. Scott wasn't able to connect the dots on this either.

Despite all the preceding identification occurrences, and at one point totally discounting Timothy as being the assailant, it wasn't until after the Hawthorne incident that their opinion had changed. It wasn't anything that they were involved in directly or an independent reconsideration of what happened that had caused them to alter their conclusion.

After Timothy's arrest on the Hawthorne incident, an article had appeared in the *Washington Post*. By happenstance, they had a mutual friend who worked for the mayor. He read the article, was aware of the Daniels' situation, and immediately called and asked them if they had read the paper. At the time, they hadn't. So, he told him of what the paper said regarding Timothy's arrest for rape and asked them, "Did you ever think it could be Timothy?" Naturally, this led to an instant flashback to the incident at the Underground and an immediate reversal in their conclusion. Apparently, the inherent contradictions of their attending the visual lineups and identifying other individuals, not to mention chasing all the men in the alley and identifying different men on the streets, no longer mattered.

After finishing up with Nelson, the next witness was Lynn Daniels. She was without a doubt the most personally challenging witness for Scott. Being married himself, hers was the most horrific situation to hear. At the time of the rape, she was three months pregnant. She and her husband had gone out to a club with some friends, returned home, had a champagne bubble bath, played around, and fallen asleep.

Scott didn't think anyone could imagine or wanted to imagine the horror of waking up in your own bed, in your own home, and finding a knife to your throat, then being made to get off the bed, knowing that somebody's going to rape you and threatening to kill you if you did not cooperate or made a noise. And then being faced with the idea that your husband will be killed if he tries to protect you.

Treating her with kid gloves was essential. Not only was it a good trial technique, but he had no personal interest whatsoever in attacking her and making her situation worse, despite obligations to his client. He would do whatever was necessary for him professionally to protect his client but would do it in as delicate and low-key manner as possible.

Again, it was necessary to go over her recitation of the incident about what she had already testified for the prosecution. She testified for the prosecution and stated:

"On Wednesday night around 7 PM, my husband and I went to bar located in the third block of Pennsylvania Avenue NE. We were there to watch the basketball game until it was over. Approximately 11:30 PM, we left the Hawk and Dove and went next door to another bar called Duddingtons where we had one glass of champagne. We were there approximately 20 minutes and then left to go home. While we were at the Hawk and Dove after the Bullets game, the bartender opened bottles of champagne and poured it all over everyone who was there. When we got home, we went into the kitchen and had soup and fed the cats. Since we got the champagne all over us, we went upstairs to the third-floor level and took a bubble bath together. Then we went to bed. We tried to have sex once we got into the bed, but he was so drunk, we couldn't. Then we went to sleep."

"I was awakened by a leather glove over my nose and mouth, and a sharp instrument on the left side of my neck. There was a voice saying, 'Don't move, don't reach for your husband, and don't make a noise or I'll stick you.' I said, "Don't hurt me because I am pregnant. Please let me breathe so my baby can breathe." At that point, he loosened his grip so that I could get some air."

"He kept saying over and over, 'Don't try to reach for your husband and don't move.' His voice was nervous, and his hand was shaking. While he was saying that he kept pushing the knife harder up toward my chin. Then I had my hand out and tapped my husband's arm. He caught me doing that and he moved the knife to the back of my neck and told me, 'I warned you not to try and wake him up or move.' All the while he was pulling my hair." "

"'Roll towards me, move slowly and roll off the bed and don't make any noise.' I could not do it because being pregnant, you just can't sit up. He kept putting the knife to my neck. I rolled toward him and he pushed my head away. Finally, I somehow got off the bed on my knees and he still had the knife to my throat. He moved it again to the back of my neck. "Don't hurt me and my baby," I said. Then he told me to put a pillow over my head. I can't remember much else. I do remember him and his body next to my buttocks. I told him again not to hurt me, and he said he wasn't going to. 'I just want to rub it against you,' he said."

"At that time, I felt his penis against my vagina. 'Just keep the pillow over your head and I won't hurt you.' Then I felt something penetrate me. Not very deeply, but just a little bit. About that time, he jumped up, leaned over the bed, and told my husband not to move or he would cut him. But I don't remember exactly what he said. I saw my husband move and the cover was bouncing. I stood up and he had a knife pushing it in the back of my neck. Somehow, he moved and at that point, I think my husband was sitting up. I reached around behind me with my left hand and picked up a very large lamp that was on the bedside table beside me. I threw it at this figure that moved away from me and was standing at the end of the bed. I think I hit him, but I'm not sure. I remember him lunging towards me and a stinging on my left arm. I just started screaming as loud as I could and don't remember much after that. Nelson was up at that time and I just don't remember anymore."

"Could you describe the subject?"

"No. The voice, I don't think I'll ever forget. He spoke as an educated man."

"Is there anything else you want to add to your testimony?"

"All he told me was that he just wanted to rub it between my legs. I said to him, "What do you want? If you want money, there's money over on the dresser.""

"Did anyone leave the bar when you left?"

"Not that I know of. We frequented those places quite often."

"Did anyone say anything out-of-the-way to you while you are at the bars, like flirtatious innuendos, or anything like that?"

"No."

One of the things dramatically different in a real trial from television is that on cross-examination, a lawyer cannot get up into a witness's face or approach them closely such that you get into their personal space without the permission of the court. "TV law" is incredibly misleading and, unfortunately, detrimental for witnesses and jurors who have watched too many court dramas.

In order to get up close to the witness, an attorney seeks the permission of the court by asking if they may approach the witness. Even then, they have to be cautious not to get too close if they are going to be very confrontational with the witness because either their lawyer will object, or the court will intercede. In either case, the attorney doesn't want to cross over that delicate protocol line. Particularly in this case, it served no useful purpose, but potentially could hurt his case and send a negative image to the jury, unless, of course, the lawyer exposes a lie and then, with cause, he goes for the jugular.

Nevertheless, as Scott often said, "You can have a good message, but your delivery sucks!" In this instance, he had a significantly negative message to deliver to the prosecution. It would be an unpleasant surprise for the prosecution *if* it worked. It was necessary and important not to do it in a manner that sucked and diverted attention from the message and minimized its impact.

The courtroom was wood paneled with a rich, medium, brown stain. The area in front of the bench where the stenographers and court personnel sat were somewhat curved. The ambience of the rear of the courtroom as you came in the front door was to give an image of softness with the curvature of the judge's bench. To the left was the jury box, which was slightly curved to fit the soft features of the courtroom. To the right, were two tables, the nearest for the prosecution and the one on the far back to the right for the defense.

Scott was up on his feet in front of the judge somewhat close to the witness stand. Slowly, while she was answering his questions, he drifted to his left, passing in front of her toward the jury box, then moving slowly backward along the front of the jury box, and ending up at the very end of the jury box as far away as possible from the witness and the judge. As he was moving, he could see in his peripheral vision some of the jurors' heads slightly following him. This was exactly what he wanted. As usual, he avoided making any eye contact. His heart began racing as he approached the dramatic point in his cross-examination that was the equivalent of "show and tell time."

Now was the moment of truth! His heart was pumping much faster. Even though he still had permission of the court to approach the witness, for effect, he again asked the court if he could approach the witness as he moved along the jury box. Had he been more experienced and attempting to create more drama and anticipation, he might've done it even slower, making eye contact with members of the jury, and slowly turning and making eye contact with Broom Hilda. But he was a bit too nervous to do any of that. He was not at all confident that this whole thing wouldn't totally blow up in his face! It was all he could do to act as casual as possible as he approached the witness, slowly reach into his suit jacket pocket, and pull out the envelope.

After the visual only lineup in December almost a year ago, when Scott had returned to his office, he was livid. In his mind, Jay had been deceived by Timothy and Timothy had lied to Scott. After all, he had been identified in the voice-only lineup by *four* people, and Scott felt totally deceived.

Notwithstanding his anger, he then explained to Timothy who the people were that came into the voice-only lineup and had identified him. Timothy naturally had denied raping Hawthorne. He did not know Roberta Wood. And he was flabbergasted that his friends, the Daniels, had accused him of rape. Neither Scott nor Timothy knew that she had been three months pregnant at the time of the rape.

Then came the stunner! Here they were in December and Timothy had been arrested and charged in one rape earlier in the year. He had just been arrested and charged for another rape. And he had just been identified in a voice-only lineup in connection with other rapes. Now, he had the gall to tell Scott that he could not understand why the Daniels would make such a charge against him. Naturally, Scott told him that's the way it was and asked, "Why do you think that they would make a charge against you?"

"I am so shocked because she just had a baby in October, and she had sent me a birth announcement in November!" Needless to say, not being able to see his own face, Scott couldn't say how he visually reacted, but he was reasonably sure that he maintained his composure. Scott's mind was racing! *Does he think I am the dumbest fucking white man he has ever seen in his life?* But Scott wasn't going to say that. He kept his cool. He went along with Timothy's version.

Then Timothy mentioned again that she had sent him the birth announcement just a few weeks earlier and he just couldn't understand what was happening. Again, Scott went along with it. What the hell! It was entertaining!

So, going along with this idiot story, Scott had asked him if he still had the birth announcement.

"I think so."

"Check and see and let me know."

Timothy left. Scott was in shock! Then, he proceeded to give Jay an earful about the results of the lineup, not to mention the cockamamie story about the birth announcement, and what he thought of the client that he had sent him.

The next morning, Scott got a call from Timothy. He had found the birth announcement. Scott's office was near the Arlington County Courthouse just across the river not far from Memorial Bridge. By then, Timothy had moved to Maryland across the Wilson Bridge, which was just below Alexandria. Again, Scott went along with the charade. Timothy told him that he would mail it. Calmly, Scott told him, "No ... Timothy, bring it by the office. I don't trust the mail."

When Timothy brought it in, Scott looked at it. It was just an ordinary birth announcement. It had blue overtones and had a note written on it. There was no way Scott knew whose handwriting it was or who might have sent it. As is, on its face, it was almost worthless. Without challenging or explaining this to Timothy, Scott asked him asked if he had the envelope. With his usual calmness, he said, "I think so. I'll look for it."

A couple of days later, Scott got another phone call. It was pretty much the same conversation as the first one. Timothy had found the envelope and he would mail it to Scott. He told him, again, "Timothy, why don't you bring it to my office. I don't really trust the mail."

Scott will never forget how shocked he was when Timothy asked him, "Could this be important?" Scott couldn't help but think that either Timothy was the dumbest son of a bitch he had ever met in his life, or he was so totally innocent and scared that he was oblivious to the significance of the birth announcement.

Again, Timothy showed up with the envelope, which was torn up, as happens when you rip an envelope open, but it was all there, with the pieces connected. It had Timothy's mailing address on it and a return address with the right names and address on it purporting to be from the Daniels. But Scott still had no way of knowing if it was her handwriting or not. All skepticism aside, it seemed reasonable and believable that the card and envelope were legitimate.

As he stood at the end of the jury box, he was more intellectually than physically tense. It was for dramatic effect that he had purposely, slowly, moved the full length of the jury box toward the witness and the judge. He wanted everyone's attention to be on him. He was conscious of everyone's eyes following him, especially the jury, and he knew he had succeeded. All things considered, he was more calm than excited.

He showed her the envelope. "Do you recognize it?"

To his everlasting relief and gratification, she replied, "Yes."

"What is it?"

"It's one of my birth announcements."

"Is that your handwriting on the envelope?"

"Yes."

"Would you take the card out?" For effect and identification purposes, he asked her: "Is that your handwriting?"

"Yes."

"Are both the envelope and the card in your handwriting?"

"Yes."

"Did you mail it to Timothy?"

"Yes."

There are attorneys whose approach at that time would have been to just tear her apart with contradictions in her and her husband's testimony regarding Timothy being the rapist. Scott could've crucified her with the contradictions of her trial testimony and other known evidence. She acknowledged that they had been to other lineups, identified other people, had at one time at the Underground thought he was the rapist and totally discounted it, never ever thought about it again, or talked about it again with each other.

And she also acknowledged something that Scott had saved for her cross–examination that he had also asked Nelson. She confirmed that they never reported the Underground incident with Timothy to the Sex Squad detective assigned to their case.

To put a nail in the coffin of her testimony, the wooden stake in the heart, would have been to ask her how she could possibly send a birth announcement to somebody who she had the slightest inkling might have been the person who raped her? But Scott felt it was neither wise to risk creating sympathy with the jury by deviating from his trial strategy and ripping her apart, nor giving her a chance to explain. Not only was it a bad trial tactic, but ironically, she made no attempt to distance herself from having sent the birth announcement or explain that her opinion about Timothy had so clearly changed. Scott already knew from her earlier testimony that it was the call from the mutual friend at the mayor's office that had been the impetus to their rethinking about Timothy.

In his opinion, there was nothing to be gained by that and it was inconsistent with his approach to treat the witnesses with respect and delicacy. One thing he was sure about, however, was that the prosecution would not do any redirect examination at all, and if they did, the last thing in the world that they would benefit from would be to ask her any questions about the birth announcement. After all, her testimony had been unequivocal and there was nothing to be gained by reinforcing her testimony or creating doubt in her credibility by trying to get her to change it. Effectively, this would be attacking the credibility of their witness and he knew there were no grounds to do that. While Scott could've objected if they did, and most likely the court would sustain the objection, if they chose that approach, it would be, in Scott's view, just laying another landmine for closing argument.

By that point, his trial strategy was working very well. His anticipation of the prosecution's reactions was on target. His confidence continued to increase exponentially!

The prosecution was aware that Scott had alleged that the Daniels had sent a birth announcement to Timothy because it was included in his Motion to Dismiss the Indictment for Abuse of the Grand Jury Process. That was one of the most significant factors that he felt should have been brought to the attention of the grand jury but wasn't. Even though it had been mentioned in the pleading, probably because Broom Hilda couldn't bring herself to treat Scott with civility or worthy of serious consideration as an opponent, she would never have stooped low enough to ask him any questions about it or if he had it. It's not something that he knew then or ever found out, but he surmised that they never expected the birth announcement to show up. Perhaps, since it wasn't submitted as an exhibit to support the Motion for Dismissal, they concluded that the defense didn't have it and they were only going to be confronted by Timothy's unsubstantiated testimony. If that occurred, it would be no credibility contest between Timothy's testimony and hers. Of course, this also led to speculation as to whether they had even asked the Daniels if it existed. Lynn Daniels didn't seem to be surprised at all, or perhaps she even expected it. In a fashion, she had been rather matter of fact about the whole issue.

Scott was very satisfied. At that point, it was near noon and the court said they would reconvene at 1:30. Judge Carrington only got off the bench about 15 minutes from her start at 8 o'clock in the morning until they finished at 5 in the afternoon. She would hear motions for an hour, conduct the trial, declare a lunch break, hear motions for 45 minutes, and then spend all afternoon on the trial. Scott was convinced that she obtained her nourishment via an IV and wore both a catheter and a urine bag.

Scott was starving and would've loved to have eaten a big lunch, but it would make him sleepy. All he had eaten for lunch that week was a light salad with a little milk. He couldn't afford to get drowsy from even a small meal. All the while, he was reminded of how clammy his hands were.

Prior to resuming the trial, Scott was sitting alone out in the long hallway looking over some notes when Broom Hilda came clomping out of the courtroom walking directly toward him. It was the only time, other than being in her office with her Major Domo, that she had ever spoken directly to him.

She told him that she noticed that Arthur was on his list of witnesses and that he was being called as a character witness. That characterization was not in any way accurate. Maybe it was her wishful thinking. He was really being called because he was a former bartender at the Underground and was believed to have slept with Hawthorne. But Scott knew that she did not know that. He expected to tie that information to the unidentified Negroid head hairs on her bedspread.

"Did you know that he is been convicted of a felony?"

"Yes, but we were unable to find out what it was, and he would not tell us. However, I expect that you going to tell me what it was."

"He was convicted of raping a policewoman."

Ouch!

At moments like that, instinctively, Scott was relying on his NITA poker face. He was determined to not let her see that it hurt. But it did! A lot! Nevertheless, he still needed him as a witness. The fact that he was not really calling him as a character witness did not mean that calling him did not help the prosecution or jeopardize Scott's presentation. Naturally, although Scott intended to call him to connect him to Hawthorne, now Broom Hilda would most certainly attack him for his credibility and bring up the rape charge. Even so, Scott felt Arthur was enough of an independent witness to survive the challenge of the rape charge. After all, it was his testimony as a former bartender at the Underground that was relevant to the case. Quickly, Scott recovered and rearranged his strategy. The policewoman rape charge was perfect for casting doubt on Timothy being the assailant.

Coincidentally, the moment she told him about the case, Scott remembered it very clearly. Arthur was in a bar in DC and had run into this off-duty policewoman. They started having some drinks and were clearly getting it on. *She* drove him to Maryland, in *her* car, to *her* apartment, and somewhere along the line after they got there, "Yes, Yes!" turned into "No, No!" Although Arthur had been convicted, he was out in a very short time, much shorter than the time usually served for rape. Scott remembered when he read the article about the offense and later the article about his conviction. He couldn't help but think that the "Blue Code of Silence" was working, and it was supported by the courts.

Scott ended up calling him as a witness anyway and Broom Hilda predictably attempted to discredit him because of the rape conviction. She even introduced a small vial that supposedly had pubic hair and when Scott looked at it, it was empty. He told her it was empty, and she looked at him like he was a fool. He did not then, nor did he ever understand in the first place, what she was doing or why she was trying to use the small bottle, purportedly with pubic hair, against Arthur's testimony.

But Scott had discovered a hidden jewel among the lab reports for the Hawthorne case. Arthur had denied any involvement whatsoever with Hawthorne. He didn't like being there all. It was not unexpected that he would be a reluctant witness and deny connection with Hawthorne given the nature of the offenses and his history. However, in reviewing all the lab reports, Scott had noticed references by the lab technician to hair samples that had been taken from the Hawthorne crime scene. The FBI lab report noted that:

"As previously reported in the FBI laboratory report dated April 11, 1979, dark brown head hairs of Negroid origin were found on the victim's bedspread. These had been compared to the head hairs of Rogers and to the head hairs of Arthur Ratliff. Accordingly, these head hairs either originated from Ratliff or from another Negroid individual whose head hairs exhibited the same microscopic characteristics as the head hairs from Ratliff. These hairs are dissimilar to the head hairs of Rogers and cannot be associated with Rogers. It should be pointed out that hair comparisons do not constitute a basis for positive personal identification."

Scott was very puzzled by the existence of the earlier lab analysis, which had never been shared with him. Even more troubling was a total lack of any connection at an earlier time between Arthur and the offenses, except that he might have dated and been involved with Hawthorne. Scott had heard about him from Timothy and he was always a potential witness, however, there was no known connection between Timothy and Arthur available to the prosecution until Arthur was listed as a potential witness in the case.

This was just one of many puzzles that Scott couldn't solve. He couldn't get a grip on why the government continued going forward with a case with so many objective, contradictory, and exculpatory facts indicating that not only was there a question as to whether all of the rapes had occurred, but was this a serial rape case, at least, in this particular set of circumstances?

Disregarding all the ethical conflicts that Scott saw with the prosecution not addressing the strongly suggestive lab results, he did understand why they would not be addressing that issue. Scott, on the other hand, had no such reservations. Since he was several days into the trial, his anxiety about surprises from the prosecution was considerably diminished. Given the source and the explosive nature of the analysis of the hair samples, he had no reservation or hesitation about proceeding to examine his own witness.

Naturally, the thrust of Scott's examination quickly revealed he was establishing a foundation for a relationship between Arthur and Hawthorne. It was safe territory because Arthur knew Hawthorne; he was also a former bartender at the Underground and was a prime candidate to have walked her home from time to time. While it appeared that his obvious motive was to establish the possibility that Arthur could've been the rapist, as the questioning unfolded, it was clear that was not what Scott was trying to do. At least it was clear to Scott. What he was really trying to do was to further expand the thought in the jurors' mind that Hawthorne was partial to black men. This laid a foundation for the argument that a black man that she knew or somebody who wanted to know her better, but had been rejected, was the rapist.

Without any warning, Scott made a sudden right turn with his questions. "Are you aware that the FBI laboratory's analyzed hair sample found in Ms. Hawthorne's apartment and they matched yours?"

Arthur was stunned by the question! Of course, as expected, he denied it. As expected, the hook was set. Talk about muddying the water! It took a lot of effort on Scott's part to not turn to see Broom Hilda's reaction, but he could sense the shock the prosecution must have been feeling.

He also suspected that Broom Hilda approaching him in the hallway was a deliberate attempt to intimidate him into not calling Arthur as a witness. The prosecution knew about this connection long before Scott because they knew Scott didn't have the earlier lab report. But they didn't know whether Scott had picked up on it from the later lab report. Obviously, it was so damaging that they needed to make the effort to ensure that it was not brought up in the trial. Not even Broom Hilda was going to get up and contest an FBI laboratory report. *The Tiger was loose again! Yet more lead in Broom Hilda's panties!*

Finally, Scott called Cindy to testify about the various versions given by James of whose idea it was for Timothy to walk Hawthorne home. Her credibility was underscored by the fact that she had been working for a year as an investigator for the District of Columbia Public Defender Service after having graduated from college before going to law school. Cindy was very low key, confident, well-dressed, presentable, sweet, well-spoken, good looking, and came across with great credibility with her very soft, feminine voice. She did such a good job that the prosecution didn't even cross examine her!

CHAPTER 22

Each day during the trial, Scott read the evening papers to see what was reported about the case. Honestly, he wanted to see how he was perceived in handling the case. It was not disheartening because he was not portrayed as being a skilled lawyer, but actually being in the courtroom, it was unnerving to read the articles in the paper and to relate it to his view of what happened in the case that day.

What was scary about reading the articles was, while they were accurate in the sense that he was getting beaten up in the mornings, which was based on what happened earlier in the day so that the article could be printed in the afternoon paper, it was the reporter's perception of what was going on in the case that disappointed him.

He understood that she was a regular courtroom reporter who was beholden to the prosecution for inside tips. That simply was part of her job and it was in her best interest to cultivate sources. But her interpretation and description of the proceedings was very inaccurate. He was at a total loss to understand how she could be writing what she was writing because her story was so misleading. Certainly, as an experienced reporter who covered the courts, even though she was relatively young, she should've understood the process, the procedures, and the maneuvering far better than she related in her articles. It was patently clear that she did not understand court procedure and trial tactics.

He thought she should stick around for the whole day and hear him fighting back and at least write an article for the next day's issue, but he knew that she couldn't do that. In this particular case, given the high-profile attention it had received because Timothy worked at the White House, it was a case that enjoyed daily coverage. Only after the trial did he become aware of the attention the case had generated around the courthouse and around town.

The trial had been going on for three days, and on the beginning of the fourth day, Thursday, they were ready for the prosecution's last witnesses. The last witnesses to be called for the prosecution were Peter Cooper and Cynthia Lockhart. At that point in the trial, Scott felt a lot better than he imagined Broom Hilda was feeling. She began her direct examination.

"Would you tell us your full name?"

"Cynthia Bradford Lockhart."

"Where do you live?"

"In Silver Spring."

"Where were you living on December 22nd, 1978?"

"SW Washington."

"In an apartment?"

"Yes."

"Located on the first floor?"

"Ground floor."

"On that date, were you the victim of an assault?"

"Yes."

"Could you tell the ladies and gentlemen of the jury, starting back earlier in the evening, what you were doing that night and then going on to what happened to you during the assault?"

"My boyfriend and I went up to a place called Duddingtons on Capitol Hill. He was there to meet a friend of ours, Bruce, who was going away. So, we were all going to get really drunk.

I went next door to the Hawk and Dove and danced, and talked with my friend, Bruce. Then we went over and met David around 1 o'clock. We left the Hawk and Dove around 2:00 in the morning, and we went home. I remember turning out the lights around 3:30 and he set the alarm for the next day. It was 4 o'clock in the morning.

When I woke up, someone had hold of my hair and was yanking me out of bed. And when I looked, he had me like this. He had my face turned away. So, when he looked up, he was yanking so hard, he had me by the robe. He said, 'If you scream, I'll kill you.' So, I didn't scream. And he said, 'Put your arms up', and I was trying to get him away from me. "Get off me, get off me!" I screamed."

'Get out of bed or I'll kill you.' But I wasn't going to get out at bed. So, seconds lapsed, and I heard him say, 'If you move, I'll kill her.' So, he realized my boyfriend was lying right next to me and he had obviously woken up and I saw him leap across me. So, when he leaped across me, I rolled out of the other side of the bed. And I ran. I just kept going. And, finally, somebody let me into their apartment in a different apartment building. Then I called the Police.

I noticed I had a scratch on my arm. He must have cut the back of my neck. I'm not sure if he had the knife behind my throat all the time because I never saw the knife, or when he was running to get out of bed, he swung at me, and he could have caught me then."

"Did you feel a knife?"

"No, I never felt the knife. In fact, I thought he must have had a knife—I thought he must have had a gun. I didn't see any—I didn't think he would break into an apartment just with a knife. I figured he must have had a gun. So, also my arms, they were all scratched up from like cracked leather gloves, like if you had a— that's why I thought he had on gloves, which he did, because there weren't any prints when the police tried to make prints. He must have been grabbing my arm to yank me out of bed."

"Were you able to get a look at the individual?"

"Well, I looked at him the whole time he was there. I never took my eyes off of him."

"How tall would you say he was?"

"I told the police I thought he was at least 6 feet tall. Very well built and I said he reminded me of a Marine. He had on a red and black ski mask."

"Covering his face?"

"Uh, huh, covering his face."

"What do you mean he reminded you of a Marine?"

"Because he just—big shoulders and when I looked up, that's the first thing I thought, a Marine with a ski mask on in my bedroom. I don't know why. He just looked so big, and his shoulders were so wide. And that terrified me."

"During the incident, did you have the feeling that you knew this person?"

"Yes. I told the police when they arrived, once I had gotten back to the apartment, after they found me; that is what I kept saying, 'I want to get out of here. I just feel like I know this man. I'm not ever coming back here again. I just feel like I know him.'"

"Was there any particular reason that you felt that you knew him?"

"At that time, there was. It wasn't the voice. It wasn't the—it was everything combined, I guess. I guess in my subconscious it was the voice. It was the size. It's like I'd seen him before. If he hadn't had a mask on, I knew the reason he wore that mask because he knew I would know him."

"Did there come a time that you learned that someone named Timothy Rogers had been charged with at least one other rape on Capitol Hill?"

"Yes."

"Where did you learn that?"

"Lynn and Nelson."

"Daniels?"

"Yes."

"And when they told you that Timothy Rogers was being charged with raping Mrs. Daniels, did you know who Timothy Rogers was?"

"No."

"Did there come a time that you discovered who Timothy was?"

"Yes, when I came down here to see the Detective Richards."

"Is that when you looked at the photographs?"

"I looked at mug shots, and I said, 'I know this man.'"

"Okay, and at that point you learned that was Timothy Rogers?"

"Yes. He goes, 'Well, this man's name is Timothy Rogers.' I said, "So."

"Where had you known Mr. Rogers from?"

"I had seen him at Duddingtons on Nard's night. Thursday nights."

"For how long a period did you see him?"

"A year, over a year."

"To your knowledge, had you ever talked to him during that period?"

"I might have said hello. I'm sure I danced with him a couple of times. But I remember not wanting to talk to him. It was because of his eyes. He scared me. When people come up and say, 'Want to dance?' I say, Okay. You know, I say alright. I'll dance. I don't care who it is, I'd dance. But I don't think I ever really talked to him, like, not a sit-down conversation. I didn't like him. I didn't like the way he—he just kind of scared me the way he looked."

"When you looked at the pictures and you realized that you knew Timothy Rogers and that he had been charged with this other rape, at that point, did it click in your mind that the voice you heard that night was the voice of Timothy Rogers?"

"No, because I hadn't spoken to him enough to remember his voice."

"On that same night that you looked at the pictures, did you listen to a tape of a police lineup?"

"Yes."

"Did you just listen to the tape?"

"Just listened."

"On that tape, you heard a number of people saying certain expressions and phrases. Is that right?"

"Yes."

"Did you recognize a voice on that tape as being the voice of the intruder in your apartment?"

"Yes."

"Now, when you heard that voice, did you recognize it only as being the intruder, or also as the known voice of Timothy Rogers?"

"Only as the intruder."

"So, you were not thinking that's Timothy Rogers's voice?"

"No, I wouldn't—I wouldn't know his voice to talk to him. I just knew that was the voice that was in my apartment."

"And would you say that you were sure that was the voice that you heard in your apartment?"

"Yes, I'm sure."

"On the police report, it mentions that on the night of the offense, or the next day, you gave them the name of a possible suspect. Was that the name of Timothy Rogers?"

"No."

"Could you describe how that came about?"

"It wasn't the name of a suspect. It was— after they drove away with David in the ambulance, they got me cornered in this chair, and they kept saying, 'Well, why do you think you know this person? Give us some names. Give us some possible names.' Well, at that point, I would have given the name of my father, my brother, anyone, just so they would leave me alone so I could go to the hospital to see how David was. And I just gave the names of people that had asked me for dates, and I had said no."

"And maybe they got a little upset over it or something like that. One name I gave them is this guy that had called me for a while, and I kept turning him down. And the last time he called, which was like a month, a month and a half before this incident, he had been a little nasty on the phone. And I just hung up on him. And he hasn't ever called back. It wasn't—it was just people I knew."

"So, these were not the names of persons that you particularly felt might be a suspect?"

"No. It wasn't names that I was saying, Yes, I know that voice belonged to this person. No."

"You said you had danced with Rogers before. Did you notice the texture of his hair?"

"No. The reason is because when I dance with people—my boyfriend goes next door because he doesn't like to dance. He says, 'Go ahead and dance.' And I'm just dancing—most of the time I dance with the person, I don't even look at him. I'm just dancing. I don't pay any attention. Just so I don't look foolish dancing by myself."

"How much light was in the room?"

"All the lights were out in the house. But, as I said, I live on the ground floor and the outside of my apartment is very well lighted. Enough light comes right in so, like, we don't have heavy drapes or anything - comes through that—once you walk—once you are in the dark, you can see perfectly well. You can—it's just like all the lights were on. So, I could—I could just look at him. Well, I really never took my eyes off his chest up because I was just so amazed at the size."

"You say there's enough light in the room for you to see, and you said that you had noticed his eyes a previous time?"

"I couldn't see."

"Did you notice his eyes that night?"

"No. No, it was—the red ski mask with the black outlines on the eyes. So, when you looked up, all the black right here, just like he was missing, you, know, eyes and a mouth."

"So, your identification was strictly by his voice?"

"Voice."

"When you spoke with the Daniels, what did they indicate to you about Timothy Rogers? Had you already been told that prior to their discussing this with you?"

"No, I hadn't. I asked them. 'I heard you all had, you know, listened to a voice lineup or something, and you all had finally found a man that could be the man who did this to you?' I said, 'Well, the same thing happened to me and I would like to talk to someone about it because the police had dropped my case and hadn't done anything about it.' They asked what happened. I told them and they said, 'Well, that sounds a lot like what happened to us. We'll give you the Detective's name.' And they said, 'You know the guy, Timothy Rogers. That's who they are saying did this.' I said, 'I don't know him.' They said, 'You know, Timothy Rogers,' but I didn't know him. Like, I didn't even know his name at that   point."

"The next day, I called Detective Richards and arranged to listen to the voice lineup. But knowing that it was Timothy Rogers, I wasn't listening for Timothy Rogers because I didn't know what he sounded like."

"How often, in your recollection, had you seen him?"

"I'd see him every Thursday night, just about, down at Duddingtons. Like, over the past year and a half. Everybody—like, mostly regulars go down there, so you notice. I see him sitting over there. He usually sits by himself, drinking a glass of red wine. He never really talked much."

"So, you had seen him. He physically fits this description of a big Marine?"

"Yes. He's pretty big."

"You say he never really talked too much? How could you distinguish his voice from a tape knowing that he's the same person?"

"No, I wasn't listening for Timothy. I didn't care who it was. I just went down there to listen to a voice, and I heard the voice that was in my apartment. I said, 'That voice belongs to the one that was in my apartment.'"

"Is this place a discotheque or something?"

"It's just a pub. But on Thursday nights, they play records. It's pretty well crammed. It's a little round bar, but you can dance around the bar. It's a place where mostly all regulars come in. You hardly ever see a strange face."

"Is Timothy Rogers a regular there?"

"On Thursday nights, I remember seeing him, but like I said, I don't talk to him."

Next up was Cooper.

"On December 22, 1978, were you the victim of an assault?"

"Yes."

"Would you tell the ladies and gentlemen of the jury what happened?"

"We were at home. A guy broke into the apartment. He came into the bedroom, grabbed my girlfriend. I woke up. I jumped on him. We scuffled. My girlfriend ran out. He cut me up in our scuffle, and he ran."

"What was he using that he cut you up?"

"A knife."

"Were you able to see the knife?"

"No."

"Did he say anything while you were struggling or as the struggle was going on?"

"Not while we were struggling. Not until I ran around to the other side of the bed. When I did that, I bent down to pick something up and I looked up, and he said, 'I'm going to kill you!'"

"What injuries did you sustain?"

"I had seven lacerations, cuts. Five on my arm, one on my side, one on my neck, and I was stabbed once."

"Where was the stab?"

"In my chest."

"On the left side of your chest?"

"Yeah."

"And were you hospitalized as a result of your wounds?"

"Yeah, for 24 hours."

"And did you have to have stitches in any of the wounds?"

"All together, I had 11."

"Did you feel that you recognized the voice of the intruder during the time that this incident was happening?"

"In the back of my mind, I felt—like, just yeah."

"That you recognized the voice?"

"Yeah."

"Did you know whose voice you thought it was?"

"No."

"Did you in the ensuing weeks think that you knew whose voice it was?"

"No."

"Did there come a time that you heard that Timothy Rogers had been charged with raping someone else in the Capitol Hill area?"

"Yeah. In January I will guess."

"And how did you learn that?"

"Well, the first time I heard about it, I didn't put the name—some friends of mine in Duddingtons, the managers who used to work there, were talking. We were talking about it and they mentioned that this guy wasn't allowed back in anymore. But at that time, I didn't think much about it. Then they mentioned his name, Rogers, and then it clicked. He had been charged in Nelson and Rosie Daniels' case and was being indicted or whatever, and then I put the name Rogers with our incident. I think I might have mentioned to them that I had to talk to them about it. It might be the same guy."

"Did you know who Rogers was at that point?"

"At that point, no."

"You didn't connect that name with a face?"

"No."

"Then did you talk with the Daniels in January?"

"Right! No, in February, early—first week of February—I talked to them and they told me more about this guy Rogers. It still didn't click to me that he worked at a television station."

"That's when you realized who Timothy Rogers was?"

"Right."

"Did you, at that point, realize that the voice you heard was the voice of Timothy Rogers?"

"Yeah."

"You felt immediately, once you knew who Timothy Rogers was, that the voice you heard that night in your apartment was his voice?"

"Uh huh."

"How long had you known Timothy Rogers?"

"He was an acquaintance more than anything. I knew him for two years—one and a half-year to two years."

"And where did you see him? In Duddingtons?"

"In Duddingtons."

"And did you ever talk with him?"

"Once, at length."

"Did you come down to police headquarters and listen to a tape of a voice lineup?"

"Yes."

"Did you recognize a voice in that lineup as being the voice of the intruder?"

"Yes."

"Were you positive that was the voice? Was the voice of Timothy Rogers, or the voice of the intruder, or both?"

"Yes."

"When you listened to that tape, were you listening to the intruder?"

"I concentrated on that because I was trying to be objective, okay. I just concentrated solely on the voice in the apartment."

"When you heard the voice that you recognized to be the voice of the intruder, did you also recognize it as being the voice of Timothy Rogers?"

"Yeah."

"You did not have in your mind Timothy Rogers's voice, but who did you have in mind?"

"The intruder."

"The intruder?"

"Yeah. I was concentrating on that."

"When you listened to that tape, did you know for certain that Timothy Rogers's voice was going to be on that tape?"

"No."

"I have no further questions."

Detective Richards was called to the stand briefly.

After the prosecution finish with his direct testimony Scott went in. "Were you present when Ms. Lockhart and Mr. Cooper listened to the tape of the voice-only lineup?"

"Yes."

"Did they listen to the tape independently of each other?"

"Yes."

"Did either of them make any identification of any voice on that tape as being the person that was involved in the incident on December 22nd?"

"They both did."

"And who did they identify?"

"No. 11."

"Who was No. 11?"

"Timothy Rogers."

"And both identified the voice of Timothy Rogers?"

"Yes."

"I have no further questions."

At the noon recess, Scott had lunch. Once again, he was back in the hallway, alone, reviewing his notes and waiting for the trial to resume. He looked up and saw Detective Stevens walking toward him. Cautiously, but deliberately, looking up and down the hallway to be sure they were alone, he approached Scott. Clearly, something was on his mind!

He obliquely mentioned to Scott the anonymous phone call. Equally obliquely, Scott spoke of it and the caller, almost in third person, and noted that he had learned that the prosecution was extremely upset about that and had put a full-court press on the relevant officers.

Glancing down the hallway, speaking to no one, he voiced that he had heard the same thing. "Luckily, I just *happened* to be sailing off the coast of North Carolina out of communication range."

Good planning!

While all this was going on, there was no eye contact. Without further words, Detective Stevens drifted off down the hallway. No one had seen them together. Scott smiled to himself and resumed reviewing his notes. Although he never revealed to the prosecution whether

Timothy would testify, it was always his plan that he would.

Timothy was a tall, handsome, well-built man of about 6'2" at the time of trial and up to 225 pounds because he had put on some weight due to stress; he was very presentable to the jury. In many cases, a defendant does not take the stand in their own defense, which is their right under the Fifth Amendment. Nevertheless, even though no comments can be made by the prosecution and the jury is admonished in their instructions that they are to infer nothing against the defendant if the defendant does not take the stand, in the real world, it does not look good for defendant to *not* take the stand.

At this point, all the objective facts pointed to Timothy not being the assailant. The prosecution's direct examination was void of any questioning of the complaining witnesses designed to influence the jury's mind that the complaining witnesses were less than firm in their identifications. Considering all the objective conflicting evidence in Timothy's favor, the prosecution did not go near the descriptions in the PD51s. To do so, obviously, would open Pandora's Box, undermining the credibility of their witnesses.

And Scott wasn't going to challenge the witnesses about the descriptions either. One of the most critical lessons he had learned in the NITA course was to establish what you want to establish in cross-examination and avoid giving witnesses the opportunity to explain contradictions or discrepancies in their testimony. Inasmuch as all the police reports were part of the evidence, Scott was reserving highlighting those discrepancies for his closing argument.

Another lawyer once told Scott that a case never gets any better than the day it walked in the door. 'They just get worse!'

But they had survived, so far; they were still in possession of a hard-core set of facts that did not point to Timothy as being the assailant; instead, the prosecution had shown the videos taken of the voice-only lineup's, and the reliability of the identifications by each of the individual victims was less than certain. Fortunately, the videos contained sound so that the jury members could actually see and hear what was going on with respect to each of the victim's identifications.

They also had in their favor that the prosecution's testimony by Timothy's supervisor had been not only impeached by his own testimony, but it left the prosecution looking rather incompetent. Although there was the obvious attempt by the prosecution to discredit the testimony from Arthur, given his rape conviction, Scott survived that episode pretty well as well as any damage from James because James himself was not too sure about earlier statements he had made to the prosecution and Cindy's very credible testimony about her conversations with James was very compelling.

Even though the FBI agent had harpooned Scott by changing his testimony significantly from their earlier conversations, it was his hope that the jury would understand that the lab reports showed that Timothy had type O blood and that he was a non-secretor. Even if the lab technician said that the samples could have been compromised, he didn't actually enter a medical opinion to that effect. Either way, it was left open for Scott to argue that point to the jury. Of course, the obvious argument was, notwithstanding what the lab technician said, if the prosecution had any hard and fast laboratory evidence connecting Timothy to any of the incidences, they would have introduced it by then.

CHAPTER 23

When detective Stevens testified in the pretrial proceedings about Hawthorne's statements to him on the morning of the incident regarding being "absolutely certain," versus being only "8 ½" on a scale of 1-10, Scott struck gold! When it came time for her to testify at trial, she was adamant that, while she was "absolutely positive" about her certainty as to the voice she heard in her room that night, the "8 ½" was not related to her certainty as to the identity of the voice in her room that night being Timothy but related to her ability to pick out his voice in a voice-only lineup.

All during the trial, Scott kept thinking about rebuttal testimony on this point. Normally, when a witness is called for rebuttal testimony, a party is calling their own witness who has already been prepped for trial. That party already knows the witness' testimony and what the answers will be to prescribed questions. They may or may not have testified previously in the case, but usually, not on the subject of the rebuttal issue. That is, precise testimony directly contradicted by known facts, as in this case, precise testimony from the investigating Sex Squad officer in their case and offered by the prosecution as a witness.

The procedural danger in calling someone other than one of a party's own witness, especially an opposing party or their witness, is that procedurally, that party is in danger of that witness becoming the calling party's witness. What this means is, the party calling that witness to testify is confined to asking direct questions as opposed to leading questions on cross-examination, and they are stuck with their' witness's testimony because they are vouching for their testimony. Unless a witness lies, the party placing them on the stand cannot impeach them. It is yet another very dangerous situation for either side calling a witness.

Obviously, the rebuttal strategy would be for Scott to recall Detective Stevens to the stand and ask him to repeat his pretrial testimony on this point. Inasmuch as his pretrial testimony was brief and he relied on his field notes, there was no risk in recalling him to the stand as long as Scott stuck strictly to the facts and did not stray outside of his previous testimony and open up the door for him to start expressing opinions.

Also, there didn't seem to be any downside to calling him to testify, his sandbagging Scott and changing his testimony, or worrying about the prosecution cross-examining him on his testimony. After all, they put them on as a witness in the pretrial hearing and the trial and his testimony was locked in. So as long as Scott stuck to the scope of his direct testimony, he was safe and would not be opening up any doors for the prosecution to question Stevens about any other matters. But keeping the door shut would be a crapshoot! Scott was also keenly aware of the danger to the prosecution of attempting to "clarify" Stevens' contradictory testimony to highlight the credibility issue.

At that point, the defense needed all the help that it could get. From a melodramatic standpoint, the obvious choice was to recall either Hawthorne's aunt or uncle whom she had called immediately after she realized the assailant had left her apartment. Their testimony against her would be devastating. As far as Scott was aware, they were present during all the interviewing process with the uniform officers who first appeared on the scene and up to and including having been there when Detective Stevens interviewed her. However, Scott was not nearly as confident about obtaining succinct testimony from them on the "8 ½" issue as he was from Stevens. Of even greater significance, her statements were made directly to Stevens and he memorialized them in his field notes, making his testimony more credible and impactful than theirs; plus, his field notes were the best evidence on that point next to his oral testimony, and trumped any testimony they might provide.

Oddly enough, as the pretrial and trial testimony unfolded, Scott became convinced that all the complaining witnesses, each and every one of them, were telling the truth, at least from their viewpoint. Each and every one of them had been through a horrific and terrifying experience that would stay with them for the rest of their lives. Also, it is human nature to seek emotional closure. In his opinion, they were not only telling the truth from their vantage point, but it was what they wanted to believe, and it was the only pathway to closure. Not to be overlooked was the helpful "support" that they had received both directly and implicitly from the police and the prosecution in forming their opinion that Timothy was the assailant, and their perception of events was accurate with respect to his being the assailant.

Obviously, the prosecution was aware of the objective contradictions in the PD 251s and the witness and identification testimony, but they chose to overlook it because they wanted a scalp on their belt; this was a serial rapist case in which they could not afford to let one case fall by the wayside. It was a too high-profile case.

After careful analysis, Scott decided to not call Detective Stevens. Although he was supremely confident that he had the "8 ½" testimony in the bag, he felt it would be much more emotionally impacting on the jury to call Hawthorne's aunt. Scott elected to call her because there was no doubt in his mind that her aunt and uncle had been very forthcoming and truthful in their testimony. Significantly, it was not for the sole purpose of the "8 ½" testimony that Scott decided to call her aunt to testify. Testimony from her aunt would be a much more persuasive and a softer way for the jury to hear testimony. Not to be lost in all this was the obvious fact that her aunt, if she gave the testimony he expected, was basically contradicting and impeaching her own niece. And, as instructed by the judge, up to that point, there were no indications that anyone had discussed their testimony and her aunt would not know her niece's version.

Although he was quite confident calling her aunt for rebuttal, he couldn't help but wonder if the prosecution knew what he was doing and why. When the aunt took the stand, Scott reminded her of her earlier testimony regarding her niece's statements when she received her phone call: her niece's description given the police early in the morning when the uniform officers arrived in which she indicated that she was "absolutely positive" that the man in her room that night was Timothy and gave his full name to the police.

He reminded her that when Detective Stevens appeared at the scene shortly after 7 AM, for reasons that were never explained, no one actually told him that she claimed to know the identity of the assailant and had identified him by name. As the conversation proceeded, Stevens picked it up that she had, in fact, identified Timothy as the assailant and knew his full name, which she gave to him.

Hawthorne's aunt readily confirmed Scott's recounting of the events as he understood them. She seemed rather relaxed and, again, was very forthcoming in her testimony. Scott was reassured and encouraged. Finishing up reviewing with her some of the preliminary earlier conversations that her niece had with the police and Stevens, Scott directed her attention toward discussing her niece's response to Detective Stevens' question about how "absolutely positive" she was in her identification.

Scott reminded her of Stevens' example of "on a scale of 1 to 10, how absolutely positive are you?" She confirmed that her niece responded that she was "8 ½" positive. He then asked her: "Does the "8 ½" represent your niece's certainty as to the identity of the voice of the man that was in her room that night that raped her, or is it related to her confidence in her ability to pick out the voice of the man who was in her room that night and raped her from a voice-only lineup?"

She responded, without hesitation, "No, the "8 ½" on a scale of 1 to 10 represents her certainty as to the identity of the voice that was in her room that night she was raped. In fact, when we first arrived, she was absolutely positive about the identity of the voice that was in her room that night, but only 2 ½ hours later, she wasn't very sure at all."

Now, Scott could breathe! He felt a great sense of relief after she finished testifying. And as he expected, the prosecution did not cross-examine! And since Hawthorne was the final prosecution witness, Scott now knew there was no bombshell and there was nothing that he had overlooked or missed.

CHAPTER 24

In Scott's zeal to cover everything, or perhaps from a subliminal panic to not overlook anything, notwithstanding the opening statement debacle, he reviewed all of his notes and realized that he *had* prepared notes for an opening statement; he just forgot to actually prepare it! Only complete distraction could explain the oversight! If there was anything that he did not want to do now, it would be to omit or even overlook a vital point in his closing argument.

For reasons unclear even to him during the review of his notes, he noticed that he had done some research and made notes to himself to ensure that he would have appropriate time to finalize his closing argument as well as to have enough time to do a full closing argument, which included entitlement to both sides to, in fact, have enough time for a full closing argument, and in the event that the time was cut short for any reason, or the request was disallowed, that he would remember to make objections on the record complete with statements of reasons enumerating the issues eliminated by a short time for argument. He even had allowed for setting times for the prosecutor's closing and rebuttal argument to prevent being sandbagged. In retrospect, he didn't understand these parts of his notes or why he did that because closing arguments are not time restricted.

As it turned out, Broom Hilda was once again up with her legal pad and many pages of notes to follow for her closing. He sat there while she went through everything. Her closing was somewhat of a repetition of the opening statement, except the tense had changed and there were no longer any references to statements prefaced with "we expect the evidence to show." Now, of course, she spoke in terms of what the evidence had shown. Understandably, she avoided the contradictions in the police reports, his client's supervisor's impeached testimony, Hawthorne's testimonial issues, the Daniels' multiple "identifications," and, no surprise, with respect to the Daniels birth announcement, the silence was deafening.

Although Scott was caught totally off guard during the opening statement phase of the trial, by this time, he was loaded for bear and very self-confident. Even more able at this point than during trial to recount all the details without notes, he still had copious notes to follow. Even though this was only his second jury trial, he remembered that at least in the first trial when he got up to present his closing argument to the jury, he could not have been smoother or more professional. The theme of his closing was that all the various pieces of information occurring on the day his client was to have embezzled government property essentially were a mosaic. The very nature of a mosaic is that it is unnecessary to have all the pieces in order for an individual to visualize the intended image. Having completed this stage extremely well once, he had no hesitancy or lack of confidence now.

His closing outline consisted of five points that he wanted to cover, reduced to five lines! And when it came time for him to get up and present his closing argument, he left his outline on the table. After all, he could recite, index, and cross-index each and every detail of the case without notes. And he felt certain members of the jury would notice the contrast between her copious notes and his no notes presentation as they did for his opening statement.

Only once did he lose his place. In an intentionally, very subtle, slow fashion, he eased away from where he was standing in front of the jury box to the defense counsel's table to look at point number four. All the while he was slowly backing up to the defense table to look at his notes, he continued speaking. He was well aware that the jury and everyone in the courtroom was watching him because, except when he looked down at his notes, unlike during the trial, he casually maintained eye contact with all the members of the jury. This was in keeping with Scott's demeanor because anytime he talked to anyone, he was what would be called "an eye contact person." He also knew from previous interaction with individuals that his eye contact could be riveting and intimidating. If nothing else, he knew it got someone's attention. He had planned to use it for all it was worth during his closing argument. And, unlike the trial, he made it a point to casually scan the courtroom.

Bobby had come to Washington for the trial and was sitting in the courtroom. Previously, during the trial, Scott had barely been aware of anyone but the principles, court personnel, the court reporter, the judge, and the jury being in the courtroom. At that point, he had weathered a weeklong jury trial, numerous motions, objections and arguments, and was in a totally different zone from the beginning.

At one point during his closing argument, while he was standing in front of the jury, he slowly turned to his left and looked straight out into the audience at his friend, Bobby. That was the first time that he recalled being aware that the courtroom was totally packed, and people were standing shoulder to shoulder against the walls. He was in a zone all by himself! Literally, he could take all the police reports, the relevant medical information, the contradictions in the various complaining witnesses' statements, and other witnesses' testimonies and compare them very precisely. Scott could slice and dice them in any way that was necessary!

He maintained sole eye contact with Bobby and spoke directly to him alone for approximately 30 seconds. Briefly, without pausing, he then glanced at other people in the courtroom and on either side of Bobby and became aware that they were so entranced in his closing that they weren't even aware that he had fixed his vision on one person in the audience. He would've thought that the people sitting on either side of Bobby would've been aware that he was staring almost, but not quite, at them.

The central theme of his closing argument was to remind the jury of the prosecution's opening statement, the promises the prosecution made in its opening statement to the jury to present certain evidence, the omissions from the prosecution's opening statement, which were favorable to Timothy, the contradictory testimony of his manager, contradictory testimony of Hawthorne, and the unfolding of evidence during the trial that not only was favorable to him, but did not support the government's theory of the case.

The government's theory was that this case was about a serial rapist and Timothy was the serial rapist responsible for each of these events. When you think about it, that was the core issue that they were required to prove. The problem was that if you start with the initial documents in each case, being the Complaint, the Event Reports, and the statements of the complaining witnesses, they objectively failed, first and foremost, to support the government's theory that the offenses were committed by the same person. This would hold true irrespective of the fact that Timothy either knew or was known by most everyone involved in these incidences, except for Wood.

Then, there were the problems with the identifications themselves. Beginning with the descriptions actually given by the complaining witnesses, the subsequent identifications at the voice and visual lineups were all tainted. In the Hawthorne case, she identified Timothy by name, but never actually gave a physical description and, apparently, the police never asked her to give one. She was, despite her credibility issues, a weak witness for the prosecution because there was a strong suggestion that she dated black men. Although it was not directly related to the offense, the presence of Negroid head hairs from several different individuals on her bedspread was serendipitous and clearly left the impression that she was somewhat "available."

Without a doubt, the greatest damage to her credibility was the unreliability of her testimony on her certainty as to who was in her room that night versus her certainty as to her ability to identify the voice of the assailant in a voice-only lineup. Only because of the way her testimony unfolded regarding the application of her "8 ½" statement could Scott be sure that neither the police nor the prosecutor had spoken with her about the conflict between her trial testimony and Stevens' pretrial testimony attaching the "8 ½" statement to her certainty as to who was in the room that night. But when considered together with the "anonymous" phone call, the revelation that the detectives were having "trouble" with her case, together with the obvious pattern of the prosecution (i.e., Broom Hilda ignoring hard contradictory exculpatory facts in their case), it was not unreasonable to conclude that the prosecution was well aware of the conflict and put her on the stand anyway and was well aware that when she testified that she lied. An incredible ethical violation!

The fatal blow to her testimony was the testimony of her aunt who clearly recalled that the "8 ½" related to her certainty as to who was in the room that night, consistent with Stevens' testimony, and not, as she had testified, to her ability to identify the assailant's voice in a voice-only lineup.

After the closing argument was concluded, Scott breathed a huge sigh of relief. The jury was allowed a short break and when they were reconvened, the judge read them the jury instructions. Although they were quite detailed, the judge went over some very important items.

The attorneys were told that they could return to their offices if they chose, which for Scott meant driving across the Potomac to Arlington. The court advised that everyone would be called when the jury reached a verdict. It wasn't long after that Scott got a call to come back to court because the jury had requested to view the voice-only video tape again, which would be done in open court.

This was an encouraging request. Notwithstanding that the burden in a criminal case is a finding of guilt beyond a reasonable doubt, Scott was less assured that the factual contradictions in the case had served them that well. After all, despite all the contradictions, the prosecution had moved forward with the prosecution, Scott had been unable to get the motion to dismiss the indictment granted, or the identifications suppressed, and at the end of the close of all the introduction of the evidence, Scott had moved for a directed verdict from the court, which as expected, had not been granted.

At least there was some encouragement that the jury was taking a long, hard look at the particulars of the identification at the voice-only lineup. It was all the more meaningful and illuminating for the jurors to view, hear, and assess the witnesses' original confidence as they went through the identification process, rather than hear them testify about their identification and describe it for the jury.

By then, Scott had known from Cindy's investigative efforts that he had been mistaken by the "cop eyes" of individuals comprising the voice-only lineup. Even though he knew they all had been criminals, none were sex offenders. Coupled with the composition of the visual lineup only of men who had facial hair when no facial hair had been observed in the Wood's case, it only underscored the efforts of the government to tip the scales of justice by stacking the voice lineup with actual criminals, but no known sex offenders who potentially were the offenders in this case. Not to mention the known sex offender identified by Nelson Daniels as a suspect in his own case.

The video of the voice-only lineup was replayed. When Lynn Daniels came in, each of the individuals repeated the phrase, "Don't make any noise. Don't try to wake him up. Now roll off the bed onto your knees. Don't move, hear, or I'll cut you, hear?" She recognized number 11.

Next, Nelson Daniels came in and pretty much went through the same process. "Don't you move, hear, or I'll cut you, hear. Okay, hear?" After they repeated the phrase, he paused and said he was not sure. Then, he asked for a repeat. Each of the individuals repeated the phrase. He thought for a moment, then said, "Not sure, possibly number 11." Next, was Roberta Wood. Again, the men behind the curtain repeated the phrase: "Rollover, take off your panties. I have a knife." She identified number 11 without much hesitation. Last, was Sheila Hawthorne. Each man behind the curtain repeated the phrase, "Keep your hands on the pillow. If you move or scream, I'll kill you. I'm going to be in here a while." Her response was, "I think it is number 11."

Scott was surprised as they watched all of the voice-only identifications at how much more uncertain they had appeared to be as they went through the process than they appeared to Scott under the stress of the trial. Without all the pressure of actually being at trial, and having positive feelings from doing a good job, there was no question in his mind now that he was a great deal more objective about the equivocal identifications. In fact, it was almost a shock to him how the witnesses seem to be so much more unsure than he had perceived during the pressure of the trial. He couldn't help but relate back to the very argument he was making to the court in his motion to suppress the identification in which he focused on, among other things, the level of uncertainty demonstrated by witnesses and the suggestiveness of the lineup and photo array procedures, not to mention the hallway collusion before the lineup. It also occurred to him, now that a lot of the pressure was off, he had missed a good opportunity when arguing his motion to suppress the identification to ask that the lineup tapes be reviewed by the court.

At the conclusion of the videotape, the jury was instructed by the court to return to the jury room and resume their deliberation. At that point, Scott made the decision to hang around the courthouse for a while because there was no big reason to go back to his office because it seemed that they were near a verdict.

Surprisingly, they were again called back to the courtroom after about only an hour with everyone in attendance, except the jury, which was still sequestered in the jury room. It seems that they were having trouble with the video equipment and the administrative office of the court was unable to find a technician to go in and either repair the equipment or replace it. Because of the malfunction, the jury had not completed its need to further review the videotape in the jury room.

At that point, everyone in the courtroom received a surprise. Broom Hilda advised the court that she knew how to operate video equipment and that she would be more than happy to assist the court and go into the jury room to run the equipment for the jury while it deliberated. Surprised? No, everyone was totally shocked at her "offer."

The judge looked at her in a perplexed/angry manner. "You're not seriously suggesting that you, the prosecutor, go into the jury room and operate video equipment for the voice-only lineup while the jury deliberates?"

Broom Hilda, back stroking and tap dancing, was unable to really recover. Scott couldn't help but smile at the stupidity of that offer. On the other hand, it was in keeping with her heavy handiness on the scales of justice.

It didn't take long for the court to be advised that a technician had been located and that the problem had been solved. Now, it was just a matter of waiting.

CHAPTER 25

After about four hours of deliberation, Scott received word that the jury had reached a verdict. It took a while to gather up all the parties, the prosecution, and the court reporter. By the time the court reconvened and called in the jury, the courtroom was packed once again. Totally standing room only! Timothy's parents had flown in from California and attended every day of the trial. The tension in the courtroom was overwhelming.

The court asked the jury whether they had reached a verdict. The foreman stood up and said, "We have Your Honor."

The court then proceeded to ask the jury foreman on each count how the jury found the defendant:

"One, as to burglary while armed in the Daniels premises on June 8, 1978, we find the defendant.......... Not Guilty."

"Two, as to rape of Mrs. Daniels while armed on June 8, 1978, we find the defendant Not Guilty."

"Three, as to assault with a dangerous weapon of Mrs. Daniels on June 8, 1978, we find the defendant Not Guilty."

At this point, Scott breathed a very big sigh of relief. They still had a long way to go, but he felt that getting by the Daniels case was extremely important because they knew him so well. Although he did not have time to think about it at that moment, it flashed through his head all the contradictions and weaknesses in their story respecting identification of Timothy as the assailant.

Next, they came to Hawthorne. It was the most gut-wrenching part of the verdict, even though there was really no pause in the courts questioning of the jury foreman. In each instance, in almost a staccato fashion, the court inquired, "As to count.... How do you find defendant?"

Hawthorne was, in his view, the most critical verdict to hear because she was the person who had direct contact with him, with only a couple of hours having elapsed between the time that they were in the bar and the time she was assaulted. And, but for the impeaching testimony of her aunt and Stevens' "8 ½" testimony, he felt she was their strongest case.

"Four, as to burglary on while armed at Hawthorne's apartment on November 8, 1978, we found the defendant Not Guilty."

The jury having found him not guilty of burglary while armed at her apartment, it was obvious that they would not find him guilty on the other charges because they had determined he was never there.

"Five, as to rape of Sheila Hawthorne while armed on November 8, 1978, we find the defendant Not Guilty."

"Six, as to burglary while armed of Roberta Wood on December 4, 1978, we find the defendant Not Guilty."

"Seven, as to the rape of Roberta Wood while armed on December 4, 1978, we find the defendant Not Guilty."

"Eight, as to burglary while armed on Cooper/Lockhart apartment on December 22, 1978, we find the defendant Not Guilty."

"Nine, as to assault with a dangerous weapon on Cynthia Lockhart on December 22, 1978, we find the defendant Not Guilty."

"Ten, as to assault with intent to kill Cooper on December 22, 1978, we find the defendant Not Guilty."

It is impossible to express the depth of relief that Scott felt. Having been through a long, arduous trial, he was physically and mentally exhausted. But he was feeling pretty good at that point. He was happy for Timothy because he had come to believe in his innocence. It distressed Scott on a very personal level that Timothy had been falsely accused of being a serial rapist.

They barely had time to speak and for Scott to congratulate Timothy when Broom Hilda advised the court that they wanted to poll the jury. Either party has the right to do that. What it means is they want the court to ask each individual juror with respect to each individual count of the verdict if the verdict read by the foreman represents their individual verdict that they gave in the jury room during deliberation.

The prosecution is hoping that an individual juror who voted "Not Guilty" in the jury room really wanted to vote that Timothy was guilty. It is hoped by the prosecution that a person who may have been pressured into voting not guilty in the jury room will avail themselves of the opportunity in the courtroom to change their verdict. So, they had to sit there while each and every juror was questioned about the verdict announced by the foreman being the way they voted.

Because it was a 10-count indictment, they sat while the court asked each individual juror on each count, or 120 total, for the entire jury, if the Not Guilty verdict represented their verdict. In order to be sure that the members intended to vote a certain way, the court did not ask if "Not Guilty" was their joint verdict so that an individual jury member could answer "yes or no," rather than respond *en mass*. The court first asked each jury member, "What was your verdict as to Count One of the indictments?" In each instance, as the court moved on to subsequent counts, it got more pleasant for Scott. There was a real sense of relief as the inquiry moved through the Hawthorne case to hear a clear and firm, "Not Guilty." The responses continued in harmony as each juror was questioned on each of the counts.

At the conclusion of polling the jury, the court thanked the jury members for their service and told them that they were dismissed. The judge then turned to Timothy and told him that he was free to go.

They were about to leave when Broom Hilda jumped up and advised the court about the SLIP charge. In the midst of the euphoria of having won a major and difficult jury trial, Scott was taken aback by her raising the issue at *this* time, in *this* court, and before *this* judge.

On a Monday morning in February, shortly after Timothy's second arrest, Scott had come to the office in a very good mood. His weekend had been great! Nikki greeted him warmly as usual. She was well-liked and highly regarded by both Scott and Jennifer. She was a secretary that any lawyer would pray to have; that is, she was very good and because they got along so well, she had his back.

In addition, they had the good fortune of her having two "aunties" in Arlington. One was a Deputy Clerk at the Circuit Court of Arlington and the other was an Arlington Deputy Sheriff. They never had to worry about the procedural details of filing pleadings or other pleading issues because the Deputy Clerk always filled in what Nikki didn't know and service was exceptionally quick. In other words, it was already set-in place that filings would be procedurally correct and as soon as it was completed, the other auntie, the Deputy Sheriff, would pick it up, pop into her police car, and go serve it immediately!

Very low-key she asked him: "Did you speak to Timothy over the weekend?"

"No."

"You didn't talk to him over the weekend?"

Now she had his attention! "No, what is going on?"

"Timothy is in jail!"

"**What!**"

"He was arrested over the weekend."

"What for?"

"Solicitation for prostitution!"

In the District of Columbia, as well as other jurisdictions, it is referred to by the acronym SLIP and is called a "SLIP charge." Exacerbating the uncomfortableness of the situation, turns out that the SLIP charge was a result of his soliciting an undercover policewoman! The details revealed that he was just joking around stopping at a stoplight and saying he only had $10. But he touched all the right bases, said all the right things, and mentioned *money*! It didn't matter that no hooker would take him on for $10, which underscored the lack of seriousness in his mind. Nevertheless, it was, in fact, solicitation!

Aside from the procedural objections, it was exceptionally awkward and embarrassing because Timothy had never advised his parents of the pending charge. They were confused. Obviously, there were some other charges involving him and the prosecution wanted some action by the court. Neither Timothy nor Scott could focus on his parents' concern now but, instead, had to focus on Broom Hilda and the court.

Broom Hilda had the floor and proceeded to advise the court about the "SLIP charge" and that she wanted him placed under a $5,000 bond pending a trial in that matter. What she was asking for was unconscionable, inappropriate, and procedurally incorrect because they were not even in the proper court to be raising the issue. In the District of Columbia, the standard disposition of a "SLIP charge" for someone without a criminal record was to receive a summons, pay a $50 fine, either at the time or mail it in, not even have to go to court, and they went home! Timothy had no criminal record.

Even more aggravating, they were in the felony trial section and the "SLIP charge" was a misdemeanor that would be heard in another court. Moreover, Timothy was already charged in the other case, had spent the weekend in jail, had paid a bondsman a fee to post a bond, and that matter would be scheduled for hearing independent of any other pending case. Clearly, she had a vendetta because she had lost a very high-profile case. Her embarrassment was evident, and it would only increase as the word spread and the results appeared in the newspapers.

"Ms. Kincaid, the "SLIP charge" is a separate matter and will be heard in the misdemeanor trial section. The court notes that he is already on bond for that case and it wouldn't be appropriate even if this court had jurisdiction to take any action in the case," the judge replied.

After the court quickly disposed of Broom Hilda's thwarted attempt, Scott and Timothy left the courthouse and went to a bar across the street for celebratory libations. Scott hadn't had a drink all week and treated himself to a very dry martini. It didn't matter to him that it was only 1 o'clock. After all, he was in Washington DC, and a two-martini lunch was commonplace!

CHAPTER 26

On Friday, January 11, 1980, the "SLIP charge" was heard before a judge of the misdemeanor trial section. Ms. Jansen, the Assistant U.S. Attorney prosecuting the case, was a petite, very attractive, young black woman.

THE COURT: "Alright, counsel."

"Your Honor, we're here before the Court on this misdemeanor. I've spoken with Mr. Rogers about it and we've discussed it in detail, and on my advice, he is going to enter a plea of guilty on this charge of solicitation."

THE COURT: "Alright! Mr. Rogers, I think you've been in the courtroom and heard me question the other gentlemen, and I'm going to basically go over the same information with you. Do you understand that?"

"Yes."

"How much education have you had?"

"Three years of college."

"Okay. Are you now under the influence of alcohol or drugs or taking medicine of any type?"

"No."

"Alright. The charge here is Sexual Solicitation; that is, you solicited a person who turned out to be an undercover policewoman for sexual purposes. Do you understand the charges?"

"Yes, sir."

"Is there any agreement with the government in any way of what the sentence will be?"

"No, sir."

"Your lawyer says you wish to admit the charge. Is that correct?"

"That's right."

"By admitting the charge, you give up your right to a judge trial; to hear the witnesses testify against you; have your lawyer question those witnesses, or to call witnesses for you at our expense, because you're presumed innocent and the government has to prove you guilty beyond a reasonable doubt. You give up those rights, plus your right against self-incrimination, because you admit the offense. You give up all the technicalities, all the appeals; the only issue is the sentence. The maximum can be $250 fine, 90 days in jail. Because you're pleading now, however, I will give you a substantial break on whatever the sentence may be. Do you understand that?"

"Yes."

"Now, you're pleading to the charge. Has anyone promised you anything or offered you anything in a plea agreement or anything?"

"No."

"At one time, I noted there was a felony, or something involved in the case. Is there any agreement with the government in any respect?"

"None at all, Your Honor," replied Ms. Jansen.

"Alright. Has anyone promised or offered you anything else?"

"No, sir."

"Anybody threatened you or harassed you in any way to get you to plead?"

"No, sir."

"Anyone told you there was a secret deal made with me about the case?"

"No, sir."

"I've never talked—I'm not sure I've ever met your lawyer, so I've certainly never talked to him about it. Are you completely satisfied with your counsel?"

"Yes, sir."

"Do you have any questions about your rights or procedures?"

"No."

"Here is a statement of facts here that says a so-called Gurstein proffer that says you engaged in a conversation with the officer in which you solicited her for sexual purposes. Did you, in fact, do that?"

"Yes."

"Alright. The Court accepts the plea. It's knowingly and voluntarily made without any and proper inducements and conditions. It's free from coercion, made with an understanding of the nature of the charges and direct consequences. It's made after advice of counsel and has a factual basis. It's provident and accepted. What is the status of the felony? It's just pure curiosity."

"Your Honor, the felony cases went to trial, and the defendant was found not guilty," stated Ms. Jansen.

"Okay."

"The government would, however, in this case, although normally in a case of this nature the government would not have allocated for the defendant to be held pending sentencing, this is a very unusual situation.

The defendant was arrested and charged for numerous counts of armed burglary, assault with intent to rape, and assault with intent to kill while armed. As I indicated to the court, the defendant was acquitted on the charges; however, we thought the court should be aware that these charges had been lodged. Moreover, there were some difficulties with voice identifications in a trial as opposed to a total lack of evidence or other reasons why the defendant was acquitted. So, in this case, we would ask that the defendant be held or at least have a third-party custodian because of the nature of those charges are of a similar nature to these charges."

"Well, he already spent three days in jail on this, didn't he?"

"He spent longer than that on one of the charges," Scott interjected.

"Well, how long were you in jail, Mr. Rogers?"

"I think about four days or five days, or something like that."

"Close to a week."

"Do you have any other prior record? I'm not talking about these other charges; I'm talking about any convictions."

"None whatsoever, Your Honor."

Scott tried to interject. "Your Honor, if I may address the Court on this --."

"I just want to go over this file. I just don't accept the government's position on this. He paid a $3,000 bond, which must have cost him $250. He had to retain counsel; he spent three days in jail on a SLIP charge. That's all it's worth. Time served!"

Ms. Jansen rose immediately in protest. "Your Honor, if I may, Ms. Kincaid wished to address the Court at the time of sentencing; and I spoke to defense counsel this morning, and he indicated to me that he was going to request a pre-sentence report. I would at least like to have the court have an opportunity here for Ms. Kincaid."

"But, if he was acquitted of the charges, I'm not going to resurrect those up to his disadvantage. Maybe the jury was dead wrong; but he, in fact, got acquitted and that shouldn't haunt him, particularly on a charge that is of such a relatively minor nature as this."

"Yes, Your Honor, but she did ask. Ms. Kincaid did ask for that opportunity."

"No. I see your point; but if someone spent-four or five days in jail, with no record, had to pay a commercial bondsman, and according to that, had to hire his own lawyer, any greater sentence of a person with no record would be vindictive and totally disproportionate to the sentencing concessions that go with pleas. I know this case that you're talking about. That had some attention around the courthouse, but things have to be in proportion. Besides, if he's a bad guy, he'll come back into the system again, and you'll get him the next time. Okay? Tell Ms. Kincaid I understand her position. I'm not putting you or her down, but I think it would be disproportionate."

"Yes, sir; I will."

"Okay," ended the judge.

Broom Hilda's hand had been in all of this, Scott knew. She would just not give it up! But all her maneuvering and manipulations in the rape case were for naught. She had pushed the boundaries, in some instances, exceeded them! She had done everything she could possibly do to tilt the scales of justice against Timothy.

Scott was disappointed that Broom Hilda had not appeared for the misdemeanor hearing in person so that she could have personally made her presentation to the judge. Scott could not help but fantasize that he may have been more forthcoming and direct regarding the propriety of her request. It was without foundation or precedent! Notwithstanding his opinion on how improper it was, Scott had taken great satisfaction in the court summarily disregarding the request.

Scott was left with no doubt that the court completely understood the maneuvering and the dynamics involved. Broom Hilda had lost the case and everyone around the courthouse knew it, and by now, it had been in all the newspapers.

Scott couldn't help but smile when he heard the court's words echoing in his head: *"The court is aware of the case, but the government lost! If he is really a bad guy, then he would be back in the system again and the government would get another chance. But not this time!"*

Which is why the court sentenced him to time served!

CHAPTER 27

A short time after the trial, Scott received some unexpected feedback. First, James was at a cocktail party in the District, which was attended by a number of Assistant U.S. Attorneys. The outcome of the case had created quite a buzz around the courthouse and was still being discussed in some circles. James didn't identify his connection to the case or participate in the conversation but absorbed the comments. One assessment of Scott's trial performance made by an Assistant U.S. Attorney was, "He wasn't that flashy, but he was very efficient," he said.

When James shared that comment with Scott, he said, "I can live with that."

The second tidbit of information Scott obtained was from his own sources within the U.S. Attorney's Office. Apparently, there was considerable ethical and intellectual conflict within the department between various factions regarding whether the case should have even gone to trial. One faction was adamant that the case should not have. Scott could only surmise that the lack of concrete evidence of which he was aware, conflicting evidence, and testimony of which he was aware, and possibly other evidentiary and testimonial conflicts of which he was not aware, but all of which this faction was aware, lead more objective observers to conclude the case was not only not a serial rape case, but Timothy wasn't the rapist in any of the cases!

The other faction, he surmised, was led by those who wanted a scalp on their belt for the publicity and could not bring themselves to accept the objective conclusion that, with one case in trouble, it was not a serial rape case at all, or he was not the rapist in any of the cases.

The third tidbit was in the last article on the trial that appeared in the paper. It noted that the reporter interviewed jurors after the verdict. They felt that the case lacked concrete evidence linking Timothy to the crimes. The article stated that the jurors had discounted the testimony of his supervisor, who also was a friend and colleague at the station. In addition to the essentially false testimony about Timothy not showing up for work the day after each of the rapes, he had also testified that Timothy once confided that he had forced a woman to have sex with him. All in all, they felt there was insufficient evidence because the three rape victims had sat together at police headquarters before the voice-only lineup and had exchanged the suspect's name.

EPILOGUE

After the trial, some were able to go on with their lives, in a somewhat normal fashion.

Cindy completed her one year at the Public Defender's office and went on to finish law school. She has a very successful practice in Maryland today. From time to time, she and Scott talk, and he's had the pleasure of dining with her and her husband.

Scott only stayed in Washington about five more years. During that time, he continued to practice criminal defense work. As he started to increase the size of his family, Jennifer and he decided that they wanted to go somewhere where the pace was a little slower to raise their children. As much as they loved the DC and Northern Virginia area, the pace was too fast, and they had too much trouble keeping in touch with people.

They lived in a neighborhood where you just "accepted" that people did what they said they did for a living and you didn't ask probing questions.

Most of the people they knew that worked on the Hill were destined to move onward and upward and become Deputy Undersecretary of something. When Ron Brown, Secretary of Commerce, was killed in a plane crash in Europe, along with a full complement of staff, the moment they heard about it, they knew that there would be someone on that plane that they knew. That's the typical position where people they knew would end up. They were publicly, nameless people, but important career staff people who really kept the government running when the political appointee heads of departments kept changing. Sadly, Jennifer's former, well-liked boss was on the plane.

When they moved from the DC area in early '83, Scott gave up practicing criminal defense work. He was all ready to do that anyway, but the previous fall before they moved from the DC area, two of their closest friends and neighbors had been murdered in their home. Only by luck, Scott was out of town and Jennifer and their firstborn child were not in the house visiting at the time. She had decided that they would wait until Scott returned on the weekend and they would all visit together.

Often through the years, in meeting new people, Scott has been asked about the kind of law that he practiced. Although he became a civil litigator, the conversation naturally turned to his early career and generally he only told people that he had done major felony defense work in Northern Virginia and DC

Invariably, in describing his early career, it led him to thinking about the victims and this case. Notwithstanding the fact that Timothy was found not guilty, he was innocent; this had nothing to do with the horrific trauma each of the victims had endured. Still, Scott has never been able to escape wondering how their lives unfolded and wishing the best for them.

As was in keeping with her demeanor, Broom Hilda did not congratulate him on the outcome of the trial. He never had any contact with her after the trial or ever saw her in person again. However, he did see her once, briefly, when he fumbled for his remote. She had become a fucking "Talking Head!!"

As for Timothy, Scott only saw him one more time and after that, he never heard of, or from him, again. Timothy still owed him almost $9,000 in legal fees. But because Scott had begun to believe in him, he broke his own rule about being paid up front, or at least requiring a client to be current. As Scott said before, James had always advised him, "In a criminal case, get your money up front. If a client cannot or will not pay you when they need you the most, they *will* not pay you!"

Shortly after the trial concluded, Timothy declared Chapter 7 Bankruptcy. There was nothing Scott could do about it and his fee was simply going to be written off. For reasons that have since escaped Scott, except to maybe glare at Timothy, since he could not address the court or object, Scott went down to the bankruptcy court in Alexandria for the discharge hearing.

At the conclusion of the hearing, Scott was walking outside, and Timothy and his lawyer came up to him. That's when Timothy's lawyer confronted and admonished Scott. "If you had just offered to let him pay out this bill in $100 a month payment, this would not have been necessary!"

In a slightly raised, irritated, voice Scott responded. "What do you mean *if* I had just offered to let him pay it out at $100 a month! That's *exactly* what *I* offered him!"

For a brief instant, his lawyer was startled, and he and Scott stared at each other. After a pause, slowly, in unison, each head turned toward Timothy. And then Scott knew.

The End!!

BLIND JUSTICE

About the Author

Charles J. McCall was born and raised in Arkansas. He attended the University of Arkansas from which he graduated with a BA in Psychology, with a minor in Chemistry. Originally, he was headed toward dental school, but elected, instead, to go to law school at the University. He received his JD degree from Arkansas, but he completed law school in Washington, DC, and later engaged in graduate law studies in Government Procurement Law, each at George Washington University.

After receiving his JD degree, he spent two years working for an aviation related lobby group and then two years in Miami working for a major land developer. After returning to Washington in 1976, he began private practice in which he represented defendants in major felony cases in Washington, DC and Northern Virginia. In 1983, he shifted his practice totally toward civil litigation.

During his years in private practice, he has been involved in complex civil litigation, acquiring land for the Appalachian Trail under government contract, and spent several years as an administrative hearing officer for the Commonwealth of Virginia. Approaching retirement, he is now engaging in an activity that has been on his mind for many years: writing.